CHARLiE BONE

AND THE SHADOW OF BADLOCK

Books by Jenny Nimmo

Midnight for Charlie Bone
Charlie Bone and the Time Twister
Charlie Bone and the Blue Boa
Charlie Bone and the Castle of Mirrors
Charlie Bone and the Hidden King
Charlie Bone and the Wilderness Wolf
Charlie Bone and the Shadow of Badlock
Charlie Bone and the Red Knight

Henry and the Guardians of the Lost

The Secret Kingdom
The Secret Kingdom: The Stones of Ravenglass
The Secret Kingdom: Leopard's Gold

The Snow Spider Trilogy

CHARLIE BONE

AND THE SHADOW OF BADLOCK

JENNY NIMMO

EGMONT

EGMONT

We bring stories to life

First published in paperback in Great Britain 2016
by Egmont UK Limited
The Yellow Building, 1 Nicholas Road, London W11 4AN

Text copyright © 2002 Jenny Nimmo
Cover illustration by Garry Walton
Cover illustration based on original works by Scott Altmann
Endpapers © Shutterstock

The moral rights of the author and illustrator have been asserted

ISBN 978 1 4052 8098 3

www.egmont.co.uk

45338/11

A CIP catalogue record for this title is available from the British Library

Typeset by Avon DataSet Ltd, Bidford on Avon, Warwickshire
Printed and bound in Great Britain by the CPI Group

Stay safe online. Any website addresses listed in this book are correct
at the time of going to print. However, Egmont is not responsible for content
hosted by third parties. Please be aware that online content can be subject
to change and websites can contain content that is unsuitable for children.
We advise that all children are supervised when using the internet.

MIX
Paper
FSC   FSC® C018306

CONTENTS

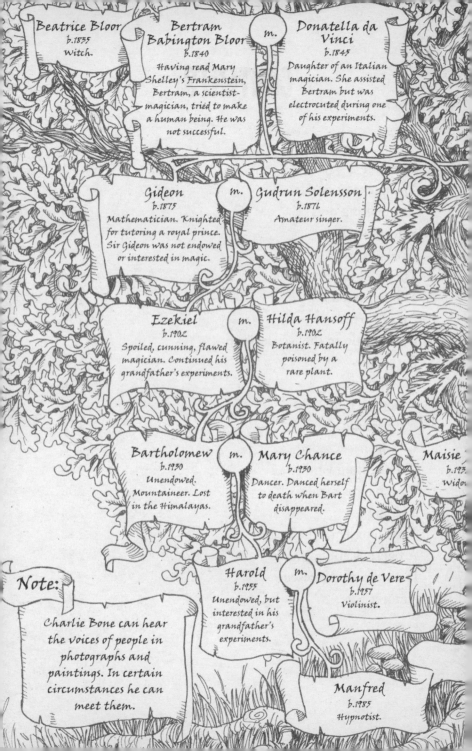

Beatrice Bloor
b.1835
Witch.

Bertram Babington Bloor
b.1840
Having read Mary Shelley's Frankenstein, Bertram, a scientist-magician, tried to make a human being. He was not successful.

m.

Donatella da Vinci
b.1845
Daughter of an Italian magician. She assisted Bertram but was electrocuted during one of his experiments.

Gideon
b.1875
Mathematician. Knighted for tutoring a royal prince. Sir Gideon was not endowed or interested in magic.

m.

Gudrun Solensson
b.1876
Amateur singer.

Ezekiel
b.1902
Spoiled, cunning, flawed magician. Continued his grandfather's experiments.

m.

Hilda Hansoff
b.1902
Botanist. Fatally poisoned by a rare plant.

Bartholomew
b.1930
Unendowed. Mountaineer. Lost in the Himalayas.

m.

Mary Chance
b.1930
Dancer. Danced herself to death when Bart disappeared.

Maisie
b.193
Wido

Note:

Charlie Bone can hear the voices of people in photographs and paintings. In certain circumstances he can meet them.

Harold
b.1955
Unendowed, but interested in his grandfather's experiments.

m.

Dorothy de Vere
b.1957
Violinist.

Manfred
b.1985
Hypnotist.

Yorath Yewbeam
b.1850
Shape-shifter.

m.

Vera Kuragina
b.1862
Hypnotist.

Grace Bloor
b.1885
Painter. Unendowed.
Lived with her son and
grandson, Paton, until
she died, aged eighty.

m.

Manley
b.1884
Soldier. Killed in 1918
in the Great War.

Yolanda
b.1900
Shape-shifter.
Inherited her father's
castle. Never married.

Henry
b.1905
Disappeared when
he was eleven.
Unendowed.

Daphne
b.1908
Clairvoyant. Died
of diphtheria in 1916.

James
b.1910
Unendowed.
Historian.

m.

Solange Sourzac
b.1912
French actress. Fell and broke
her neck in mysterious
circumstances while visiting
Yolanda's castle in 1964.

Monty Bone
b.1937
Pilot. Died 1963.

m.

Grizelda
b.1937
Unendowed.

Lucretia
b.1942
Matron.
Unendowed.

Eustacia
b.1947
Clairvoyant.

Venetia
b.1952
Designer
of magic
clothes.

Paton
b.1957
Power-
booster.

Amy Jones
b.1967
Store assistant.

m.

Lyell
b.1962
Pianist.
Disappeared in
1994.

Note:

When James Yewbeam's
wife, Solange, died, his four
daughters went to live with
their evil great-aunt,
Yolanda, who turned them
against their father. Yolanda
also tried to steal Paton,
but James resisted her.

Charlie
b.1992
Picture
traveller.

THE CHILDREN OF THE RED KING, CALLED THE ENDOWED

Manfred Bloor — Talents Master at Bloor's Academy. Previously head boy. A hypnotiser. He is descended from Borlath, eldest son of the Red King. Borlath was a brutal and sadistic tyrant.

Naren Bloor — Adopted daughter of Bartholomew Bloor, Naren can send shadow words over great distances. She is descended from the Red King's grandson who was abducted by pirates and taken to China.

Asa Pike — A were-beast. He is descended from a tribe who lived in the Northern forests and kept strange beasts. Asa can change shape at dusk.

Billy Raven — Billy can communicate with animals. One of his ancestors conversed with ravens that sat on a gibbet where dead men hung. For this talent he was banished from his village.

Lysander Sage	Descended from an African wise man. He can call up his spirit ancestors.
Tancred Torsson	A storm-bringer. His Scandinavian ancestor was named after the thunder god, Thor. Tancred can bring rain, wind, thunder and lightning.
Gabriel Silk	Gabriel can feel scenes and emotions through the clothes of others. He comes from a line of psychics.
Emma Tolly	Emma can fly. Her surname derives from the Spanish swordsman from Toledo, whose daughter married the Red King. He is therefore an ancestor to all the endowed children.
Charlie Bone	Charlie can travel into photographs and pictures. Through his father he is descended from the Red King, and through his mother, from Mathonwy, a Welsh magician and friend of the Red King.
Dorcas Loom	Dorcas can bewitch items of clothing. Her ancestor, Lola Defarge, knitted a shrivelling shawl whilst enjoying the execution of the Queen of France in 1793.
Idith and Inez Branko	Telekinetic twins, distantly related to Zelda Dobinski, who has left Bloor's Academy.

Joshua Tilpin	Joshua has magnetism. He is descended from Lilith, the Red King's oldest daughter, and Harken, the evil enchanter who married her.
Una Onimous	Mr Onimous's niece. Una is five years old and her endowment is being kept secret until it has fully developed.
Olivia Vertigo	Descended from Guanhamara, who fled the Red King's castle and married an Italian Prince. Olivia is an illusionist. The Bloors are unaware of her endowment.
Dagbert Endless:	Dagbert is the son of Lord Grimwald who can control the oceans. His mother took the gold from drowned men's teeth, and made them into charms to protect her son. Dagbert is a drowner.

The endowed are all descended from the ten children of the Red King: a magician-king who left Africa in the twelfth century, accompanied by three leopards.

PROLOGUE

The winds of Badlock were the cruellest in the world; they came from every quarter, screaming against the giant's broad back, tearing his hair and lashing his eyes, so that he could barely open them. At every step great gusts swept around his long legs until, at length, he was forced on to his knees.

Behind the giant lay a vast plain of wind-torn scrub and ever-shifting stones. It had taken him and his child a night and a day to cover this inhospitable terrain. They had come from the range of snow-capped mountains that surrounded the plain like a massive wall.

The giant drew his cloak tight about the boy in his arms. They had been making for a little hollow, where a shelter of trees could be seen, and the gleam of water.

'Forgive me, Roland,' moaned the giant. 'I can go no further.'

'You are tired, Father,' said the boy, twisting out of the giant's arms. 'If I walk you can move more easily.'

The giant marvelled at his little son's spirit. It must come from the boy's mother, he thought. It shamed him to see

Roland still so unafraid after their long ordeal. Gathering his strength, the giant got to his feet again and battled forward, while his son staggered bravely at his side.

'Look!' Roland suddenly sang out. 'I see a light in the hollow.'

'The moon,' murmured his father.

'No, Father. A flame.'

The giant brushed a hand across his eyes and blinked. Yes, there was, indeed, a light flickering at the edge of the hollow. But how could he tell if it meant danger? They were unlikely to find help in such a godforsaken place.

All at once, Roland suddenly sprinted ahead. He had always been inclined to rush headlong into things that excited his curiosity.

'Wait!' called the giant.

But Roland, his arms wide as if embracing the wind, forged through the swirling gusts, whirled away towards the trees and disappeared from view.

When the giant arrived at the hollow, he found his son talking earnestly to a boy of about ten with startling snow-white hair. The stranger raised his rush-light the better to see the form that stood at the lip of the hollow, and the giant noted his large violet-coloured eyes. A goblin, thought the giant. What fairy tricks has he come to play on us?

'Roland, come here,' the giant commanded, stepping closer to the pair.

Of a sudden, as if from nowhere, another figure moved

into the circle of light: a tall young man with raven hair and a cloak of some dark shiny stuff.

'Don't be afraid,' said the dark young man. 'White-haired Owain is no fairy. He has sought you for many months.'

'For me?' The giant's eyes narrowed.

'You are Otus Yewbeam?' asked the boy.

'That is my name.'

The boy made a deep bow. 'I am so happy to find you, sir. No one could tell me where you had gone. It was an old woman in your village who, nearing the end of her life, overcame her fear of punishment, and told me that you and your son had been taken prisoner by a knight all in green.'

'Count Harken.' The giant gave a snort of loathing.

'But you have escaped,' said the dark youth.

'We would have rescued you,' said Owain, 'however fiercely you had been guarded.'

Roland, who had been leaping up and down with excitement, could contain his news no longer and burst out, 'Owain is my cousin, Father, and he,' he pointed to the dark young man, 'he is my uncle Tolemeo.'

The giant frowned. 'Can this be true?'

Tolemeo said, 'Let us go further into this hollow where we can speak more easily.' For they had been shouting in sentences devoid of warmth or feeling, as the wind snatched their words and scattered them into the air.

Tolemeo led the way, followed by Owain, whose

flaring torch caused Tolemeo's cloak to sparkle with ever-changing colours, from vivid blue to green to deepest purple.

He is wearing feathers, thought the giant, and a small thread of unease ran through him. Yet I must not expect them to be ordinary, he told himself, for they are the Red King's children and my own dear wife, Amoret, was a child of the magician-king.

They reached a cluster of rocks at the bottom of the hollow and, easing himself on to a wide slab, the giant asked, 'Have you news of my wife?'

He did not get an immediate answer. Owain looked at the ground. The white-haired boy seemed, all at once, nervous and uncertain.

'Forgive me, sir,' said Tolemeo, 'but you are not my idea of a giant.'

'No,' said Owain, with an edgy laugh. 'I always imagined a giant's head to be swallowed by the clouds.'

Otus smiled indulgently. 'I am not a true giant, though I come from a race of giants. My father stood two fathoms high. I am only two-thirds his height. My brothers are even smaller. Perhaps our descendants will be a more manageable size.' He glanced at Roland and then said urgently, 'But please, have you news of my wife?'

Tolemeo lowered his gaze. His slight uncomfortable shrug caused the giant's heart to miss a beat.

'Tell me, please,' cried Otus, 'even if it is the worst a man can expect.'

'Your wife went to her brother Amadis . . .' Tolemeo began.

'Yes, yes,' broke in the giant. 'We heard that Count Harken was on his way. I thought she would be safe with Amadis. She had a mirror, made by her father, the king, and she used it – for travelling.' Otus looked into the faces that stared up at him. They didn't seem surprised. 'You know of the mirror?'

'We do,' Tolemeo affirmed. 'And we know that it is what Harken craves.'

The giant's mouth twisted in a bitter smile. 'Count Harken may be an enchanter but he craves everything the king, your father, ever made or owned. They surrounded our house, Harken and his army of trolls and thugs. Amoret tried to take our baby with her, she thought the mirror would transport them both but, somehow, it would not work for Roland. He fell into my arms just as his mother vanished. Minutes later, Harken broken into the house and captured us. They brought us here to Badlock and for two years we have been imprisoned in one of his many towers. Three days ago I kicked out at the wretched troll who brought our food and while he was still reeling from the pain of my boot, clever Roland pushed him into a cupboard and locked the door.'

'And then I untied my father's bonds,' said Roland. 'They didn't know I had grown so strong, or they would have chained me to the wall, like my poor father.'

The giant lifted his son into his arms. 'We have been

travelling ever since, but with these accursed winds it is hard to make progress. If we can reach the coast and get a boat, we'll find my wife no matter what. I've heard her brother, Amadis, has a fine castle, on an island in the western sea.'

The silence that greeted this remark was so profound it seemed like a dark chasm where the giant's mind refused to go.

'Tell me,' he whispered.

'Your wife is dead,' said Tolemeo steadily. 'Owain will tell you the rest, for he was there.'

Roland buried his head in his father's neck, his shoulders heaving with quiet sobs. I have known this all along, thought Otus. How could I have hoped to avoid the truth? 'Tell me,' he said.

Owain slipped off his rocky perch and passed the torch to Tolemeo. Then, clasping his hands together, he looked steadily into the giant's face and began, 'It was my own uncle, your wife's older brother Borlath. You must know that he is one of Harken's allies. He found my father's island and the castle he had built. The loveliest castle in all the world, they said. Borlath wanted it. He brought an army of mercenaries and tried to starve us out, but my father, who could speak with animals, called to the wolves, the bats, the birds and the rats. The rats were especially useful, they ate all Borlath's supplies. When winter came the mercenaries grew sullen, they wanted to leave, and that's when Borlath used his awful power. I saw it myself from the battlements; fire came from his hands, flames from every finger.' Owain held up his hands, his fingers spread wide. 'In a second a ring of fire had encircled us. My father lifted me down. "Run, Owain," he cried. "Run to the well as fast as you can, and don't come out until I tell you." So I ran. And as I went I looked up and a bright mirror came flying over my head, and I caught it, and far, far away, I heard Amoret call out, "Give the mirror to my son." And I went down the well, and my raven came with me. He was my friend, you see, and I talk his language.

'From the depths of the well we listened, Raven and me. We listened to screams, to roaring flames, to beams tearing and crashing, to moans and cries and boulders falling. And I smelt fire, and worse than fire.' Owain lifted his glistening eyes to the sky and his chest rose and fell, as though he were fighting for breath. Tolemeo put a hand on his shoulder, and the boy continued, 'And then it was quiet, very quiet, and I knew my father could never tell me to come out; I knew I would never hear his voice again. So I came out anyway. And they were all dead. Everyone.'

The giant's mouth had fallen open, but his cry was silent. Roland turned his head to stare at Owain. Horror had dried up his tears.

Owain said gently, 'When I came out it was snowing, and the castle walls were as shiny as glass, so shiny I could see my face in them.'

'It was the work of a magician,' said Tolemeo, 'my father's friend, Mathonwy. He sent a cloud of snow to smother the flames. But his help came too late to save Amadis and Amoret. I was in Toledo, my mother's city, when it happened.'

Owain clasped Tolemeo's hand. 'I sent my raven to find him, and since the day Tolemeo arrived, we have been searching for you.' He put his hand into his jerkin and drew out a mirror set in a jewelled frame. The glass was so brilliant it was as if the sun had touched their faces.

The giant gasped, and turned his head away. 'Amoret,' he murmured.

Tolemeo took the mirror from Owain and thrust it into the giant's hands. 'Take the mirror, Otus Yewbeam,' he said sternly. 'You have lost your wife but you still have your son.'

The giant was about to reply when Tolemeo suddenly spun on his heel, his nostrils flaring, his eyes wide and alert. 'They are upon us,' he cried.

'I heard nothing,' said the giant.

'Nevertheless.' Tolemeo lifted Roland on to his shoulders. 'We have but a moment.' He began to stride round the lake. 'Otus, make haste. They approach.'

The giant stood, clutching the mirror to his chest. He looked up to the rim of the hollow, and there they were – a long line of shadows weaving through the trees. A deep, nasal roar filled the giant's ears as Harken's troll army began to run down the steep bank. Their tiny eyes and scribble mouths were all but hidden in the fleshy spread of their huge noses. They wore scaly breastplates of dull metal, and tall, ridiculous helmets that disguised their lumpy heads. Their weapons were cudgels, spears and deadly slingshots, and behind them came a group of hideous beings that were neither troll nor human.

The giant began to run, his long legs easily clearing the rocks at the lake's edge. Ahead of him, he could see Roland's small face gazing back from Tolemeo's shoulders. 'Run, Father, run,' called the little boy.

The trolls' bellowing filled the hollow. Rocks and spears began to rain down from every side, and now the giant could see that they were surrounded.

'The Count is angry,' a thick, rasping voice announced. 'He punished me for your escape, Otus Yewbeam. And now I shall punish you.'

The giant recognised Oddthumb, leader of Harken's guards. He was bigger than the others and his face was a corpse-like grey, but what marked him out was the thumb of his right hand, a huge, gnarled, stumpy thing, wider than his palm.

Otus ducked as a rock came winging from Oddthumb's slingshot.

'The mirror, Father,' cried Roland. 'Use the mirror to save yourself. Mother would have wished it.'

Tolemeo stopped and called back, 'It's the truth, Otus. Give them the mirror. It will slow them down. I will save your son, but you will have to fend for yourself.'

'Save Roland,' cried the giant, and he threw the mirror high into the air.

Every troll face was raised in fear and astonishment as the shining circle spun to earth, its radiance piercing their weak eyes and momentarily blinding them.

A howl of pain and fury went up. The mirror dropped at Oddthumb's feet. He felt its weight but couldn't see it.

'Farewell, Otus!' called Tolemeo.

The giant turned.

Tolemeo was rising from the ground with Roland and Owain clasped in his arms. Higher and higher. Now they were over the lake, and the feathered cloak billowed around them, while the dark water shimmered in the breeze. When they were higher than the trees that rimmed the hollow, two great wings spread behind Tolemeo. He swung in the air and lay like a swimmer, while the wings beat gracefully above him. He might have been a great bird soaring through the starlit sky, if you chose not to see the two small figures clasped to his chest.

A joyous smile lit Otus Yewbeam's face, and in the long, solitary years that were to follow, the smile would return every time the giant remembered that moment.

The trolls had recovered their sight. They ran down to the lake, swinging their cudgels, grunting and swearing. The giant knew it would be useless to run. He saw that Oddthumb had picked up the mirror. The shadow would have what he wanted at last.

THE PACKAGE IN THE CELLAR

'Pretty Cats!'

In the hall of number nine, Filbert Street, a small boy stood at the foot of the staircase. He looked sickly and too thin. Scraping a tangle of dull brown hair away from his face, he stuck out his tongue. 'Flames! That's what they call you, isn't it?'

The three cats, sitting on the rail, stared down from the landing above. They had fiery coloured coats: copper, orange and yellow. The orange cat hissed; the yellow cat lifted a paw and flexed his dangerous claws; the copper cat gave a deep, threatening growl.

'Why don't you like me? I'm smarter than you. One day,' the boy raised his fist, 'you'll be sorry.'

A door opened behind him and a voice called, 'Eric, what are you doing?'

'Come and look.'

Two women stepped into the hall. They would have been identical if there had not been twenty years between them. Both were tall and dark-eyed, with thin, chilly mouths and long, narrow noses. But whereas one had bone-white hair, the other's was as black as a crow's wing.

'Look!' Eric pointed up at the three cats.

The older woman uttered a throaty snarl. 'What are they doing here? I've forbidden them, *expressly*.'

The younger woman, Eric's stepmother, grabbed his hand and dragged him back. 'I've told you never to approach those creatures.'

'I didn't,' said Eric. 'I'm down here and they're up there. And anyway, they can't hurt me.'

'Of course they can,' his stepmother retorted. 'They're wild creatures.'

'With leopards' hearts,' her sister added. Raising her voice, she called, 'Charlie! Charlie Bone, come here, this minute.'

A door opened upstairs and a moment later a boy with tousled hair leaned over the railing. The yellow cat walked up to him and rubbed its head against his arm. The other cats jumped down and circled his legs.

'What is it, Grandma?' Charlie stroked the yellow cat's head and yawned.

'Lazy lump!' said his grandmother. 'Have you been asleep?'

'No,' Charlie replied indignantly. 'I've been doing my homework.'

'Did you let those cats in?'

'They're not doing any harm,' said Charlie.

'Harm?' Grandma Bone's dark eyes became angry

slits. 'They're the most harmful creatures in this city. Get them out.'

'Sorry, Sagittarius.' Charlie lifted the yellow cat off the banisters. 'Sorry, Aries and Leo,' he said to the cats winding themselves round his legs. 'Grandma Bone says you've got to go.'

Whether it was Charlie's tone of voice or his actual words was not clear, but the cats appeared to know exactly what he was saying. They followed him into his bedroom and, when he had opened his window, they jumped through it, one by one, on to the branch of a chestnut tree that stretched close to the sill.

'See you at the Pets' Café,' Charlie called as the Flames leapt on to the pavement. They bounded up the street with a chorus of mews that made a dog, on the other side of the street, stop dead in its tracks.

Charlie smiled and closed the window. Returning to the landing, he found his grandmother, his great-aunt Venetia and Eric still staring up at him.

'Have they gone?' Grandma Bone demanded.

'Yes, Grandma,' Charlie said wearily.

At this point a third woman emerged from the sitting room. With her sharp features and abundant grey hair she was clearly related to the other two women. She was, in fact, Charlie's great-aunt Eustacia. She was carrying a flat rectangular object covered in brown paper. It was about a metre and a half long and, perhaps, just under a metre wide.

Charlie knew there was no point in asking about the package. He would be told to mind his own business. But he had a fairly good idea what it was. He began to feel unaccountably excited.

'What are you staring at?' Great Aunt Eustacia grunted at Charlie.

'Get back to your homework,' ordered Grandma Bone.

Eric's thin little mouth twisted into an unpleasant smirk. 'Goodbye, Charlie Bone!'

Charlie didn't bother to reply. He went back to his room and closed the door with a loud click. But then, as quietly as possible, he opened it, just a fraction. He wanted to know what was going to happen to the object Eustacia was carrying. Surely, it had to be a painting.

It was two years since Charlie had discovered his extraordinary endowment. It had begun when he heard voices coming from a photograph. Over the next few months Charlie found himself travelling into photographs and talking to people who had died many years before. When he turned his attention to paintings, the same thing had happened: he could meet the subjects in old paintings, people who had lived centuries before. Charlie often tried to avoid these situations; it was one thing to go into the past, quite another to leave it. Once or twice he'd been lucky to get out alive.

For some reason, the rectangular object with its covering of wrinkled brown paper aroused Charlie's intense curiosity. He put his ear to the crack in the door and listened.

'Why you've brought it here, I can't imagine.' Grandma's voice crackled with irritation.

'I told you,' whined Great Aunt Eustacia, 'my basement's damp.'

'Hang it on your wall, then.'

'I don't like it.'

'Then give it to –'

'Don't look at me,' said Great Aunt Venetia. 'It gives me the creeps.'

'She made me take it,' Eustacia said fretfully. 'Mrs Tilpin isn't someone you can argue with.'

Charlie stiffened. He hadn't heard Mrs Tilpin's name mentioned for some time. Once, she had been a rather pretty Music teacher called Miss Chrystal, but she hadn't been seen since she had been revealed as a witch.

'They won't keep it at the school,' went on Eustacia. 'Even Ezekiel is wary of it. He says it steals his thoughts, it draws them away like a magnet – he says.'

'Joshua Tilpin is a magnet,' said Eric.

His stepmother uttered a short, dry laugh. 'Huh! The witch's son. So he is.'

At this everyone began to talk at once, and Charlie had difficulty in making out what was said, but it seemed that Grandma Bone had finally agreed to allow the painting, or whatever it was, to be stored in her cellar. Strictly speaking, it wasn't *her* cellar, because she shared the house with her brother, Paton. Charlie and his other grandmother, Maisie, had been permitted to live there until Charlie's parents returned from their second honeymoon, and their house, 'Diamond Corner', had been restored.

There began a succession of bangs, scrapings and irritated exclamations as the painting was presumably carried down into the cellar. Finally, the cellar door was shut and, after more discussions, bangs and clicks, Grandma Bone, her two sisters and Eric left the house.

Charlie waited in his room until he heard everyone bundle into Great Aunt Eustacia's car. Then, with much mis-firing and a painful scraping of gears, the old Ford lurched down the street.

After another five minutes had passed, Charlie slipped out of his room and ran downstairs. When he reached the cellar he found that the door had been locked. Luckily, Charlie knew where all the keys were kept. He went into the kitchen and pulled a chair up to the dresser. Standing on tiptoe, he reached for a large blue jug patterned with golden fishes.

'And what might you be up to?' said a voice.

Charlie hesitated. The chair wobbled. Charlie uttered a shaky yelp and steadied himself. He hadn't noticed Grandma Maisie folding the washing in a corner.

'Maisie, are you spying on me?' asked Charlie.

Maisie straightened up. 'I've got better things to do, young man.'

Charlie's other grandmother was the very opposite of Grandma Bone. Maisie wasn't much taller than Charlie and battled hard to keep her weight down. Being the family cook didn't make this easy.

'Now, I wonder why you were trying to get those keys?' Maisie's face was too round and cheerful to look stern. Even frowning was an effort. 'Don't deny it. There's nothing else up there that would interest you.'

'I think Great Aunt Eustacia has put a painting in the cellar.'

'What if she has?'

'I . . . well, I just wanted to . . . you know, have a look at it.' Charlie clutched the fish jug and drew out a large, rusty-looking key.

Maisie shook her head. 'Not a good idea, Charlie.'

'Why?' Charlie replaced the jug and jumped down from the chair.

'You know *them*,' said Maisie with meaning. 'Those Yewbeam sisters are always trying to trick you. D'you think they didn't know you'd be just itching to take a look at . . . whatever it is?'

'They didn't know I was listening, Maisie.'

'Huh!' Maisie grunted. 'Course they did.'

Charlie twiddled the key between his fingers. 'I just want to take a look at the outside of it, the shape of it. I won't take the paper off.'

'Oh no? Look, Charlie, your parents are watching whales on the other side of the world. If something happens to you, how am I going to . . .?'

'Nothing will happen to me.' Before Maisie could say another word, Charlie walked briskly out of the kitchen and along the passage to the cellar. The key turned in the lock with surprising ease. But as soon as the low door opened, Charlie knew that there was really no doubt – something would happen to him. He could feel it already: a light, insistent tug, drawing him closer; down a set of creaking wooden steps, down, down, down, until he stood in the chilly gloom of the cellar.

The package was propped against the wall, between an old mattress and a set of rusty curtain poles. Charlie couldn't be certain but he thought he could hear a faint sound coming from beneath the crumpled wrapping paper.

'Impossible!' Charlie clutched his hair. This had never happened before. He had to see a face before he heard its voice. But this sound was coming from something out of sight. As he stepped towards the package a deep whine whistled past his ears.

'Wind?' Charlie reached out a hand.

At his touch the paper rustled and creaked. The whole package seemed suddenly alive and Charlie hesitated. But a second of doubt was immediately overcome by his burning curiosity, and he began to tear at the wrapping. Strips of paper flew into the air, borne by Charlie's frantic fingers and the unnatural wind that blew from who knew where.

The painting didn't even wait to be entirely revealed. Long before every corner was free of the paper, a dreadful landscape began to seep into the dim cellar. This was not how it should happen. Charlie was mystified. He waited for the familiar tumbling sensation that usually overwhelmed him when he travelled into paintings. It never came. He watched in astonishment as the brick walls of the cellar were swallowed by a vista of distant mountains. Tall, dark towers appeared in the foreground; one swam so close to Charlie that he could smell the damp moss that patched the walls. Ugly scaled creatures scuttled over the surface, pausing briefly to stare at Charlie with dangerous glinting eyes.

It has to be an illusion, Charlie told himself. He put out his hand – and touched the horny spine of a black toad-like thing. 'Ugh!' Leaping away from it, he tripped and fell on to his back. Beneath him he could feel rough stone cobbles, slippery with grey-black weeds. Above him purple clouds rushed through an ash-coloured sky, and all about him the wind roared and rattled, howled and sighed.

'So I'm there already.' Charlie got to his feet and rubbed his back. 'Wherever *there* is.'

In brief intervals, when the wind died to a low whine, Charlie could hear the tramp of heavy feet and a low muttering of voices. 'It's here,' one said. 'I can smell it.'

'It's mine.' This voice glooped like a sink full of dishes. 'I know how to catch it.'

'Oddthumb knows,' came a chorus of low, tuneless voices.

Charlie backed round the tower as the marching feet drew closer. There appeared to be no windows in the building and Charlie was just beginning to think that it was without a door, when he was suddenly seized round the waist and lifted high in the air. A huge fist closed over his mouth and a voice, close to his ear, whispered, 'Boy, your life depends on your silence.'

Shocked and speechless, Charlie was swung backwards through an open door and set down. He found himself on the lowest step of a stone staircase that spiralled upwards before disappearing into the shadows.

'Climb,' whispered the voice, 'as fast as your feet will take you.'

Charlie mounted the stone steps, his heart beating wildly. Up, up and up, never stopping until he had reached a door at the very top. Charlie pushed it open and went into the room beyond. A narrow window high in the wall shed a dismal light on to the sparse furnishings beneath: the longest bed Charlie had ever seen, the highest table and the tallest chair, and . . . could that be a boat, hanging on the wall? He turned quickly as the owner of the room ducked under the lintel and walked in, closing the door and locking it.

Charlie beheld a giant, or the nearest thing to a giant he had ever seen. The man's white hair was coiled into a knob at the back of his head, and a fine, snowy beard reached a neat point just above his waist. He wore a coarse shirt, a leather waistcoat and brown woollen trousers tied at the ankle with cord.

The giant held a finger to his lips and then, raising his

arm, pushed open a small panel set between the rafters of the roof. Without a word, he lifted Charlie up to the dark space revealed. Charlie rolled sideways and the panel was immediately replaced, leaving him in a dark, stuffy hole with his knees drawn up to his chest and his arms wrapped around his legs.

'They'll not find you. Trust me,' whispered the giant, whose head was perhaps only a foot below the rafters.

There was a tiny hole right beside Charlie's ear and when he turned his head, he could see directly into the room below. He had just positioned himself as comfortably as possible when he heard voices echoing up the stairwell.

'Otus Yewbeam, are you there?'

'Have you seen the boy?'

'Caught him, have you?'

'He's ours.'

'Mine,' came Oddthumb's husky snarl. 'All mine.'

A battery of fists and cudgels began to thump against the door.

'Patience, soldiers,' called Otus. 'I was sleeping.' One step took him to the door, which he unlocked, with much sighing and rattling.

A crowd of squat, ugly beings rushed in and surrounded the giant. They wore metal breast-plates over their patched leather jerkins, and strapped to their heads were tall helmets like metal top hats. Axes, knives, catapults and cudgels hung from their belts, though some had bows slung over their backs, and quivers bursting with

21

shiny arrows. Most came well below the giant's waist, but there was one, somewhat larger than the others, who looked familiar to Charlie. Couldn't be the same carved stone troll that had once sat outside Great Aunt Venetia's gloomy house?

'Why did you lock the door against us?' this larger being demanded.

'Not against you, Oddthumb,' said the giant, 'against durgles.'

'Durgles!' spat Oddthumb.

'Durgles are very destructive,' said Otus. 'Many a day they have eaten my bread whilst I slept.'

'Liar,' said Oddthumb. 'A durgle can no more unlock a door than a diddycock. You have got him, I know it.'

'Who?' Otus enquired in a mild tone.

'The boy,' snarled one of the smaller beings. 'He's here. The Watch see'd him a'coming from far off. Caught he was, by the Count's guile.'

'Enchanted,' said the being beside him.

'Spell-brought,' chorused the others.

There was a loud creak as Otus lowered himself on to his bed. He was now out of Charlie's sight, though he could still see a long leather-bound foot.

'Respected soldiers, I have seen no boy,' said Otus. 'Search this room if you must.'

'We will,' grunted Oddthumb. 'Up, giant!'

Otus had barely risen from the bed, when Oddthumb and his crew had pushed it over. They slashed at the

22

blankets, battered the straw mattress, tore off a cupboard door, turned over a thin rush mat, poked up the chimney, pulled charred wood from the fire, and hacked at the floorboards. The frenzied attack lasted no more than ten minutes and, from his hiding place, Charlie saw a growing pile of ash and straw, broken pottery and chunks of bread.

'Squirras!' cried one of the soldiers suddenly.

Charlie couldn't see what he had found. It must have been on the far side of the room.

'Greedy, greedy,' said Oddthumb. 'Six squirras for your brekfass, Otus?'

'I'm a giant,' sighed Otus.

'We'll leave one – the smallest,' Oddthumb said spitefully.

'I thank you,' said Otus.

A soldier with a warty face came and stood directly under Charlie's spyhole. 'No boy here, General,' he said. 'In forest maybe?'

'No boy, eh? No boy.' Oddthumb paced across the room. He stopped beside Wart-face and looked up.

Charlie found himself staring into a stony grey eye. He dared not blink. He dared not breathe. His own eye began to ache as he held it wide open and unmoving. Could Oddthumb see him? Did he sense Charlie's presence, lying above? An urge to sneeze overcame Charlie. He pressed his lips together, brought his fingers slowly up to his face and clamped them over his nose.

'Dreaded creatures up there,' whispered Wart-face.

'Blancavamps maybe. Let us leave here, General.'

'Blancavamps?' Oddthumb stroked his chin with a grotesque thumb, as big as his hand. 'Have you got blancavamps, Otus?'

Charlie had difficulty in stifling a gasp.

'Sadly,' said the giant. 'They steal my sleep.'

Oddthumb threw back his head and gave a hideous burbling chuckle. In a second the room was filled with gurgling laughter, as the soldiers echoed their general. The dreadful sound stopped abruptly the moment Oddthumb closed his mouth. Without another word, the general marched out, followed by his troops.

Charlie listened to the stamp of heavy feet receding down the steps. A door at the foot of the tower clanged shut and the soldiers began to march down the street. Charlie waited breathlessly. He dared not move for fear one of the soldiers remained in the room below. He could hear Otus settling his room to rights after the rough intrusion.

Long after the footsteps had faded, the giant came and grinned up at Charlie. 'You are safe, boy. Be not afeared, I will get you down.'

'Thanks,' Charlie said huskily.

The giant pushed back the panel, saying, 'Step on to my shoulders.' He held up his arms and Charlie thrust his legs through the hole. Otus gently lifted him down and set him on the bed.

Charlie wriggled his aching shoulders and rubbed his

arms. 'I'm not sure how I got here,' he said.

The giant pulled his chair up to the bed and sat down. Putting his head on one side, he regarded Charlie quizzically. 'Your name?' he asked.

'Charlie Bone, sir.'

'You are a traveller?'

'I . . . yes, I am sometimes. I can travel into photos and paintings.' Observing the giant's puzzled frown, Charlie added quickly, 'Photos are a bit difficult to explain, but I expect you know what a painting is.' The giant nodded. 'Anyhow, this time it was different, my travelling, I mean. This time a painting has . . . kind of . . . captured me.'

'Mm.' The giant nodded again. 'My wife had a mirror that took her a-travelling.'

'A mirror?' Charlie said excitedly. 'My ancestor, Amoret, had a mirror. It caused a bit of trouble. Someone wanted it . . . an enchanter.'

'Amoret was my wife!' The giant clutched Charlie's hand in his huge fist. 'My name is Otus Yewbeam.'

'Then . . . you're my ancestor, too.' Charlie's gaze slid over the giant's long frame, from the crown of his head to the tip of his long foot. 'Maybe I'll grow a bit.'

The giant smiled. 'I was this high when I was a boy.' He held his hand about six feet from the ground.

'Oh,' said Charlie, a little sadly.

'What is your century?' asked Otus.

'Um . . . twenty-first,' said Charlie, after a bit of thought.

'There are nine hundred years between us.'

Charlie frowned. 'I don't get it. I've never, ever come into the past this way. I was just looking at a painting; I saw mountains and towers, but no people, and then, suddenly, it was all around me.'

'He is powerful,' Otus said gravely. 'He wanted you in Badlock.'

'Who?'

'Count, enchanter, shadow of Badlock; he has many names. He brought me here as a captive, twenty years ago, when my wife fled to her brother's castle.' The giant's large eyes clouded for a moment, and he looked up at the fading light in the window. 'He wanted Amoret. He wanted all the Red King's children. Five he won easily, they already walked the path of wickedness. The others – Amadis, Amoret, Guanhamara, Petrello and Tolemeo – they fled the evil. It was Tolemeo who rescued my son, Roland, and for that the shadow punished me. His soldiers relish torture. Now they let me bide in peace. I am forgotten, almost.'

Charlie reminded the giant that, today, the soldiers had not let him bide in peace. 'I've put you in danger,' he said. 'If they catch me . . .?'

'No,' the giant leaned forward earnestly. 'They will not catch you.' He got up and strode over to a hearth set into a wide chimney breast. 'Presently, we shall dine on squirra, boy.'

'Oh, good.' A note of anxiety crept into Charlie's voice.

What was a squirra, he wondered.

The giant opened a small door in the wall and brought out a black rat-like creature with an extremely long, hairless tail. 'Only one,' Otus sighed. 'But it will suffice.'

Charlie's stomach lurched. 'If that's a squirra, what's a blancavamp?'

Otus chuckled. 'They are what we, in our world, know as bats, but blancavamps are white as snow. The people of Badlock believe them to be ghosts. But I am not afeared of them.'

'Nor me.' Charlie darted a quick look in the giant's direction. Otus was already skinning the squirra and, hoping it was something *he* would never need to do, Charlie looked quickly away. 'Have you ever tried to get home again?' he asked the giant.

Otus gave a rueful smile. 'My wife's brother, Tolemeo, tried a second time to rescue me, but Oddthumb and his ruffians caught us. Tolemeo was lucky to escape with his life. And, knowing my wife had perished, I cared less and less how and where my life should end.'

Charlie recalled the fleeting image of a beautiful woman smiling out from a mirrored wall, and a near-impossible plan began to take shape in his mind.

'Badlock is a country no one from our world can find,' the giant continued. 'No one but clever Tolemeo. It is an awful place. There is the eternal wind, and then, in winter, there is a deluge. Water fills the land between the mountains, a fathom deep.'

'It *is* a boat, then.' Charlie nodded at the wooden boat-shape hanging on the wall.

'Indeed, a boat. There is no other place to live but in a tower.'

'And where does the Enchanter live?'

'In a dark fortress, a scar on the mountain. I'll show you.' Dropping the meat into an iron pot, Otus wiped his hands on a rag tucked into his belt and, before Charlie could protest, lifted him up to the high window.

Night was falling fast, but the mountains were sharply outlined against a ribbon of pale green sky. Close to the top of the tallest mountain, flickering red lights could be seen and, behind them, a black shape capped with steep turrets.

'He is seldom there,' said the giant, 'but the fires burn constantly to remind his subjects that he is watching them.'

Charlie shuddered. It had only just occurred to him that he might be trapped in this hostile world forever. He was about to be lowered to the ground when he shouted, 'Stop. I see something.'

A few feet away from the base of the giant's tower stood a large yellow dog. It was staring up at the window. When the dog caught Charlie's eye, it began to bark.

'Runner Bean!' cried Charlie.

How had his best friend's dog followed him into a painting? It couldn't happen.

But it had.

THE MELTING DOG

A few minutes after Charlie had travelled into Badlock, his best friend, Benjamin Brown, a small, tow-haired, anxious-looking boy, left his house at number twelve, Filbert Street, and crossed the road to number nine. His dog, Runner Bean, trotted behind him.

When Benjamin rang the bell at number nine, the door was immediately opened by Charlie's grandmother, Maisie.

'Benjamin, love,' cried Maisie, drawing him into the hall. 'I hope you can do something. Charlie's gone.'

'Gone, Mrs Jones? Gone where?' Benjamin dutifully wiped his shoes on the doormat.

'If I knew that I wouldn't be standing here asking you to do something, would I?' Maisie closed her eyes and scratched the back of her neck. 'Whatever am I going to tell his parents?'

'I don't expect you'll have to tell them anything,' said Benjamin. 'Perhaps my mum and dad can help, being detectives.'

Benjamin instantly regretted saying this. His parents

were working on a very important case. They had just left the house, Mrs Brown disguised as a man, and Mr Brown disguised as a woman. Benjamin didn't much like it when his parents dressed like this; they hadn't even explained the circumstances that demanded the fake moustache (for Mrs Brown) and the blonde wig (for Mr Brown), they had just told Benjamin to go over to Charlie's house, where Maisie would give him lunch.

'I'm sorry, I don't think my parents can help,' Benjamin apologised.

'I'm pretty sure they can't.' Maisie turned away and led Benjamin down a dim passage. 'This is one of those disappearances that normal people couldn't hope to solve.'

'But I'm normal,' Benjamin reminded her.

Maisie sighed. 'Well, I know. But you're a friend, and you could get one of the others: the endowed ones – or whatever they call themselves.'

'Children of the Red King,' Benjamin said quietly.

They had reached the cellar door, which stood wide open. Maisie beckoned to Benjamin and pointed into the cellar. Benjamin looked down into the murky underground room. Maisie nodded encouragingly. Benjamin didn't like cellars, nor did Runner Bean. The big dog began to whine.

'Do I have to?' Benjamin asked.

'It's down there,' said Maisie in a hushed voice.

'What is?'

'The painting, dear.'

Benjamin uttered a very slow 'Ooooh' as he realised

that Charlie must be travelling. 'He hasn't *really* disappeared then.'

'This time he has,' said Maisie solemnly.

Benjamin stared into the cellar. He descended three, four steps until he could see the whole room. A dim light, hanging from the ceiling, showed him a disused cupboard, broken chairs, curtain poles, piles of newspapers and magazines and large black plastic bags filled with bulging objects. And then he saw the painting. It was standing against one of the walls, beside an old rolled-up mattress.

A small shadow flickered over it, and Benjamin saw that a white moth was hovering round the light bulb. All at once, the moth swung away and vanished. Benjamin went to the bottom of the steps and walked over to the painting. Runner Bean scrabbled down after him. He was panting very heavily and occasionally emitted a nervous whine.

The painting gave Benjamin the shivers. He was, as Maisie had admitted, a normal boy, so he experienced none of the insistent tugs that Charlie had felt, nor did he feel or hear the moaning Badlock winds. He did, however, get the impression that the almost photographic reality of the painting showed a place that had not been imagined but copied faithfully. It existed. Or did, once. With its dark towers, sunless sky and looming mountains it was certainly a hostile, sinister country.

There was a green scrawl in the bottom right-hand corner of the painting. '*Badlock.*' If Badlock really was a place, it was not somewhere that Benjamin would have wanted to visit. So why did Charlie 'go in'? It was deserted and, as far as Benjamin could remember, Charlie had always needed first to hear a voice, and then to focus on a face, before he entered a picture. And in all the time Benjamin had known about his friend's endowment, Charlie had never actually disappeared. His physical presence had always remained in the present, while his mind roamed the world behind the pictures.

'What d'you think's going on, Ben?' asked Maisie from the top of the steps.

Benjamin shook his head. 'Don't know, Mrs Jones. Where's Charlie's uncle?'

'Paton? Bookshop,' said Maisie. 'Where else?'

'Think I'll go over there. Mr Yewbeam will know what to do.' Benjamin turned towards the steps.

Runner Bean didn't follow his master, but stood before the painting in an odd attitude, his head on one side, as though he were listening to something. He gave a low, mournful howl. And then, before Benjamin's very eyes, the yellow dog became a smaller, paler version of himself.

'Runner?' Benjamin leapt towards his dog. He touched the tip of Runner Bean's tail, which was standing out, as stiff as a broom, but in less than a second the tail had melted away and with it the whole of Benjamin's beloved dog.

Benjamin shrieked, 'RUNNER!' just as the front door slammed.

'Oh, my giddy aunt!' Maisie clapped a hand over her mouth.

She was roughly pushed aside by Grandma Bone, who had suddenly appeared beside her.

'What on earth is going on?' demanded Grandma Bone.

Benjamin stared up at the two woman. Maisie was shaking her head, her eyes were very wide and her eyebrows were working furiously up and down. She seemed to be warning him. Distraught as he was, Benjamin began to think, fast. It was always understood by Charlie and himself that Grandma Bone must know absolutely nothing about what went on, especially if it had anything at all to do with Charlie's travelling.

Grandma Bone had caught sight of Maisie's eyebrow-wriggling. 'What's the matter with you, woman?' she snarled.

'*Surprise*,' said Maisie. 'So surprised. Thought we heard a rat, didn't we, Benjamin?'

Benjamin nodded vehemently.

'*I* thought I heard a bark.' Grandma Bone glared suspiciously at Benjamin. 'Where's your dog?'

'He . . . he didn't come with me today,' said Benjamin, almost choking with distress. Could Grandma Bone see the unwrapped painting from where she stood? He didn't think so.

'Unusual. Not to bring your dog. Thought it was your shadow?' The tall woman turned on her heel and walked away, adding, 'I'd come out of that cellar if I were you.

It's more than likely the rats'll get you. Where's Charlie, by the way?'

'Gone to the bookshop,' Maisie said quickly. 'And that's just where Benjamin's going, isn't it, Ben?'

'Er – yes.'

Benjamin dragged himself regretfully up the cellar steps. He felt that he was betraying Runner Bean, leaving him trapped inside the awful painting. But what else could he do? Charlie's Uncle Paton would provide an answer. He usually knew what to do when things went wrong.

Maisie saw Benjamin to the door. 'Take care, dear,' she said. 'I don't like to think of you alone in the city, without your dog.'

'I *am* eleven,' Benjamin reminded her. 'See you later, Mrs Jones.'

'I hope so, dear.' Maisie closed the door.

Benjamin had taken only a few steps up the road when he became acutely aware that part of him was missing. The dog part. He'd been without Runner Bean before, when his parents took him to Hong Kong. But this was different. This was in a city where almost nothing was ordinary. Without warning, people could suddenly disappear, street lights could explode, snow could fall in summer.

Ingledew's Bookshop wasn't far from Filbert Street, but today it felt as though there was a huge chasm between Benjamin and safety. He was halfway down the High Street when he saw two children on the other side of the road. Joshua Tilpin, a small, untidy, sullen-looking boy, shambled beside his taller companion, a boy with a pale greenish complexion and an odd lurching walk. Dagbert-the-Drowner.

Pretending he hadn't seen them, Benjamin walked nonchalantly on, but from the corner of his eye, he saw Dagbert nudge Joshua and point across the road.

Benjamin lost his nerve. Instead of continuing up the road, he darted into a side street. For a few minutes he stood in the shadows, watching the two boys. He was being silly, he told himself. Why should he be afraid of two boys from Charlie's school? He hardly knew them. All the same, they gave him the creeps. Joshua had a reputation for making people do things against their will; not hypnotism, exactly; they called it magnetism. As for Dagbert, he drowned people. Recently, he'd tried to drown Charlie in the river.

Glancing up the street behind him, Benjamin was relieved to find that he knew where he was. He began to run.

'What's up, Benjamin Brown?' called a voice. 'Lost your dog?'

Benjamin didn't look back. Joshua and Dagbert must have raced across the road and followed him.

'You're not frightened of us, little Ben, are you?' Dagbert shouted. 'Where's Charlie?'

Almost falling over his own feet, Benjamin bounded into a cobbled square. In the centre of the square stood an old detached house. It was surrounded by a low wall and a weedy garden. Nailed to the gate was a weathered board that read, 'Gunn House'. The rest of the board was filled with music notes: crochets, quavers, minims and semibreves, though one hardly needed the musical notation to know that a family of musicians lived here. The noise coming from within the house made it obvious. The walls shook with the sound of drums, violins, flutes, cellos and singing voices.

Benjamin pressed the doorbell and a deep recorded voice announced, 'DOOR! DOOR! DOOR!'

The Gunns' door-voice always unnerved Benjamin, but then a tinkling bell would have been drowned by the music, and visitors would have waited on the step in vain.

The door was opened by Fidelio Gunn, a violin in one hand and a bow in the other. 'Hi, Ben, where's Charlie?' said the freckle-faced boy.

'Oi!' came a shout behind Benjamin.

'Charlie's – er . . . Can I come in, PLEASE?' asked Benjamin.

Catching sight of Benjamin's pursuers, Fidelio said, 'You'd better.'

Benjamin leapt into Gunn House and Fidelio slammed the door.

'What's going on, Ben?' Fidelio led the way into a chaotic kitchen. A grey cat was eating the remains of a breakfast that still hadn't been cleared from the table, and a woman in a long colourful skirt was singing at the sink. A small freckle-faced girl tuned her violin beside her.

'Pianissimo, please, Mum!' Fidelio shouted. 'Mimi,

take your violin somewhere else.'

Mrs Gunn looked over her shoulder. 'Benjamin Brown,' she sang. 'What a surprise! Can't believe my eyes! Where's the dog of impressive size?'

'Where's Charlie Bone?' asked Mimi, plucking a string.

'Look, Benjamin is a person in his own right,' said Fidelio. 'He doesn't have to have an appendage.'

'A what?' said Mimi, plucking another string.

'An attachment,' replied her brother. 'Benjamin's dog is not permanently attached to him, nor is Charlie. Sit down, Ben.'

Benjamin pulled out a chair and sat down. Feeling hungry, he picked up a piece of dry toast and took a bite out of it.

'Pudding has just licked that,' Mimi informed him.

Benjamin eyed the grey cat and sadly replaced the toast.

Fidelio took a chair beside him and leaned forward, his elbows on the table. Mimi stopped plucking at her violin and perched on the other side of the table. Mrs Gunn hummed softly while she scraped at something in the sink.

'What's happened, Ben?' asked Fidelio. 'It's not just those morons outside, is it?'

'No.' Benjamin looked at Mimi.

'Mimi always knows what's going on,' said Fidelio. 'You can't keep secrets from her, but she *can* keep a secret, can't you, Mims?'

'My lips are already sealed.' Mimi gave Benjamin a big, sealed smile.

'OK.' Benjamin began his story rather slowly, but then the drama of Runner Bean's disappearance got the better of him and he poured it all out in a tearful rush.

'I can't believe it.' Fidelio sat back. 'Charlie's never taken a dog with him before. I didn't know he could.'

'He didn't take him,' wailed Benjamin. 'Runner Bean vanished long after Charlie went in. At least I think so. But Charlie's never gone right into anything, has he? He always stays outside. It's only his mind that goes in.'

'Until now,' Fidelio remarked. 'Perhaps his endowment is developing.'

Benjamin shook his head. 'Something's wrong, Fido.' He got up and walked over to a window that overlooked the square. 'My stalkers have gone. I think I'll take a chance and run up to the bookshop. Charlie's uncle will know what to do.'

'Has he . . . has he . . . has he . . . popped the question?' sang Mrs Gunn.

'Pardon?' said Benjamin.

'Uncle Paton, Mr Yewbeam,' Mrs Gunn dropped her musical tone temporarily. 'He's surely going to make an honest woman of Miss Ingledew. How can he resist? He really ought to marry her. The whole city is waiting.'

'You mean *you're* waiting, Mum,' said Fidelio. He turned to Benjamin. 'I'll come with you, Ben. Don't like to think of you alone in this city without your dog.'

'I *am* eleven,' sighed Benjamin.

'And I'm twelve,' said Fidelio firmly. 'There's a difference.'

After weeks of dark skies and frosty winds, today a few rays of frail sunshine had begun to filter into the city. They did nothing to lift Ben's spirits. He felt quite resentful towards Charlie for doing something so risky. But that was Charlie all over. He was always rushing into situations without thinking them through.

Fidelio, who seemed to have read Benjamin's mind, said, 'It's possible that Charlie never meant to go into that painting. He might have been sucked in, against his will, just like your dog.'

'Hm,' Benjamin grunted.

The boys were now entering the narrow cobbled street that led to the cathedral. On either side of them, half-timbered houses with ancient crooked roofs leaned over the cobbles at dangerous angles. The bookshop stood directly opposite the great domed cathedral; a sign above the door read INGLEDEW'S in olde worlde script and, in the window, two large leatherbound books were displayed against a curtain of dark red velvet. Miss Ingledew sold rare and precious books.

If the boys had paid attention to the gleaming black car that stood outside the shop, they might have had second thoughts, but they were in such a hurry they rushed straight in. A small bell, attached to the inside of the door, tinkled pleasantly as they entered the shop. The sight that met their eyes, however, was not at all pleasant.

Sitting in a wheelchair beside the counter was Mr Ezekiel Bloor, the owner of Bloor's Academy. Mr Ezekiel, as he liked to be called, was a hundred and one years old and his head was as close a thing to a living skull as you're ever likely to see. He was covered in a tartan blanket and wore a red woollen hat pulled well down over his large wrinkled ears. There was very little flesh covering his large nose with its high knobbly ridge, or the sharp cheekbones and long chin. Mr Ezekiel's eyes, however, were another matter. They glittered beneath the protruding forehead as black and lively as the eyes of a ten-year-old.

Behind the ancient man's wheelchair stood a burly, bald-headed man: Mr Weedon was the school porter, chauffeur, handyman and gardener. There was nothing he would not have done for Mr Ezekiel, including murder.

Fidelio and Benjamin would gladly have stepped backwards out of the door, but it was too late to escape. They reluctantly descended the three steps into the shop.

'Aha!' croaked Ezekiel. 'What have we here? Odd customers for a rare book, I'd say. I bet you haven't got a hundred pounds to spare, Fidelio Gunn, not coming from a family of eight. You can't even afford a pair of shoes, I'd say.' He directed his mocking gaze at Fidelio's shabby trainers.

Fidelio shifted his feet self-consciously, but he was not the sort to be outdone, even by the owner of Bloor's Academy. 'I save my best for school, sir,' he said, 'and we've come to see Emma Tolly.'

'Girlfriend, is she?' snorted Ezekiel. 'The little bird?'

'Not at all, sir,' Fidelio said calmly. 'She's a friend.'

'And who's the scrawny lad trying to hide in your shadow?' Mr Ezekiel twisted his head to see Benjamin, who was, indeed, trying to hide behind Fidelio. 'Who are you, boy? Speak up!'

Benjamin was now in quite a state; desperate to get help for Runner Bean, he could scarcely concentrate on anything else, yet he knew he couldn't mention his dog's disappearance to Mr Ezekiel.

'Come on, you half-wit!' spat the old man.

Fidelio said, 'He's Benjamin Brown, sir. Charlie's friend.'

Mr Weedon decided to enter the conversation. 'So where's Charlie Bone today?' he asked, with a sneer.

Benjamin croaked, 'Busy.'

Mr Ezekiel gave a nasty chuckle. 'I know who you are. Your parents are private detectives. Hopeless sleuths. Where's your dog, Benjamin Brown?'

Benjamin screwed up his face, gritted his teeth and sent Fidelio a helpless look of despair. 'E – rr . . .'

Fidelio came to his rescue. 'He's at the vet. Benjamin's very upset.'

Mr Ezekiel threw back his head and cackled lustily. Weedon joined in with a deep chortle, while the boys watched them in baffled silence. What was so funny about a dog being at the vet?

The curtains behind the counter parted and an elegant woman with chestnut hair appeared. She was carrying a heavy gold-tooled book, which she laid very carefully on

41

the counter. 'Hello, boys. I didn't know you were here,' said Miss Ingledew.

'They're after your little bird,' Mr Ezekiel sniggered.

Miss Ingledew ignored his remark. 'I think this might be what you want, Mr Bloor,' she said, turning the book so that he could see its title.

'How much?' snapped the old man.

'Three hundred pounds,' Miss Ingledew told him.

'Three hundred.' Mr Ezekiel slammed a mottled hand on to the valuable book, causing Miss Ingledew to wince. 'I only want to know a bit about marquetry. Mother-of-pearl inlaid boxes in particular, dates and sizes, et cetera.' He began to flip the pages over with his long, bony fingers. 'Help me, Weedon.'

While the old man was occupied with the book, the two boys moved swiftly across the shop and round the counter. Mr Ezekiel began to whine about the small print as they stepped through the curtains and entered Miss Ingledew's back room.

Here, there were even more books than in the shop itself. They covered the walls from floor to ceiling: old, faded, mellow books; large on the bottom shelves and very small at the top. They gave the room a musty, leathery smell that was rather comforting. But it was, after all, a sitting room, so there were several small tables, a sofa, two armchairs, an upright leather chair and a desk. Hunched over the desk was a black-haired man who, even sitting down, seemed exceptionally tall.

The man paid no attention to the boys but continued to pore over the papers in front of him.

Fidelio cleared his throat.

Without looking up, the man said, 'If you want Emma and Olivia, they've gone to the Pets' Café.'

'Actually, Mr Yewbeam, it's you we wanted,' said Fidelio.

'Ah,' said Charlie's uncle. 'Well, I'm busy.'

'This is urgent,' Benjamin blurted out. 'Charlie's gone into a painting, and so's my dog, and they won't come out.'

'They will.' Uncle Paton continued to scrutinise the papers. 'Eventually.'

'You don't understand,' said Fidelio in as urgent a tone as he could muster. 'This time Charlie's gone *right* in he's disappeared – vanished.'

Uncle Paton raised his eyes to peer at them over the top of his half-moon spectacles. 'Vanished?'

'Yes, Mr Yewbeam. Completely gone,' said Benjamin, on the edge of tears. 'There was this painting in your cellar, and Charlie's grandma, the nice one, asked me to go down and help because Charlie had disappeared. So I went down and Runner Bean followed me, and then he . . . went in, too.'

Uncle Paton frowned. 'What sort of painting was this, Benjamin?'

'Horrible,' said Benjamin. 'Lots of dark towers and mountains. It had a name at the bottom. Badlock, I think it was.'

'*Badlock!*' Uncle Paton sprang up so rapidly his chair fell over and all the paper fluttered off the desk.

'Is it a dangerous place?' Benjamin asked breathlessly.

'The worst place in the world,' said Uncle Paton. 'Though I can't be certain that it was ever actually *in* this world.'

Benjamin's mouth fell open. He gaped at Paton Yewbeam, trying to make sense of what he had said. Even Fidelio was lost for words.

'No time to lose. Come on, boys.' Uncle Paton brushed aside the curtain and marched into the shop, quickly followed by Fidelio and Benjamin.

SQUIRRA STEW

Julia Ingledew was anxiously watching Ezekiel Bloor as he thumbed through her precious book. She didn't like to wrest it away from him in case even more damage was done. When he saw Paton Yewbeam, however, the old man looked up.

'Aha! Paton Yewbeam!' Ezekiel declared. 'Thought you didn't go out in daylight.'

'I go out when I please,' Uncle Paton retorted, snatching his fedora from a hat stand in the corner.

'Hm,' sniffed the old man as Paton strode to the door. 'I suppose that's why this *oldey worldey shoppey* is so dark. You could do with a bit of electricity in here, Mrs Books.'

Uncle Paton stopped mid-stride, causing Benjamin to walk straight into him. 'Watch your tongue, Ezekiel Bloor,' growled Paton.

'Or else . . .?' sneered Ezekiel. 'I hope you're not thinking of asking this good lady to marry you, Paton. She'd never have you, you know.' He broke into a fit of cackling.

The boys watched uneasily as both Miss Ingledew and

Paton Yewbeam turned very pink. Ezekiel had let go of the book to wipe his mouth and Miss Ingledew took the opportunity to slide the rare book away from him. Mr Weedon pulled it back again.

Recovering his composure, Paton said, 'Kindly keep your nose out of my business, Mr Bloor.'

'And you run along about yours.' Ezekiel waved his wet hand dismissively.

Paton hovered, glaring at the old man. 'I hope you're not damaging a rare book.' He looked at Miss Ingledew. 'Ju . . . Miss Ingledew, do you want me to . . .?'

'No, no,' said Miss Ingledew, still very pink. 'You go, Pa . . . Mr Yewbeam. I can see it's urgent.'

'It is rather.' Paton was now in an agony of indecision. He clearly wanted to stay and protect Miss Ingledew, but Benjamin was already halfway up the steps, and tugging at his sleeve.

'I'll ring you,' Miss Ingledew picked up her mobile, 'if anything goes wrong.'

'You do that.' Paton gave her a meaningful look and stepped through the door that Benjamin was impatiently holding open.

'What are you going to do, Mr Yewbeam?' asked Fidelio, as they sped down the street.

'It depends what is called for,' said Paton.

'Look!' Benjamin pointed down the street.

Running towards them were two girls: Emma Tolly, in a blue anorak with her blonde hair flying over her face, was struggling with a large basket, while beside her, Olivia Vertigo also carried a basket, this one smaller and obviously easier to hold. Olivia looked quite spectacular in an outsized sweater with STAR picked out in gold sequins on the front. She also wore a sparkly white hat and a gold scarf. Her hair was a deep purple.

'Mr Yewbeam,' called Olivia. 'You've got to help.'

'Please, please, please,' cried Emma. 'Something awful has happened.'

The two parties met in the middle of the street.

'We're extremely busy, girls.' Uncle Paton brushed past them and continued on his way.

'What's your awful happening?' asked Benjamin, stopping in spite of himself.

'The Pets' Café has been closed,' wailed Emma. 'Permanently. It's awful. We could see Mr Onimous sitting at a table. His head was in his hands. He looked *so* depressed.'

'We can deal with that later, Em.' Fidelio stepped round the girls. 'Something worse has happened to Charlie.'

'And Runner Bean,' Benjamin added. 'They've both gone. Vanished. Utterly disappeared into a painting.'

Emma lowered her basket, from which a loud quacking could be heard. 'What are you going to do?'

'We won't know till we get to Charlie's house,' said Fidelio, anxiously watching the departing figure of Uncle Paton.

'We'll come!' Olivia was never one to be left out of

things. 'Let's leave our pets at the bookshop, Em.'

'Wouldn't go in the shop if I were you,' Fidelio called over his shoulder. 'Old Mr Bloor is there.'

The two boys ran on while the girls stood making up their minds. Eventually, Emma decided she couldn't leave her Auntie Julia alone with Mr Bloor. She carried on up the street with her pet duck, Nancy, while Olivia hastened after the boys with her white rabbit, George.

It was a tricky time for Uncle Paton. He had emerged into the High Street, where lights blazed in every shop window. Paton pulled the brim of his black hat well down over his face, trying vainly not to glance at the windows. But today was Saturday and the High Street teemed with shoppers. Leaden clouds had covered the sun and raindrops were beginning to fall, softly at first, and then with a vengeance. Umbrellas were hastily put up and, being so tall, Paton was immediately at risk. 'Watch it!' he gasped, as he nearly lost an eye. Leaning sideways, he found himself looking into a window full of prancing mannequins.

'BANG!' The plate glass window shattered.

Amid screams of shock and disbelief, Paton hurried on. He failed to notice a red light as he sailed over the crossing, and a blue Volvo almost ran him down. 'Sorry, sorry,' called Uncle Paton, glancing at the car's side-lights. This time the explosion was quieter, a mere pop. The driver didn't even notice, and Uncle Paton was able to reach the kerb undetected.

Unfortunately, another car, unable to brake fast enough, had crashed into the back of the Volvo. Both drivers leapt out and ugly words rose into the damp air.

Suspecting that Uncle Paton might have something to do with the cracked window, the two boys pushed their way through the crowd and were just in time to see Paton, bent almost double, running away from the scene of his latest 'accident'. He had nearly reached number nine, Filbert Street, by the time they caught up with him.

'Was that you, Mr Yewbeam?' asked Benjamin. 'The window thing, I mean.'

''Fraid so, Benjamin. I'd be grateful for your silence in the matter.'

'Course, Mr Yewbeam.'

They ascended the steps of number nine, Uncle Paton leading the way. As he opened the door, he raised a finger to his lips and whispered harshly, 'Not a sound. My sister may be at home.'

'She is,' Benjamin whispered back.

There was a shriek from the street and Olivia came flying up to them, the basket swinging wildly from her hand. 'Wait for me!' she called.

'Ssssh!' hissed the boys.

'Sorry,' said Olivia, catching her breath. 'Is the demented grandma about?'

Benjamin nodded. Olivia scrambled up the steps and hopped into the hall with the others. Uncle Paton quietly closed the door, and Olivia plonked her basket beside the coat-stand.

They tiptoed into the kitchen, where Maisie was waiting anxiously. 'Nothing's happened,' she said. 'Not a sign. I keep taking a look, but the wretched picture just sits there, looking back at me. D'you know what? I can feel a kind of smugness coming from it.'

'We'll take a look.' Uncle Paton removed his hat.

Benjamin's stomach gave a loud bleat.

'Goodness,' Maisie exclaimed. 'I've even forgotten lunch. That's a first. I'll get a bit ready while you lot go down into the cellar.'

Uncle Paton thought it unnecessary for them all to visit the cellar. Telling Fidelio and Olivia to wait in the kitchen, he chose just Benjamin to accompany him. Benjamin had, after all, seen Runner Bean vanish, and he could tell if the painting had changed at all.

Paton lit three candles in a tall candelabrum that stood on the dresser. 'Don't, whatever you do, turn the light on in the cellar,' he told Benjamin.

'Course not, Mr Yewbeam,' Benjamin said emphatically.

Paton descended the steps backwards with the candelabrum in his right hand. Benjamin followed.

'Ye gods, what a grim place!' Paton declared as the flickering candlelight played over the surface of the painting.

Benjamin shuddered. Badlock had looked sinister before. In candlelight it looked terrifying. He could hardly bear to think what might have become of Runner Bean in such an awful place. And then he saw it. At the bottom of the painting, peeping round the corner of one of the towers, was a dog. Runner Bean. His mouth was open in a silent howl.

Benjamin screamed.

'What the –' Uncle Paton almost dropped the candelabrum.

'Look, look, Mr Yewbeam!' Benjamin pointed a shaking finger at Runner Bean.

Paton bent closer to the dog's head.

Benjamin's scream had brought the others rushing to the cellar door.

'What is it? What's happened?' Maisie demanded.

'Can I come down, *please*?' begged Olivia. 'I can't stand not knowing.'

'Runner's h-h-here . . .' Benjamin quavered.

'Here?' said Fidelio.

'Here . . . but, not *here*. *There*,' moaned Benjamin.

'In the painting.' Uncle Paton's tone gave the already tense atmosphere an edge of menace. This was too much for Olivia, who began to scramble down the steps. She was stopped by a shout from the hall.

'RABBIT!' screamed Grandma Bone.

Grandma Bone was scared of most animals, but harmless rabbits were her bêtes noires.

Olivia reluctantly climbed back, while Fidelio said calmly, 'It's all right, Mrs Bone. It won't hurt you.'

'It's EVIL,' shrilled Grandma Bone, and then she saw Olivia. 'What are you doing here, you harpy?'

Olivia had never been called a harpy before. She was rather pleased. Her rabbit, George, had escaped from his basket and was now halfway up the stairs, happily grazing the carpet. Grandma Bone was standing at the top; one of her small black eyes was screwed shut, the other watched the rabbit's progress in horror.

Olivia leapt up the stairs, grabbed her rabbit and carried him back to his basket. 'He honestly wouldn't hurt a fly,' she said, fastening the basket lid.

'I asked you what you were doing here.' Feeling safer, Grandma Bone slowly descended the stairs.

Before Olivia could think of a reply, Uncle Paton emerged from the cellar and said, 'I think it's about time you answered a few of *my* questions, Grizelda.'

'Such as?' Grandma Bone tossed her head imperiously.

'Such as – what is that painting doing in the cellar, and where has it come from?'

'None of your business.' With a wary glance at George's basket, Grandma Bone swept down the stairs and crossed the hall into the sitting room. Uncle Paton followed her and the three children trooped after him. Maisie, however, sank on to the hall chair with a baffled sigh.

'It *is* my business,' Uncle Paton insisted.

Grandma Bone settled herself in an armchair and picked up a newspaper.

'Are you listening to me, Grizelda?' roared Uncle Paton,

and then, to the concern of the three children hovering by the door, he said, 'Your grandson has vanished into that painting.'

Benjamin muttered, 'We're not supposed to tell . . .'

Grandma Bone lowered her newspaper. Her long, grumpy face was momentarily transformed by a look of pure delight. 'But that's what he does,' she said.

In the giant's tower, Charlie gave Runner Bean a brief wave, before being lowered to the floor by Otus.

'A dog?' said Otus. 'Their like is ne'er seen in Badlock.'

'We must rescue him before those awful troll-things come back,' said Charlie, making for the door.

'Boy, wait!' commanded Otus. 'This is not as simple as it seems.'

'Nothing here is simple.' Charlie began to run down the stone spiral.

'STOP!' The giant's huge roar echoed down the stairwell and Charlie was forced to obey. 'It is most likely a trick, Charlie, to force you into the open. Come back, I beg you.'

Charlie reluctantly trudged back to the giant's room. The situation would be hopeless, he realised, if both he and Runner Bean were caught. 'I feel so guilty,' he told the giant, 'leaving him out there all alone, specially now he's seen me.'

'I know, I know.' Otus lit a candle and set it on the table. 'But all about us there are towers and watchers.

Soon the darkness will come, a darkness like no other, Charlie. No stars shine in Badlock and moonlight is – scarce. So we will creep down our tower and rescue the poor dog then.'

The giant stirred the pot hanging over his stove. 'I had a dog once, in the world we come from. It was a fine dog and we were scarce parted. Here in Badlock there are no dogs or cats. There are only bugs and slimy, creeping, cold-blooded things called durgles. And the birds fly on bony featherless wings, and they have long, fearful beaks.'

Charlie climbed on to the giant's bed. 'Why are there no dogs or cats?'

'The shadow and his people consider a creature's use is solely for the food it can provide, or for the pelt that can become a cloak, a jerkin, or even shoes. Every warm-blooded creature has been hunted, almost to extinction. Only squirras survive; they breed like demons, that is the reason, perhaps.'

'What about blancavamps?' asked Charlie.

'Aha, the blancabats.' Otus smiled. 'They dare not touch the blancavamps, for they are ghosties.' He ladled several dollops of steamy stew into two wooden bowls. 'Come to the table, Charlie-my-descendent, and eat your supper.'

Charlie hauled himself off the bed and on to the tall chair, while the giant tore a round loaf in two and placed a piece beside each bowl. He then half-sat on the table and began to swish the bread into the stew, using it as a kind of spoon. Charlie did the same. Squirra stew was surprisingly good, but then Charlie was very hungry.

They ate in silence for a while. Charlie kept thinking of the dog outside the tower. How frightened he must be. And then the warm stew settled in his stomach and he could only think how comforting it was. Occasionally he glanced at his ancestor's face. He could see no resemblance between the Yewbeams he knew and the giant. Grandma Bone and her sisters had tiny black eyes and thin lips, while Otus had grey eyes, and a wide, generous mouth. But, of course, many generations had come between them.

'Tell me about your life,' said the giant, scraping the last morsel from his bowl.

Charlie licked his fingers until every delicious trace of the stew was gone, and then he began. He told the giant how his father had been hypnotised by Manfred Bloor, and lived for ten long years in the school called Bloor's Academy, while no one knew he was there. He went on to say how he, Charlie, had discovered his talent for travelling into pictures. He described Grandma Bone and her terrible sisters, and his friends, the normal boys like Fidelio and Benjamin. 'Only Fidelio isn't really normal,' Charlie added. 'He's a musical prodigy and one day he'll be famous.'

And then Charlie recounted some of his adventures with those other children, the endowed, descendants of the Red King, like himself. Emma, who could fly, Billy, who understood animals, Lysander, who could call up his

spirit ancestors, Tancred the storm-bringer, Gabriel the
clairvoyant, 'And there's Olivia.' Charlie gave a chuckle.
'She's an illusionist, but the Bloors don't know about her.
She's kind of our secret weapon.'

'So this ancient man, Ezekiel, keeps you prisoner in his
Academy for the . . . the?' The giant looked at Charlie
questioningly.

'Gifted, I suppose you'd call it,' said Charlie. 'And
we're not really prisoners.'

'But under his control.'

'Sometimes we disobey.'

'Good! Good!' cried Otus, clapping his hands. He
glanced up at the window. 'Darkness has come. The dog
can be rescued.'

'Runner Bean!' Charlie had almost forgotten poor
Runner Bean while he'd been talking to the giant.

Otus led the way down the tower. He held the candle
in an iron dish. It smelled like burning fat and cast huge
leaping shadows on the stone walls. When they reached
the outer door, the giant stopped and listened. Charlie
waited beside him, scarcely able to breathe.

Otus had barely opened the door, before Charlie rushed
out. He was met by such an overpowering blackness, he
felt he might have been blinded. And through the terrible
dark came the winds, first from one side, then another,
driving him against the wall of the tower, dragging his
legs, howling in his head.

'RUNNER!' Charlie screamed into the wind.

He waited for an answering bark. But nothing could be heard above the winds.

'Best return, boy,' called Otus. 'He has been taken.'

'No!' Charlie ran blindly forward. Suddenly, he was falling. He landed with a groan on to hard, rocky ground. Putting out a hand, he felt a damp wall. Something scuttled over his fingers and he screamed again.

There came a deep, throaty bark and, even in his dangerous position, Charlie felt a surge of joy. 'Runner!' he called.

The giant's voice drifted above the wind. 'Cursed giant that I am. I should have warned you of the pits. Where are you, boy?'

'Here!' cried Charlie. He heard the thud of boots. A giant hand touched his, and then he was being hauled up the side of the pit. As he reached the top, a shaft of weak, ragged moonlight showed him a large yellow dog perched on the rim. 'Runner!' he shouted.

Runner Bean barked delightedly as the giant bundled boy and dog towards the tower. 'Hush, dog!' he said, pushing them both through the door.

Charlie grabbed the excited dog's collar, while Otus closed the door and drew two heavy bolts across it.

'Faith, that dog will have us all in chains before night has passed,' the giant muttered.

'Did someone hear us?' Charlie stroked Runner Bean's head, calming him down.

'I fear my neighbour,' Otus admitted, as he ascended

the stone staircase. 'His tower is close, and he is not a kind man.'

Now that Runner Bean had found Charlie, he seemed reluctant to climb the shadowy steps. Charlie had to coax him up with strokes and promises of bones, though he had no idea if any would be found once they reached the giant's room.

The giant had thought ahead. By the time Charlie had enticed the nervous dog to the top of the stairs, Otus had fished two bones out of the cooking pot. Flinging them across the floor, he chuckled, 'Chew on those, brave dog.'

'I don't think he feels very brave,' Charlie remarked as he watched Runner Bean ravenously gnawing the bones.

'Charlie, you must flee from here,' Otus said gravely. 'We cannot hope to hide that dog. Soon my neighbour will alert Oddthumb and his crew. You will hear the horn, and then you must be gone.'

'But how?' Charlie gazed round the giant's room. 'I can't,' he said in a strangled voice. 'I don't know how I got here. When I travel I have a wand . . .'

'A wand?' The giant's eyes widened. 'Truly, you are a magician, then?'

'No, no.' Charlie shook his head. 'It's just something that I inherited from my other ancestor, a Welsh wizard. It'd take too long to explain.'

Too long, indeed, for, at that moment, the eerie sound of a wailing horn echoed round the giant's tower.

'Oh, mercy, what's to be done?' The giant strode round

and round, clenching his fists and glaring at the high window. 'I shall defend you with my last breath, Charlie. But I am only one. I cannot prevail. Oddthumb will take you. Oh, poor boy, what is to become of you?'

The giant's mournful voice was too much for Runner Bean. He leapt up with a dreadful howl – and something astonishing happened. From inside one of the dog's ears, a white moth fluttered out. She came to rest on Charlie's arm.

'Claerwen,' breathed Charlie. 'My wand.'

'In my day, we called such things moths,' said the baffled giant.

'Yes, yes. She is a moth, but she was once a wand,' Charlie told the giant. 'Mr Yewbeam, Otus – we can go now. Thank you, thank you . . .'

'Then go,' said Otus, 'for I can hear troll feet. Swiftly, swiftly, Charlie Bone.'

'Maybe I could take you with me, Otus?'

The giant sadly shook his head. 'An impossibility. Go now, Charlie.'

Charlie flung his arm round Runner Bean. 'I'll came back, Otus, I promise. I'll find a way to get you out of Badlock.' Gazing at the moth, he cried, 'Claerwen, take me home.'

The room about him began to jerk and jolt. Defying gravity, the table, chair and bed tumbled sideways, then became airborne. Charlie was treading air. Now he was upside down. His ears were bombarded with a thousand sounds. He felt Runner's coarse hair melting under his fingers and tried to grip it tighter, but something, or someone, was trying to tear the dog from his grasp. And then his hand was empty and he was whirling away.

Charlie caught one last glimpse of his ancestor's kind, incredulous face before he was thrust through time, through a sparkling, shifting web of sounds, smells and sensations.

He landed with a light bump on the cold cellar floor of number nine, Filbert Street. The painting of Badlock stood against the wall behind him. Giving it one brief glance, Charlie ran to the steps and climbed up to the hall. He could hear voices arguing above him.

'Mercy on us!' yelled Maisie, jumping out of her chair. 'Charlie's back!'

There was a sudden silence in the sitting room. Uncle Paton stepped out, followed by Fidelio, Benjamin and Olivia.

'Charlie!' cried Benjamin. 'Have you got Runner?'

Charlie still felt unsteady. Grasping the banister for support, he said, 'Bit of a problem there, Ben.'

GREEN VAPOUR

'Charlie Bone, I hate you!'

Benjamin's sudden explosion was so out of character Charlie could only stare at his friend in astonishment.

'You're always doing it,' yelled Benjamin. 'You're always losing my dog. That time he nearly drowned, and that other time when the Enchanter came and –'

'Benjamin Brown,' roared Uncle Paton, 'control yourself.'

Benjamin's mouth closed in a grim pout. His usually pale face had turned an angry red and his eyes were filled with tears.

Charlie stared miserably at his feet. 'I'm sorry, but I tried to bring Runner with me, I really did.'

'You saw him?' Benjamin almost choked on his words. 'How come you got out and he couldn't? He's trapped in that awful place . . . and . . . and . . .'

Uncle Paton put a hand on Benjamin's shoulder and gently propelled him towards the kitchen. 'Come and sit down, all of you. We need to discuss things carefully.'

A voice called from the sitting room. 'Oh, what a to-do!'

'I suppose this is some devilish plan of yours, Grizelda?' Uncle Paton retorted.

'Mine?' came the plaintive cry. 'I know nothing whatever about it. That painting was all wrapped up. How did I know Charlie would start prying?'

'You knew all right,' muttered Uncle Paton. Having got everyone into the kitchen, he slammed the door.

'I'll make some sandwiches,' said Maisie in her soothing, matter-of-fact voice.

Everyone sat at the kitchen table while Maisie started slicing bread. Uncle Paton paced up and down, pinching his chin and scratching his head.

'Charlie, aren't you going to tell us what happened?' Olivia demanded.

Charlie looked at Benjamin, sitting hunched at the end of the table. 'OK . . . if you all want to know.'

'Course we do,' said Fidelio. 'That's why we're here.'

'It was weird,' Charlie began, with another glance in Benjamin's direction. 'I was just standing there, looking at the painting, when I felt myself being kind of dragged towards it. It was all wrapped up, but I heard a sound coming from it – the wind.'

'The wind?' Uncle Paton stopped pacing and came to sit at the table.

'Go on,' urged Olivia.

'So I unwrapped the painting, just a bit, and then, suddenly, I was there. I hardly travelled at all. It was as if the painting reached out and sucked me in.' Charlie looked round at the expectant faces. Even Benjamin was staring at him.

'Yes,' said Uncle Paton, 'and then?'

'And then I met the giant.'

'A GIANT!' everyone exclaimed, including Maisie, who squeaked as well, having accidentally slammed her fingers in the fridge.

'A sort of giant,' Charlie amended. He went on to tell them about Oddthumb and the troll army, about the squirras and blancavamps, the black fortress on the mountain and, finally, how Runner Bean had arrived, with Charlie's moth hidden in his ear.

Not once during Charlie's long account did anyone say a word and when he came to the end, such a deep silence had fallen in the room, no one seemed inclined to break it, until Benjamin said, very softly, 'What will happen to Runner if the trolls want his pelt?'

Before anyone dared to make a guess, Maisie put a huge plate of sandwiches on the table, saying, 'Have some food, kids.'

'I hope that applies to me, too,' said Uncle Paton, reaching for a sandwich with apple and walnut clearly visible along one side. 'Charlie,' he continued, 'you told us that you saw a black fortress in Badlock.'

'In the distance.' Charlie spoke through a mouthful of cheese and pickle. 'The Enchanter's fortress. Just looking at it gave me the creeps.'

'Hm.' Uncle Paton smoothed back a long lock of black

hair that he had almost eaten with the sandwich. 'It occurs to me that Harken the Enchanter is at work again.'

'He can't be,' Fidelio argued. 'Charlie and the others got rid of him when they chanted that spell around the King's tree.'

'He *must* have gone,' cried Olivia, jumping up and down in her seat, 'because Charlie's mother was saved and . . . and his father woke up, and . . . and Joshua's mother, the witch, has vanished.'

'And he doesn't live in Kingdom's Department Store any more,' Benjamin assured them, 'because Mum and Dad met the new owner when they were on a shop-lifting case there, and they said he was quite normal, except for being overweight, in Mum's opinion anyway.'

'Nevertheless,' Uncle Paton turned to Charlie. 'Is there still a shadow in the King's portrait?'

Charlie confessed that there was. The portrait hung in the King's Room at Bloor's Academy, and Charlie had often tried to enter it, but always a dark shadow behind the King prevented Charlie from meeting his famous ancestor.

'I rest my case,' said Uncle Paton.

Olivia raised an eyebrow. 'What does that mean, Mr Yewbeam?'

Uncle Paton sighed. 'It means, my dear Olivia, that if there is a shadow in the King's portrait, a shadow remains in our lives; it's very faint,' he added, observing the children's anxious faces, 'but it's a shadow, nevertheless. It seems to me that someone is still communicating with

Harken the Enchanter, hence the arrival of that painting, and the unusual manner of Charlie's journey into Badlock.'

Uncle Paton found the five pairs of eyes trained expectantly upon him rather disconcerting. Realising that he would have to come up with something better, he said, 'But who, or what, or why . . . I can't yet fathom. Unless,' he scratched his chin, 'unless someone is using the mirror.'

'The Mirror of Amoret was cracked,' Charlie said slowly, 'when Joshua stole it from me.'

'Perhaps it's been mended,' Benjamin suggested, as he tried to wish away the awful vision of a starved dog chained to a block of stone while Oddthumb the troll approached with a large pair of shears.

The Mirror of Amoret had not been mended. Mrs Tilpin, née Chrystal, might have been a witch, but she had her limitations. She had tried every spell she could find in *The Collected Charms and Bewitchments of Steffania Sugwash* (a book she had inherited from her uncle, the notorious Silas Sugwash), all to no avail. So she had decided to enrol some of the endowed students at Bloor's Academy, in a small weekend class, where she hoped their special powers could be combined to mend the precious, but sadly damaged, Mirror of Amoret.

With Manfred Bloor's assistance, Mrs Tilpin had managed to hide herself away in the basement of Bloor's Academy. Here she lived with her son, Joshua, who resented every moment spent in the two damp and dingy rooms, while his mother chanted and hummed and burned herbs in iron bowls and sometimes made him dance horrible dances with her. But she was his mother, and he didn't blame her; oh no, he blamed Charlie Bone, who had caused his mother to reveal herself, Charlie who had stolen the Mirror of Amoret and made Joshua break it.

Not many children would choose to spend their Saturday afternoons in a dank basement room at Bloor's Academy, but Dorcas Loom and the Branko twins, Idith and Inez, were keen admirers of Fairy Tilpin, as they liked to call her. This description might once have applied but not since Mrs Tilpin had been communicating with Harken the Enchanter. Joshua was, of course, in attendance, but the last member of the group, Dagbert Endless, was less enthusiastic. While the others leaned over Mrs Tilpin's table, listening with rapt attention, Dagbert preferred to pace in the shadows. Occasionally, he would glance at the little group with a slightly superior expression on his face. This annoyed Mrs Tilpin, but she never once criticised Dagbert, for she knew that he was the most powerful of all the children, and if she were to bring Harken the Enchanter back into the world, then Dagbert would be an invaluable ally.

Today, Mrs Tilpin was feeling especially optimistic. The children were ready to progress. She put *The Collected Charms and Enchantments of Steffania Sugwash* into a cupboard and locked the door with the small silver key that she kept in her pocket.

'Aww! Aren't you going to tell us about Steffania today?' One of the Branko twins sent a spindly chair teetering across the room.

'Petulance will get you nowhere,' admonished Mrs Tilpin. 'Who did it?'

'I did,' said the twin who was responsible.

'Yes, but *which* twin are you?'

'Can't you tell, Mrs T?' The voice came from the shadows beside a looming cupboard. 'And I thought you knew everything.'

Mrs Tilpin decided to ignore Dagbert. 'If you don't tell me which twin you are, then the lesson is over.'

The Branko twins, sitting close to each other, stared at Mrs Tilpin from under their deep black fringes. Their round porcelain-white faces showed not a trace of emotion, but then one of them suddenly cried, 'Inez, Fairy Tilpin. I'm Inez.'

'No you're not, you're Idith,' said Dagbert.

This time he had gone too far. 'Dagbert Endless, if you don't stop sabotaging my class, I shall have no alternative but to dismiss you.'

'OK.' Dagbert strode towards the dilapidated planks of wood that served as a door to the so-called classroom.

'Stop!' Mrs Tilpin commanded.

Dagbert reached the door and glared back.

Mrs Tilpin eyed the sullen-looking boy with distaste. He smelled of fish, his face had a greenish hue, and his lanky hair put her in mind of seaweed. But she needed him.

'I didn't say you *were* dismissed,' said Mrs Tilpin in a slightly wheedling tone. 'I'm sure we can get along if we try a little harder. There's something I wanted to show you in particular, Dagbert.'

'Why Dagbert?' asked Joshua.

'Well, all of you,' said his mother and, with a dramatic flourish, she reached under the table and produced a gleaming, jewel-framed mirror. Holding it out so that each one of them received an almost blinding flash from its shining surface, she announced, 'The Mirror of Amoret.'

'It's cracked,' Dagbert observed.

'Exactly.' Mrs Tilpin smiled.

'What do you mean – exactly?' asked Dorcas Loom in her monotonous voice.

Mrs Tilpin wasn't completely without feeling. She felt sorry for Dorcas, with her large pink face and drab over-permed hair. 'Well, dear, the reason I'm showing you the mirror is *because* it's cracked. I thought if we combined our considerable powers, then we might, just might, be able to mend it.' She laid the mirror on the table, noting with satisfaction that Dagbert had moved closer.

The three girls leaned eagerly over the table and peered into the silvery glass. Expecting to find themselves reflected in the mirror, they were surprised to see a mist of subtle colours swirling over the surface.

'It's like water,' said Inez.

Dagbert stepped closer and looked over Joshua's shoulder.

'Why can't we see ourselves?' asked Dorcas.

'Because you are not there,' murmured the witch.

Dagbert directed a sceptical look at her. 'We're here,' he stated, 'so we should be there.' He pointed at the mirror.

'Ah. But this is the Mirror of Amoret,' said Mrs Tilpin. 'I can see that you don't know the story, Dagbert. I shall enlighten you. Nine hundred years ago, the Red King, whom we, in this room, acknowledge to be our ancestor, had –'

'Not the only ancestor,' Dagbert pointed out.

'Ssshhh!' hissed everyone.

Mrs Tilpin continued as though the interruption had not happened, '. . . had ten children. Lilith, his eldest daughter, married Harken the Enchanter and I am descended from their union.'

'Phew!' Dagbert whistled.

'Amoret, the King's youngest daughter, married a . . .' Mrs Tilpin waved her white fingers in the air, 'a giant, I believe.'

Dagbert whistled again, but everyone ignored him.

'The King made a mirror for Amoret, a mirror that enabled her to travel. She had only to look into this mirror and think of the person she wished to see, and there she would be, beside them.'

At this point Joshua took up the story that, by now, he knew only too well. 'But Amoret died and Count Harken inherited the mirror.'

'Really? Inherited the mirror, did he?' Dagbert gave a very slight snort of disbelief.

Mrs Tilpin's grey eyes flashed. 'Yesss! Inherited!'

'I wish you wouldn't keep interrupting, Dagbert,' Idith complained. 'It spoils it for the rest of us.'

'*So* sorry!' Dagbert shrugged and walked away.

'Wait!' commanded Mrs Tilpin. 'I brought Harken back with this.' She grabbed the mirror and held it up.

'But Charlie Bone got it, and we had a fight, and I broke it,' said Joshua, 'and then he found a spell to send the Enchanter back into Badlock.'

'And there he stays until the mirror can be mended,' continued Mrs Tilpin. 'But we can do it, can't we, children? You and I together, so that Harken can walk among us once again.'

They gazed up at the sallow-skinned, beetle-browed woman, who had once been so blonde and pleasant-looking. Her hair was now lank and colourless, her eyes ringed with black shadows, even her lips had shrunk to a thin purple line. Was this what happened when you gave in to witchery? wondered the girls.

Dagbert Endless moved restlessly towards the make-shift door. 'I drown people,' he said. 'I don't see how I can mend glass.'

'Look!' ordered Mrs Tilpin, desperately waving the mirror. 'Be surprised, Dagbert Endless! Be awed, wonder-struck, amazed.'

Dagbert obliged her with a cursory glance at the jewel-framed mirror. And then he looked again. His eyes widened and his jaw dropped. For there, among the constantly shifting shapes and colours, a figure was forming. First a bright emerald tunic, then an olive-skinned, but oddly featureless, face appeared beneath a cloud of golden brown hair. Gradually, in the oval of the face, two dark green eyes emerged; they seemed to be staring directly at Dagbert and, under their fierce, compelling gaze, he found himself moving towards the mirror.

But Mrs Tilpin's moment of triumph was stolen by an earsplitting crash. The rotten wood of the door suddenly gave way and a small white-haired boy fell into the room. He lay face-down on the shattered panels, and everyone stared at him in astonished silence, until Mrs Tilpin found her voice.

'Billy Raven!' she screamed. 'Spy!'

'Snoop!' cried Joshua.

'Eavesdropping snitch!' said Dorcas.

'Nosy-parker!' shouted the twins.

'How did you find us, Billy?' asked Dagbert, who had shaken himself free of the dark green gaze.

Billy Raven got to his feet a little awkwardly and adjusted his spectacles. 'I was looking for the dog,' he said.

'That scabby old Blessed,' snorted Joshua.

Mrs Tilpin laid her mirror very gently on the table and walked over to Billy. 'Why are you not staying with Charlie Bone?' she asked in a cold voice.

'He forgot to ask me,' sniffed Billy, picking a splinter out of his palm.

'*Forgot*,' said Mrs Tilpin. 'That's not very nice. I thought he was your friend.'

'He is,' Billy mumbled, 'but sometimes he's busy.'

'Aww!' said Dorcas. 'Poor Billy.'

Billy chewed his lip and darted a furtive look at the table. A vaporous green cloud was rising from the mirror and curling up towards the damp ceiling. Everyone turned to watch it, their mouths open and eyes wide.

'What's that?' Billy whispered.

Mrs Tilpin clasped her hands with a look of ecstasy. 'That, Billy Raven, is a message from my ancestor. It seems that you have disappointed him.'

'Me?' The chill that ran down Billy's spine had nothing to do with the temperature in Mrs Tilpin's room. The sight of the green vapour so terrified him, he even failed to hear the snap of wood as someone stepped over the broken door.

Suddenly Billy's shoulders were grabbed from behind and the small boy gasped with shock.

'What are you doing here?' Manfred Bloor swung Billy round to face him. 'Why aren't you staying with Charlie Bone?'

Billy looked into the cruel black eyes gazing down at him. He had always been mortally afraid of Manfred Bloor; with his bony face and narrow shoulders, he looked more like an old man than a youth of nineteen. His long hair, tied in a ponytail, was already streaked with grey, and his tight black sweater only emphasised his scrawny frame.

'Well?' snarled Manfred.

'He . . . he didn't ask,' faltered Billy.

'Didn't ask. That's no excuse.' Manfred glanced disdainfully at the children seated round the table, and then he noticed Dagbert and he gave a brief half-smile.

All that remained of the green vapour was a thin cloud that clung to the brick ceiling like a mildewy cob-web. Manfred didn't appear to have seen it. 'Scoot, kids!' he barked. 'I want a private word with Mrs Tilpin.'

With a chorus of 'Yes, Manfred,' Dorcas, the twins and Joshua gathered up their notebooks and made for the door. Dagbert said nothing, but he followed the others as they stepped over the splintered planks. And then he looked back briefly and murmured, 'She wants to let an enchanter loose on the world. What d'you think of that, Manfred?'

'I think it's an excellent idea,' Manfred replied, with another of his sinister smiles.

'Really?' Dagbert raised his eyebrows and stepped into the dark passage.

'You too,' said Manfred, addressing the white-haired boy, who seemed to be in a trance.

Billy shook himself. He looked around the room, as though he had no idea how he had got there, and then walked slowly through the doorway.

'Tell Mr Weedon to come and mend the door you broke,' Mrs Tilpin called after him.

'Yes,' said Billy weakly.

Manfred lifted two of the wooden planks and laid them across the draughty gap. Rubbing his hands free of dust, he came and sat at the table. 'Very satisfactory,' he said, his wide grin revealing a row of long, yellow teeth.

'You're very pleased with yourself,' Mrs Tilpin remarked.

'Oh, I am, Titania. Didn't you notice?'

'Notice?' Mrs Tilpin appeared to be more interested in her mirror than anything Manfred had to say.

'It's coming back!' Manfred gripped the edge of the table and leaned forward. 'My endowment, Titania. Remember, you said it would return if I was patient. "Relax," you said, "try it out occasionally but don't force it." Well, I've just hypnotised Billy Raven. Didn't you notice?'

'I suppose so.' Mrs Tilpin frowned into her mirror. 'He's not happy,' she mumbled.

'When those leopards attacked me I thought I was done for, but it's quite the reverse. I'm stronger than ever.' Manfred spread out his long thin arms.

'I expect it was anger,' said Mrs Tilpin, without taking her eyes from the mirror, 'anger and fear, both powerful agents. They can channel the forces that lie dormant within us.'

'Is that so?' Manfred frowned at the mirror. 'What's going on, Titania?'

Her gaze still held by the mirror, Mrs Tilpin said, 'He was expecting the albino. And I haven't given you permission to use my first name.'

Manfred shrugged. 'Apologies, Fairy Tilpin, but it suits you so well.'

Mrs Tilpin grimaced. She had never known how to accept a compliment. 'I feel it when he's angry, right here.' She jabbed her stomach. 'He expected Billy today. When Eustacia Yewbeam took the painting she assured me that the albino would be with Charlie.'

'What's the hurry? We'll make sure the kid sees the painting next Saturday. He'll start talking to the dog and Harken will have him.'

'The dog might not last a week,' Mrs Tilpin said sullenly. 'Trolls eat dogs, you know.'

'Poor doggie.'

Mrs Tilpin stamped her foot. 'Don't be so frivolous. Have you forgotten the Enchanter is doing this for you? He has promised to hold the boy until that wretched will is found and destroyed. What do you imagine will happen if Lyell Bone returns and remembers where the will is kept? The game will be up, Manfred Bloor. Billy Raven inherits everything, remember: this house, the ancient castle, even the treasures hidden under old Ezekiel's bed.'

Manfred lost his smile and a look of such icy cunning entered his face, Mrs Tilpin found herself holding the mirror tight to her chest, as though the green figure swirling in the glass could protect her from the youth's deadly stare.

'Lyell Bone will never return,' said Manfred. 'We'll see to that.'

THE PETS' CAFÉ
IS CLOSED

Long after his friends had left Charlie still wandered the house. Up and down the stairs, in and out of his room and down into the cellar, where he would stare at Runner Bean's image, at the strands of white hairs on his yellow beard, his shiny black nose and reproachful brown eyes that gazed into Charlie's.

'I'm trying to get you out of there, Runner,' Charlie would murmur, but try as he might, he couldn't reach the dog trapped in Badlock, a place that might not even exist in the real world. Someone had created a barrier between Charlie and the poor creature he longed to rescue. Charlie had a very good idea who it was, for he met the same impenetrable wall whenever he tried to enter the Red King's portrait.

Uncle Paton had retreated to his room to consider the problem. In his opinion Billy Raven was the one to unlock the mystery of Runner Bean's incarceration. For there was a chance that the albino could somehow communicate with the dog in the painting.

But Billy was imprisoned in Bloor's Academy, and there was no likelihood of his being released at this late hour on a Sunday. They would have to wait for next weekend, when Charlie must make sure that Billy came home with him.

'A week might be too long,' Charlie declared, thinking of Oddthumb and his partiality for dog meat.

Maisie, her usually cheerful face creased with worry, put on the kitchen television. 'There's nothing we can do for now, Charlie,' she said, 'so we might as well cheer ourselves up.'

Charlie couldn't agree. He was about to go back to the cellar when Grandma Bone came downstairs, dressed up for an evening out with her sisters. Charlie stood by the cellar door, watching the tall figure stride to the front door. Knowing it would be useless, Charlie couldn't stop himself from calling out to her.

'Grandma! Please, please, do you know why my friend's dog got locked in that painting?'

Grandma Bone hesitated.

Charlie walked towards her. 'If you know why it's happened, can you tell me how I can get Runner Bean out of there?'

'I hope you've done your homework,' said Grandma Bone. 'School tomorrow.' She turned the door handle.

'*Please*, Grandma!' begged Charlie.

Without another word his grandmother opened the front door and swept out, leaving the wind to slam the door behind her.

'Thanks, Grandma!' Charlie muttered.

He had only taken a few steps back to the cellar when the doorbell rang. Had Grandma Bone forgotten her keys? Charlie was tempted to ignore the bell, but it continued to ring in a rather frantic way. Whoever it was, with their finger glued to the bell, they weren't going to give up until someone answered.

Charlie trudged back to the front door. He had hardly turned the handle, when a small brown-haired woman in a man's tweed suit and cap burst into the hall. Charlie just about recognised Benjamin's mother, Mrs Brown.

'Charlie, where's your uncle?' Mrs Brown demanded.

'He's busy.' Charlie knew that Uncle Paton hated to be disturbed at dusk, when all the lights came on. 'If it's about Runner –'

'Of *course* it is!' cried Mrs Brown. 'What have you done? Benjamin's distraught, inconsolable . . .'

'I know . . .' Charlie began.

'You don't know, Charlie Bone, or you wouldn't have done it.'

'But I –'

'Paton!' Mrs Brown called up the stairs. 'I know you're there. I saw your candle in the window. I *must* speak to you.'

A door opened and Uncle Paton appeared at the top of the stairs. 'What is it, Patricia?' he said brusquely.

'What is it? You know very well,' cried Mrs Brown. 'You've got Benjamin's dog in here, and we want him back.'

'He's not exactly in –' Charlie tried to tell her.

Apparently, Mrs Brown would rather Charlie didn't exist. 'Be quiet,' she said. 'I'm talking to your uncle. Where is Runner Bean? I want to see him.'

'If you insist.' Uncle Paton went back to his room and reappeared with a candle. 'Kindly refrain from switching on the lights,' he said as he descended the staircase.

'I wouldn't dream of it,' said Mrs Brown.

Uncle Paton led her down into the cellar, while Charlie followed, a few steps behind. When Mrs Brown saw Runner Bean's painted image, howling silently out of the nightmarish landscape, she gave a shriek and clasped her face in her hands.

'What happened?' she gasped. 'Benjamin was incoherent. I couldn't make sense of what he told me.'

Charlie began to explain and this time Mrs Brown allowed him to tell the whole story, or at least Runner Bean's part in it. Charlie omitted most of the details about Badlock and didn't disclose that the man who rescued him was a giant.

'What are you going to do?' asked Mrs Brown at last. 'How are you going to get our dog out of there?'

'I was hoping you'd help, Patricia,' Uncle Paton said wryly. 'You being a detective.'

'Don't be flippant, Paton,' she snapped. 'I can't deal with . . . with all this magic stuff. Oh, sometimes I wish Benjamin and Charlie had never become friends. I shouldn't have let it go on, once I knew that Charlie was . . . different.'

Paton glared at her. 'You let their friendship continue because Maisie looks after your son while you're gallivanting round the country disguised as Sherlock Holmes.' He walked away from the painting and began to climb the steps. 'Come on, Charlie.'

Charlie dumbly followed.

'I'm sorry,' called Mrs Brown, scrambling after them. 'I shouldn't have said those things. I'm just so worried about Ben.'

Maisie popped out of the kitchen. 'Would you like some coffee, Trish?' she asked gently.

Mrs Brown glanced at Paton's stern face. 'I . . . Well, yes. That would be nice. If we could discuss things a little more calmly . . .'

Maisie had already lit several candles and the kitchen surfaces twinkled with a friendly light. A plate of chocolate biscuits sat invitingly on the table and Uncle Paton was persuaded to join Mrs Brown and Maisie. 'Though I prefer cocoa to coffee,' he said.

'Me too,' said Charlie.

The tense atmosphere improved a little, but Mrs Brown could not seem to rid herself of the worried frown that creased her forehead. 'I should be used to it,' she said. 'I know this city is different from others. I know our houses are built on ancient battlefields, and in places where magic spills out when it's dark. I know things happen that no one can explain, mysteries the police don't even try to solve; evils they dare not acknowledge. And it's daunting, sometimes, for normal people like Mr Brown and me – and Benjamin. But something keeps us in this city. I suppose it's because, in spite of everything, we feel there is a great goodness here.'

'The Red King,' Charlie said quietly. He felt their eyes on him and, self-consciously, he added, 'He's still here.'

'His spirit, you mean, Charlie,' said Uncle Paton.

Charlie shook his head. 'No, more than that. I've seen him. I told you, Uncle P: a knight with red feathers on a silver helmet, who wears a red cloak and rides a white horse. He saved me, twice.'

For a while no one spoke. Even Uncle Paton couldn't find words to explain the Red Knight, but at last he said, 'It might not be the king, Charlie.'

'Then who?' asked Maisie. 'Who would dress up like that, and ride around at night on a white horse?'

Paton shrugged. 'That, I do not know.'

Mrs Brown got up and put on her tweed cap. 'I came here about the dog. And now I'm more confused than ever.'

'Charlie thinks that Billy Raven might be able to help,' said Maisie.

'Billy Raven?' Mrs Brown said crossly. 'How can he . . . Oh, of course, he communicates –'

'With animals,' said Charlie. 'I just thought he might be able to understand what Runner Bean is trying to tell us. But we'll have to wait till next weekend.'

Mrs Brown sighed. 'He's our only hope, then. So be it. I'd better get back. I don't think Benjamin will go to school tomorrow.' She cast a last angry look at Charlie and, before anyone could say another word, marched out.

'I forgot to ask her why she was wearing a man's suit,' said Paton.

'Just as well,' said Maisie.

Charlie went upstairs to pack his bag for school. Being a weekly boarder meant that he had to take pyjamas, wash-bag and a set of clean clothes. Woe betide any pupil who forgot their toothbrush. The Matron, Charlie's Great Aunt Lucretia, gave detention for the slightest oversight.

On Monday morning a blue school bus picked Charlie up from the top of Filbert Street. He was wearing a blue cape, the uniform for Music students, and carried a blue bag for his clothes and a brown backpack for his books. Fidelio, also in a blue cape, had saved a seat for Charlie as usual. Behind them sat Gabriel Silk, a boy with a long face and floppy brown hair.

'Have you heard about the Pets' Café?' asked Gabriel, leaning over the back of Charlie's seat. 'It's a disaster.'

'Have they really closed it?' asked Charlie.

'Permanently,' said Fidelio gloomily.

'It was Councillor Loom, Dorcas's dad,' Gabriel told them. 'He said there'd been complaints about the noise.'

The Pets' Café was a favourite meeting place for Charlie and his friends. He couldn't imagine what they would do without it. Or what poor Mr and Mrs Onimous, the owners, would do without customers.

When the blue bus drew into the square in front of Bloor's Academy, a green bus pulled up beside it, and Art students in green capes began to climb out. Emma was among them. Behind her came Tancred Torsson and Lysander Sage. Both fourteen and almost inseparable.

'Hey, Charlie,' called Tancred. 'How was your weekend?'

'Don't ask,' said Fidelio.

Tancred walked up to them. His spiky blond hair was hidden by a denim baseball cap, and his green cape billowed out in a breeze that was all his own. 'Has something happened?'

As they walked up the steps to the Academy, Charlie began to tell Tancred about Runner Bean. He had hardly begun when he became aware that on his other side the tall African, Lysander Sage, was bending his head, in order to hear Charlie's low voice.

They passed between two towers, crossed a cobbled courtyard and ascended another set of steps, up to huge oak doors studded with bronze figures. This morning the doors stood open, but once all the children were through, they would be closed and bolted until Friday afternoon.

Charlie came to the end of his account just before they stepped into the great hall. Lysander patted Charlie's shoulder, saying, 'We'll come and get him out of there, won't we, Tanc?'

'We'll try,' said Tancred in an undertone.

They were now in the great flag-stoned hall, where

silence was the rule. Charlie, Fidelio and Gabriel made their way to the blue cloakroom, where a pair of crossed trumpets hung above the door. Tancred and Lysander walked towards the crossed paintbrushes that denoted the green cloakroom.

On their way, Charlie noticed that the great hall seemed emptier than usual. And then he realised, there was not one purple cape in sight. The Drama students were all missing.

It was not until first break that they found out what had happened. In the wide, frosty field behind the Academy, purple capes could now be seen on children jogging round the perimeter, talking in groups or playing football at the far end. The Academy capes were made of thick wool, and the hoods were particularly comforting on cold winter mornings. Olivia, her purple hood pulled well down over her matching curls, rushed up to Charlie and Fidelio, with Emma hot on her heels.

Olivia breathlessly gave them the news. 'There was an accident. It was awful. The Onimouses were on their bike, you know how they ride. Mrs Onimous in front, pedalling, and Mr Onimous on a little seat behind her. Well, a mysterious motorcyclist went into them and they both fell off. The motorbike disappeared, but a car, trying to avoid them, backed into the bus. There was glass everywhere, and we all had to get out and walk to school.'

'But the Onimouses!' Charlie exclaimed.

'Well, Mrs Onimous stood up. I saw her,' said Olivia.

'She was a bit shaky, but OK, I think. Not sure about him, though. He was lying as still as a stone.'

Gabriel and Billy had joined the group. Billy began twisting his hands together. 'What about my rat?' he cried. 'What about Rembrandt? Who's going to feed him?'

Olivia said sternly, 'I'm sure your rat is perfectly capable of looking after himself. It's the poor Onimouses we should be thinking about. We don't even know if Mr Onimous is alive.'

Billy looked sheepishly at his feet. 'Sorry,' he muttered. 'I've had a bad weekend.' Billy's remark pricked Charlie's conscience. He should have invited Billy home with him. He was about to mention the following weekend when the sound of a horn rang out over the field. Break was over.

The small group began to drift towards the school door, and Fidelio said, 'What we should be asking ourselves is, who knocked the Onimouses off their bike?'

'And why?' added Emma. 'Mrs Onimous is a brilliant cyclist.'

Charlie was about to say that Norton Cross, the Pets' Café doorman, owned a motorbike. But the idea that Norton could have caused the accident was preposterous.

Just as Charlie was going into his French class, he was roughly pulled aside. 'I want a word with you,' said Manfred Bloor.

'But I'll be late for Fr–' Charlie began.

'Not now,' said Manfred. 'Come to the King's

Room five minutes before Homework.'

'Yes, sir.' Charlie eased himself out of Manfred's painful grip and rushed into the French Room. Madame Tessier was about to begin the lesson and Charlie was lucky to avoid her beady French eye as he sneaked to his desk at the back.

For the rest of the day Charlie's thoughts kept turning to his forthcoming meeting with Manfred. The Headmaster's son was now the Talents Master. He'd been head boy when Charlie entered the school eighteen months earlier. A head boy who used his hypnotic power to terrorise the younger children. Charlie had been one of his victims. But gradually Manfred's power had waned until Charlie had begun to feel almost safe looking into those coal-black eyes. And yet, today, he'd noticed an odd glint in Manfred's gaze, and he began to dread the evening ahead.

'What's wrong, Charlie?' asked Fidelio. 'Don't you want your fish cakes?'

Charlie shook his head. 'You can have them. I feel kind of queasy.'

They were sitting at one of the long tables that ran the length of the dining hall. The supper had been particularly good. Rice cakes with bubble and squeak. All around Charlie there were murmurs of approval and enjoyment. 'Mm,' Yum-yum,' 'Aaah!' Plates were scraped and one or two surreptitiously licked. But Charlie had lost his appetite. His gaze constantly slid to the staff table on the dais at the end of the room, where Manfred sat between Mr Paltry, Flute, and Mrs Marlowe, Drama.

'*Charlie! Charlie!*' Charlie gradually became aware that Billy, on his other side, was whispering to him.

'What did you say?' asked Charlie.

Billy, trying not to move his lips, whispered, 'Mrs Tilpin is still here.'

Fidelio overheard him. 'Do you mean Joshua's mum? The witch?'

'Shhh!' begged Billy. 'I'm already in trouble. They said I was spying on them.'

'Who?' said Charlie.

'Dorcas, Dagbert and the twins, and Joshua, of course. They were in this dark old room in the basement. And then Manfred came in.' Billy threw a frightened glance at the staff table. 'I think something's going on between them; Mrs Tilpin and Manfred, I mean.'

Charlie gave a moan. 'Manfred wants to see me alone after supper.'

'I'll come with you, if you like,' Fidelio offered.

'You can't,' said Charlie mournfully. 'You're not endowed. I've got to meet him in the King's Room, and you won't be allowed anywhere near it.'

Fidelio grimaced. 'Oh well. He can't eat you, Charlie.'

'Maybe not,' said Charlie, 'but I've got a feeling he can hypnotise me.'

It was no good trying to put off the meeting. Charlie knew he would only get detention if he was late. After supper, he collected his books from his desk and trudged up to the King's Room. The other endowed children would be arriving very soon, he thought, so Manfred might not have time to do anything too unpleasant.

In a circular room on the third floor, a portrait of the Red King hung between shelves of ancient-looking books. The king's features could barely be discerned in the cracked and darkened paint, but a gold crown glinted on his black hair, and his red cloak fell about him in soft velvet-like folds.

'Charlie Bone,' said Manfred as Charlie sidled through the tall black doors.

Manfred was standing opposite Charlie, on the other side of a large round table. 'Sit down, Charlie!' he commanded.

Charlie took the nearest chair and sat down, facing Manfred. The Talents Master continued to stand, and Charlie immediately felt at a disadvantage.

'Why didn't you invite Billy Raven home with you last weekend?' asked Manfred.

Charlie struggled to understand why he was being asked such a simple question. What lay behind it?

'Have you fallen out with Billy?' Manfred persisted.

'No,' said Charlie.

'You always invite Billy home.' Manfred put his hands on the table and bent forward. 'So what went wrong?'

'I . . . nothing.' Charlie was now thoroughly bemused. 'I just forgot.'

'You *forgot?*'

Was it a crime forgetting to ask a friend home? Now Charlie was suspicious.

'You won't forget next time, will you, Charlie?' Manfred's eyes glinted. The coal-black irises were quartered with lines of blazing light.

Charlie felt an intense pain in the centre of his forehead. Why is he doing this? he wondered. He doesn't have to hypnotise me. I would have asked Billy home, anyway. Having to resist Manfred's gaze made Charlie angry. It had happened before and Charlie had discovered that he could block the hypnotist. He had to look beyond the black glare and into the mind of Manfred Bloor.

Images swam before Charlie's eyes: a knight in a green cloak, a stone troll and, last of all, far, far out on a furious grey sea, the sail of a tiny boat.

'No!' cried Charlie. The pain in his head increased. He thought he could bear it no longer. He would have to let go.

'*You will . . .*' came the words. '*You will . . .*'

'Will . . .?' Charlie murmured. He felt his head sinking forward. And then another image cut through the darkness in his head: a knight on a white horse, red feathers streaming from his silver helmet, and a sword whose blade flashed like rays of the sun.

The dark figure on the other side of the table began to sink. Charlie heard a distant roar, and then the doors behind him opened and he was surrounded by moving, murmuring forms. Charlie sat up and rubbed his eyes.

'You OK, Charlie?' asked Tancred, taking the seat beside him.

'Yes,' said Charlie confidently. 'I'm great.' He looked across at Manfred, who had dropped into a chair. His head lolled forward as though he were asleep.

Dorcas and the twins clustered round the Talents Master. Joshua tapped his shoulder and Manfred lifted his head. He clutched the edge of the table and pulled himself to his feet. 'Get on with your homework,' he said. His speech was thick and slurred. Avoiding Charlie's eye, Manfred limped out of the room.

Dorcas, Joshua and the twins took their usual places opposite Charlie. A few moments later, Emma, Lysander and Gabriel arrived and sat beside each other, beyond Tancred. Billy rushed in and made straight for the empty place on Charlie's right. The small boy seemed nervous and even more disorganised than usual. Books kept falling out of his grasp, his spectacles slipped off his nose and, reaching for them, his chair tipped sideways and he fell on to the floor.

Charlie had no doubt that the Branko twins were responsible. They often tormented Billy with their kinetic powers. He was an easy victim. Dorcas and Joshua began to snigger.

'Pathetic!' Lysander glared at the twins. 'Is that how you get your kicks? Tormenting people who can't defend themselves? Try it on me, Idith. Come on, Inez, knock *my* chair over.'

The twins lowered their eyes and opened their books. The ghostly African warriors that Lysander could call up were not something that they wanted to contest.

Dagbert Endless came in late. He sat alone, halfway between the two groups. 'Where's the Talents Master?' he asked.

'He was taken unwell,' said Dorcas, 'when Charlie Bone was with him.'

'Is that so?' Dagbert looked at Charlie with interest.

THE POISONED NET

The long, cold dormitory with its single dim light had become so familiar to Charlie . . . that he almost felt at home. But tonight he found it impossible to sleep. On one side of him Fidelio hummed in his dreams, and on the other, Billy Raven twisted and moaned in a tangle of bedclothes.

'Billy, are you awake?' Charlie whispered.

Billy stopped moving and sat up. 'I'm worried about Rembrandt,' he said. 'Who's going to look after him?'

'You heard Olivia. She said Mrs Onimous wasn't injured. She'll be back at the Pets' Café right now, I bet.'

'But Mr Onimous? He . . . he must be . . .' Billy's voice trailed off.

'We'll ask Cook about it in the morning,' said Charlie. 'She'll know.' He closed his eyes and turned over, and then he found himself asking, 'Do you want to come home with me next weekend?'

'Course I do,' said Billy.

'That's settled then.'

Fidelio had drifted out of his musical dream and slumbered peacefully. Billy lay quiet and still, at last, and Charlie should have found it easy to sleep. But another problem had presented itself.

Why was Manfred so eager for Billy to visit Charlie's home? Did it have something to do with the painting of Badlock? Charlie realised he had told Billy nothing about the painting. Billy's concern for his rat had quite put it out of Charlie's mind.

The soft light of his white moth flickered above Charlie, and he was glad she had followed him to school. As he watched Claerwen loop and swing through the darkness, he began to feel drowsy, but as he finally fell asleep a voice in his head seemed to be warning him: *Don't let Billy go into Badlock.*

From a bed at the end of Charlie's row, Dagbert Endless followed the white moth's dance across the ceiling. He put his hand under his pillow and brought out a small golden fish and five tiny golden crabs. Clutching them in his fist, he murmured, 'Sea-gold,' and a smile crept into his face.

The bare walls of the dormitory were bathed in blue-green colours, veined with rippling silver light. As the watery shades washed above him, Dagbert thought of his mother. She had given him the sea-gold creatures a month before her death. She had found the gold in wrecks so deep they had been declared forever lost. But not to her. For Dagbert's mother was a mer-woman, as much at home in the sea as in the castle her husband had built for her. She made the gold into rings and bracelets and golden chains. But the five crabs and the fish were special charms to give her gifted son a power that would exceed his father's. There was also a golden sea urchin, somewhere in Tancred Torsson's possession. The storm-boy had stolen it, to weaken Dagbert's power.

When Dagbert was five years old his mother had been caught in a net and crushed to death beneath a ton of fish, creatures she had always considered to be her friends.

Dagbert let the sea-gold charms trickle between his fingers. The loss of his sea urchin angered him. Its theft was a slur on his mother's memory. But watching Charlie Bone's moth had given him an idea. Manfred wanted that white moth for, without her, Charlie Bone couldn't travel. But if Dagbert caught the moth, he would be helping himself as well. *Tancred would surely return my charm in exchange for Charlie's moth. Dorcas Loom will make me a net*, thought Dagbert – *she's clever with her fingers. We'll soon see who's the strongest.*

The following day Charlie found an opportunity to tell Billy about Runner Bean. Billy often wandered up to the ruined castle in the woods. He felt safe behind the massive red stone walls, with the open sky for a roof and the comforting sense that the Red King and his queen might still be close.

Charlie watched Billy wander up to the top of the field and began to follow him. He found Billy sitting on a stone seat between two of the five arches that led deeper into the castle. The white-haired boy was staring at a huge flagstone that was cracked down the centre and bordered with fresh earth. When Charlie approached Billy said, 'That's where Mrs Tilpin found the mirror, isn't it?'

Charlie looked at the stone. 'Yes. Where the shadow buried it.'

'D'you think she'll try to use it again, to bring the shadow back?'

'Yes, I do.' Charlie sat beside Billy. 'There's something you've got to know, Billy.'

'Oh?' Billy's claret-coloured eyes widened with anticipation. 'Have you been picture-travelling again?'

'How did you guess?'

'You look like you have. I didn't notice before, I was thinking about Rembrandt so much. I still haven't seen Cook.'

'Your rat's going to be OK,' said Charlie. 'Look, Billy, you've got to know everything that happened last weekend, and I might not get another chance to tell you before Friday.'

'I *want* to know,' said Billy.

So Charlie told Billy everything: from the moment he heard the wind sighing out of the painting, to the appearance of Runner Bean in Badlock. Billy shuffled and gasped, he pulled his hood up and hunched himself down, as though he were trying to block out Charlie's words, yet desperate to hear more. When Charlie described how he had escaped from the painting with

Claerwen's help, Billy gave a sigh of relief and said, 'That's all right, then. But you'd better not go near that painting again, Charlie.'

'It's not all right,' said Charlie. 'I couldn't get Runner Bean out. He's stuck in that awful place, and none of us knows how to –'

'Can you *see* him?' asked Billy.

'Yes. It's horrible. He's howling.'

'Maybe I can, kind of, connect with him,' Billy suggested.

Charlie hesitated. 'It might be dangerous for you, Billy.'

Billy was silent for a while. He swung his legs and looked through the great arch to where distant figures could be seen running over the field. 'Benjamin must be in a state,' he said.

'He is,' Charlie admitted. 'I don't think he'll talk to me until I've rescued his dog.'

Billy looked thoughtful. 'I can still come home with you, Charlie, can't I? Even if I don't look at the painting?'

'Course you can.'

As they left the ruin, Charlie's moth fluttered out of his pocket and settled on his shoulder.

'We'll be OK if your moth's with us,' Billy said with a grin.

Charlie didn't reply. Claerwen had saved him from Badlock, but she hadn't managed to do the same for Runner Bean.

When the sound of the horn blew across the grounds,

the boys began to run back to the school. Neither of them saw Dagbert Endless moving out of the trees, close to the castle entrance.

Charlie's trumpet lesson always finished early. Señor Alvaro now taught all the Brass Band students, and was generally very successful. He was young and cheerful, with an interesting moustache and smiling almond-shaped eyes. In Mr Alvaro's opinion, Charlie could have played the trumpet tolerably well if he put his mind to it. But the boy with riotous hair seemed unable to concentrate.

Today Charlie was happy to be released ten minutes before lunch.

'Do you think it eez possible you spare some time to practise this week?' asked Señor Alvaro pleasantly.

'Erm, yes, sir,' said Charlie, who was already wondering how he could snatch a moment alone with Cook.

'Gracias,' called Señor Alvaro as Charlie pounded down the corridor.

Finding Cook was not as difficult as Charlie had imagined. She was sitting at one of the tables in the blue canteen, having a cup of tea with a white-haired robust-looking man: Dr Saltweather.

'A trifle early for lunch, aren't we, Charlie Bone?' Dr Saltweather remarked. 'Shouldn't you still be in a lesson?'

'Señor Alvaro let me go. I hadn't practised enough,' Charlie confessed.

Dr Saltweather sighed. He was Head of Music and felt responsible for Charlie's lack of progress. Charlie's father was the cathedral organist and a brilliant musician, but Charlie seemed to have inherited none of his father's talent. Dr Saltweather was aware of Charlie's extraordinary endowment, however, and had a certain amount of sympathy for the boy.

'I wanted to ask Cook about Mr Onimous,' said Charlie.

'Mr Onimous?' Cook's rosy face took on an anxious look. 'He's not too good, Charlie. He's in hospital. Concussion. Poor Mrs Onimous is beside herself.'

'And . . . and the animals?' asked Charlie.

'Well the Flames can look after themselves,' Cook said confidently, 'and you can tell Billy that his rat is quite safe. He's with Mrs Kettle.'

'And the boa?' said Charlie.

'Same place, Charlie. The Kettle Shop.'

Dr Saltweather stood up and pushed in his chair. 'I hear the Pets' Café has been closed,' he said.

Cook nodded. 'My poor friends. Councillor Loom was responsible.'

'A bad business.' Dr Saltweather strode towards the door. 'Something must be done about it,' he boomed.

The Music teacher's commanding tone gave Charlie a surge of hope. 'D'you think Dr Saltweather can do something about the café?' he asked Cook.

'He'll certainly try. But he'll be up against some pretty powerful people, and I wouldn't like him to put himself in danger.' Cook carried the two mugs to the counter and

Charlie followed with a teapot and two empty plates. 'There are certain people in this city who've been just waiting to finish off the Pets' Café,' Cook went on. 'They don't like you children meeting up at the weekend and hatching plots.'

'We don't hatch plots,' Charlie said indignantly.

'No? Think about it, Charlie. Oh, I know your plots are all for the best reasons, but *they* don't like it.'

'But the Pets' Café is a good place, Cook. It's a happy place. Where else can pets meet and enjoy great food? It's not just useful to us, hundreds of people love it.'

'You don't have to tell *me*, Charlie.' Cook lifted the lid from a pan of fish stew on the counter and sniffed. 'I'd better pop into the kitchen and see what my dinner ladies are up to.'

Charlie stood by the counter, patiently waiting for someone to come and ladle out the stew. Other Music students began to arrive and by the time one of the dinner ladies turned up, a long queue had formed behind Charlie.

When he had been served, Charlie went to his favourite table in the corner of the canteen. Before long, he was joined by Gabriel, Billy and Fidelio. The stew was soon gone and, as they queued for their puddings, Fidelio remarked that Dagbert Endless was missing.

'Probably ate too much fish at the weekend,' Gabriel remarked.

Charlie wouldn't have laughed so heartily if he had

known what Dagbert was up to. In fact, he wouldn't have laughed at all.

It wasn't until the end of Homework that Charlie began to miss his moth. She often disappeared for a few hours; perhaps she slept in the folds of a curtain, or nestled behind a picture frame. Charlie never knew. But in the evening she would usually flutter on to his arm, or his shoulder, as if she were reassuring him that she was near; and then she would fly off again.

This time Claerwen's absence worried Charlie. As he left the King's Room he asked Billy if he had seen the moth.

'Not since she was on your arm this morning,' said Billy.

Gabriel hadn't seen her, nor had Emma.

'She'll turn up,' said Lysander. 'Probably eating a spider somewhere.'

'Or being eaten by a bat,' said Tancred.

Lysander dug him in the ribs. 'Cut it out, Tanc. Charlie loves that moth.'

Dagbert Endless passed them silently. Charlie noticed that he wore a slight smile. Had he been listening to the conversation?

Dagbert didn't go straight to the dormitory, like the others. He slipped down the main staircase and crossed the hall.

Dr Saltweather chose that moment to leave the staff room. 'Where do you think you're going, Dagbert Endless?' he demanded.

'I've got to show the Talents Master some work,' Dagbert said casually.

'Be quick about it, then,' said Dr Saltweather. 'It'll be Lights Out in fifteen minutes.'

'Yes, sir.' Dagbert ran down the passage to his classroom. He went to a desk at the back of the room and opened the lid. Inside the desk lay something resembling a fine white handkerchief. Dorcas had done her work well. On Dagbert's instructions she had gone to the sewing-room during her lunch hour and run up a nice little net. It was made of the finest muslin, and fixed to a long bamboo cane, helpfully provided by Weedon. Just to make sure the net would do what Dagbert intended, Dorcas had impregnated the muslin with the juice of a rare herb: stillwort. She had never used the herb before and was interested to see if it had worked.

It had worked very well. The moth inside the net lay so still it appeared to be dead.

'Did you catch it?' Dorcas peered round the door.

'It was easy,' said Dagbert. 'I've taken it off the pole. Come and look.'

Dorcas crept over to Dagbert's desk. He picked up the muslin net and laid it across his palms. Inside the net the white moth's wings rose and fell, just once, as though it were taking its last breath.

'It's not dead, then,' said Dorcas, disappointment clouding her plump face.

'It will be soon,' Dagbert told her. He laid the net

on his desk and went to the stationery cupboard. Mr Carp, the English teacher, kept a thick crystal tumbler on the top shelf for his personal use.

Dagbert brought the tumbler over to his desk and eased the opening of the net round the top of the glass. The white moth fell into the tumbler.

'There,' said Dagbert. 'Now I'll take it to Manfred.'

'You will tell him I helped, won't you?' said Dorcas. 'I mean, I did make the net, and the poison and everything.'

'Of *course* I'll tell him, Dorc. You're a genius, you know that?'

'Yes, I do.' A smile dimpled her cheeks.

Dagbert covered the tumbler with the muslin and carried it to the door. Dorcas rushed to open it for Dagbert, who sailed through with a muttered 'thanks' and continued across the hall. Dorcas flew ahead of him and opened the small, ancient door that led to the West Wing.

'You will tell him, won't you?' begged Dorcas.

'I said I would,' Dagbert replied, stepping into the dark passage behind the door. 'Better get to bed, Dorc, or Matron'll come down on you.'

'And Manfred will tell Fairy Tilpin about me, won't he?' Dorcas went on. 'She'll be *so* pleased.'

'*Yes!*' Dagbert gave the door a backward kick and it slammed in Dorcas's face.

Students seldom came to the West Wing. It was home to the Bloor family and they didn't like staff or children intruding. At the far end of the passage a dim light could be seen in the room at the base of the Music Tower. Dagbert made his way towards the light. The walls on either side of him gave off the damp, earthy smell of old brick, and moss grew in the cracked slate floor.

Halfway down the passage, a bookcase stood in a small recess. Holding the tumbler tight against his body with his left hand, Dagbert used his right to remove two books from a shelf. He knocked on the bare wood behind them.

'Who is it?' called a voice.

'Dagbert, sir. I've got something to show you.'

'Oh, yes,' said Manfred in a bored voice.

'A moth.'

'A moth?' Manfred sounded interested. 'You'd better come in.'

The bookcase swung back, revealing a small study. Manfred Bloor was sitting behind a desk where green bottles, earthenware jars, rusty tins and wads of yellowing papers had been set out in groups.

'I hope it's *the* moth, Dagbert Endless.' Manfred beckoned Dagbert over. 'I'm extremely busy, as you can see.'

'It is the right moth, sir.' Dagbert turned the tumbler over in his hands and laid it upside down before Manfred. Now the moth's wings were barely distinguishable from the white muslin beneath her.

Manfred peered through the thick crystal. 'You're sure?'

'See the silver on its wings? I know it's Charlie's. I caught it in the Corridor of Portraits. Thought it was so clever, lying on a bunch of white lilies. Thought it wouldn't be seen.' Dagbert wrinkled his nose. 'Funny-looking person in that portrait.'

Manfred gave him an icy look. 'The person in that portrait was my great-great-great-grandmother, Donatella, a very brave woman. She was accidentally electrocuted in an experiment.'

'Sorry,' said Dagbert.

'Did anyone help you to do this?' Manfred tapped the tumbler.

'No, sir.' Dagbert felt Manfred's black eyes boring into his, and he had to steady himself against the desk. 'That is – only Dorcas. She made the poisoned net.'

'That girl has extraordinary talent,' Manfred said with satisfaction. 'You can go now, Dagbert.' He stood up and pointed to the door.

'About the moth,' said Dagbert. 'I know you want it so Charlie Bone can't travel safely, but I didn't catch it just for that.'

'No?' Manfred looked at the trapped moth.

'No. I want to bargain with it. Tancred Torsson stole my sea urchin, and without it I can't . . . can't . . .'

'Drown people?' Manfred suggested.

'Not exactly.' Dagbert frowned. 'I'm just not myself without all my sea-gold creatures.'

'Oh, I can deal with Tancred Torsson,' said Manfred. 'Don't worry, I'll return the moth when I've studied it a little. But make sure Charlie Bone never gets it.' He waved his hand at Dagbert. 'Now, off you go. You'll get your charm back, never fear.'

Charlie was standing in the bathroom, feeling very queasy. He wondered if someone had poisoned him. He clung to the basin while the room spun around him. First one way, then the other.

'You OK, Charlie?'

A voice broke through the buzz in Charlie's head. He turned painfully and saw Fidelio standing by the bathroom door.

'Feel a bit funny,' said Charlie. He staggered through the door and Fidelio helped him to his bed.

Dagbert Endless came in and stood staring down at Charlie. 'Not feeling well?' he asked.

Charlie looked away from Dagbert's startling sea-coloured eyes. He felt his strength leaving him. He was so weak he could barely lift his arm. Vague forms moved through the mist that clouded his vision, and he heard Fidelio say, 'Matron, Charlie's ill.'

The matron's words came booming close to his ear, a deep, indistinct, underwater sound. 'Trying it on, are you, Charlie? There's nothing a good night's sleep won't cure.'

The light went out. Charlie lay in the darkness while familiar images tumbled into his head: a knight in a green cloak, a stone troll and a furious grey sea. But the knight with red feathers streaming from his silver helmet was absent. And all that remained of the boat was the tip of its mast, sinking slowly into a heaving sea. And then Charlie saw Claerwen lying in a crystal tomb, while the silver sparkle drained from her white wings. With all that remained of his strength, Charlie raised himself on to his elbows and cried, 'CLAERWEN!'

Every sleeping boy in the dormitory was now wide awake. Others, who had not yet fallen asleep, began to shout out.

'Shut up!' 'What's he on about?' 'He's off his head!' One of the first-formers snivelled, 'What's the matter with him?' Someone else burst into tears.

'Calm down, everyone,' said Fidelio. 'Charlie's just had a nightmare. It can happen to anyone. Are you OK now, Charlie?'

Charlie sat up. The buzzing in his head had gone. The dizziness had passed. He felt almost his old self again. 'Yes. I'm OK, thanks. I feel great, actually.'

Manfred Bloor had put away his great-great-great-grandfather's tins of desiccated snails, his bottles of aspen oil and monkey tears, his jars of seaweed and nightshade, and the sheaves of yellowing paper, covered in beautiful looping script. Manfred had hoped they might be put to use, sealing the crack in the Mirror of Amoret, but there was nothing in Bertram Bloor's notes about the mending of mirrors. He was more concerned with creation, with resurrection and revival.

Manfred locked the door of his ancestor's carved oak cupboard and slipped the key into his pocket. Returning to his desk, he began to study the moth in her crystal tumbler. 'I have you now, Moth, Wand, whatever you are.'

The moth appeared to be fading. Its silvered wings had lost their sparkle, its soft head looked crumpled.

'Dead,' Manfred pronounced. 'But we can still use you.'

A small sound came from the glass. A tiny clink. Manfred sat back. Half-closing his eyes he scanned the tumbler for a fracture, a minute flaw. He was about to look closer when, with a deafening crack, the tumbler burst apart. A dozen gleaming shards flew straight at the window. The thick crystal shattered the pane and glass fell in a shower on to the cobbled yard outside.

The bed of white muslin lay empty on Manfred's desk. The moth had gone.

AN EVIL WIND

'Weedon! Weedon!'

Charlie heard a voice screaming in the courtyard below the dormitory. Leaping out of bed, he ran to the window. There were already several boys pressed up against the pane.

'It's the Talents Master,' said an excited first-former.

'Look at all the glass,' another boy observed.

'Someone's thrown a brick through the window,' said Bragger Braine, a large second-former.

'Idiot,' muttered Dagbert. 'The glass would be on the inside, not the outside, if that had happened.'

'You think you're so clever, don't you?' twittered Rupe Small, Bragger Braine's devoted slave.

A glistening quilt of broken glass lay across the courtyard. Manfred moved slowly round it, kicking the glass with his toe, then squatting down and poking the fragments with a pencil. 'Weedon!' he shouted again. 'Come here, this minute!'

The headmaster, Dr Bloor, opened one of the windows above Manfred's study. 'What on earth's going on?' he shouted.

'Look!' screamed Manfred, getting to his feet. 'Look at all this!' He threw out an arm, indicating the broken glass.

'How did it happen?' demanded his father.

Charlie saw Manfred hesitate. Whatever it was that had caused the accident, it was going to remain Manfred's secret, for the time being. 'How should I know?' he shouted, his voice taking on a hysterical note.

'I suppose it was one of your experiments,' said Dr Bloor.

'It was NOT!' shrieked Manfred. 'Where's Weedon?'

'He's tidying my study. Where else should he be?' Dr Bloor suddenly caught sight of the faces in the dormitory window. 'Get back to bed!' he bellowed. 'Or you'll all get detention.'

There was a frantic scramble away from the window. Twelve boys bounced back on to their beds and drew the covers over their heads. They waited for Matron to storm in, but tonight she had other things on her mind.

Claerwen lay hidden in the rotting leaves between two flat cobbles. She made herself as small as she could, while Weedon swept up the glass fragments that covered her. He groaned with fatigue as he bent and brushed the tiny shards into his dustpan.

'Put it all in here, Weedon.' Manfred held out a clear plastic bag.

'Wot you gonner do with it?' asked Weedon. 'Make one of them installation art things?'

'Never you mind,' snapped Manfred, who was doing

his own bit of sweeping. 'And let me know if you see anything unusual.'

'Wot sort of unusual?'

'Oh, you know,' Manfred said impatiently. 'Anything that isn't glass: a fly, maybe, or a moth.'

'Ah!' grunted Weedon. 'Now I get it.'

The porter continued to sweep for another half hour, but the temperature was falling fast and soon the cobbles began to sparkle with frost.

'It's no good, Mr Manfred,' Weedon grumbled. 'I can't tell glass from frost. I'm giving up.' He poured his final haul into the plastic bag and went through a door into the West Tower.

Manfred straightened up, rubbing his back. His leg still ached from the wound the leopards had given him. But he wasn't prepared to give up just yet. He refused to believe the moth had escaped him entirely. Limping round the edge of the courtyard, he stared at each and every cobble. Not one eluded his piercing coal-eyed gaze.

Claerwen waited. She might have been a dead thing: the vein of a leaf, a thread of grass. When Manfred had given up his search at last, she crawled out of her hiding place and moved towards the wall of the chapel. There she lay, in the pool of bright colours that fell from the stained glass window. She knew she must reach Charlie before he was tempted to travel again, but the route to his dormitory was steep and perilous for the tiny caterpillar that she had become. To escape Manfred, Claerwen had changed shape once more. It would take her some time to became a moth again.

On Friday afternoon, when the children went to pack their bags for home, Claerwen was still missing.

Charlie had used every spare minute to search for his moth but there was no sign of her. And then, as he and Billy lined up behind the great oak doors, waiting for Weedon to open them, Tancred came flying up behind Charlie and whispered, 'Charlie, Dagbert says he's got your moth.'

'What!' Letting his bag fall to the floor, Charlie swung round and searched the line of children behind him.

'He's not here,' said Tancred. 'He's having an extra lesson with the Talents Master.'

'I don't care where he is,' Charlie said loudly.

'Ssh! You'll get detention,' Tancred warned. 'Wait till we're outside.'

Weedon had appeared. Puffing and groaning, he drew back the huge iron bolts and rattled the oversized key in the lock. At last the doors were open and the sullen porter stood aside while children swept past him and out into freedom.

The three buses were waiting in the square. Charlie stood by the steps while the other Music students climbed, ahead of him, into the blue bus. When Tancred appeared, Charlie grabbed his arm.

'So where's my moth, then?'

'I told you,' Tancred hitched his green cape further on

to his shoulders. 'Dagbert said he'd got it. He's offered to swap it for his sea urchin.'

'What d'you mean?' cried Charlie.

Striding towards the green bus, Tancred said, 'I mean that he'll exchange your moth for that gold charm I took, the night he tried to drown you.'

'So when are you going to swap it?' Charlie dogged Tancred's steps until they reached the green bus.

'That's just it, Charlie. I don't think I can let him have his sea urchin. He's not so dangerous without it.' Tancred began to climb into the bus.

'You've got to,' Charlie leapt on to the bottom step.

'You'll miss your bus,' Tancred told him. 'Get off quickly, Charlie. This one goes in the wrong direction.'

'I don't care.'

'We'll find another way to get your moth,' said Tancred as he moved to the back of the bus.

'Get off, blue-cape,' ordered the driver, 'or I'll get the school porter to remove you.'

Charlie jumped off the step as the green bus rumbled out of the square. His own bus had already started moving and he only just managed to catch it. He was hauled inside by Gabriel and Fidelio, and lay in the aisle breathing heavily, while the driver complained about lads who didn't have the sense they were born with.

Gabriel lifted Charlie's bag on to the rack, while Charlie pulled himself to his feet and fell into the seat beside Fidelio.

'What's going on?' Billy's anxious face peered round the back of Charlie's seat.

'Tell you later,' said Charlie, sinking back. He turned to Fidelio and whispered, 'Dagbert's got my moth, but he's offered to swap it for something Tancred took.'

Fidelio stared at Charlie. 'I wish there was somewhere we could all meet. I've got rehearsals with the Youth orchestra, all weekend, but I'll be free on Sunday night. What are you going to do now the Pets' Café is closed?'

From the seat behind them, Gabriel said, 'Get the café to open again. I'm going to see Mr Onimous.'

'But he's . . .' Charlie began.

'Not dead yet,' said Gabriel solemnly.

The bus meandered round the city, while children jumped off at their home stops and disappeared into the dusk. The street lights had come on, but even they couldn't penetrate the dark, winding alleys that led off the High Street.

Gabriel lived on the Heights, a steep cliff road that overlooked the city. He was usually the first to leave the bus, getting off at a stop at the bottom of the cliff road, but today he waited until they reached the narrow street that led to the Pets' Café.

'Mum will be there,' he said. 'She wouldn't leave Mrs Onimous on her own after everything that's happened.'

Charlie watched Gabriel turn in to Frog Street and begin to run. Of all of them, Gabriel was probably the closest to the Onimouses. His mother helped in the café, and his large family of gerbils was always welcome there.

Charlie and Billy left the bus at the top of Filbert Street, and walked down to number nine. As they drew closer, Charlie saw Benjamin standing on the top step of number twelve. He was staring across the road at Charlie's house. As soon as he saw Charlie, he went inside and slammed his front door.

Charlie sighed. 'He's not going to speak to me until he sees Runner Bean again.'

'Maybe I could just take a look at the painting,' said Billy.

'Forget it, Billy. If you got caught in Badlock, I'd never get you out. Not without Claerwen.' And then Charlie thought of the giant. Without Claerwen he could never reach his ancestor again.

The two boys stepped into the hall and headed straight for the kitchen. Maisie was cooking something that smelled so delicious their mouths were already watering.

Unfortunately, Maisie wasn't the only person in the kitchen. Grandma Bone sat in the rocking-chair beside the stove.

'Ahh!' Grandma Bone's grim face broke into a smile. 'Billy Raven, at last. I wondered when you would be coming to see us again.'

'Hello, Mrs Bone,' Billy said nervously.

'Hang your capes in the hall, boys.' Grandma Bone pointed to the door. 'And take your bags upstairs. We don't like bringing the outdoors into our cosy kitchen, do we, Maisie?'

'Doesn't bother me,' said Maisie, heaving a large dish out of the oven.

Grandma Bone scowled at her. 'Nevertheless.' She waved the boys away.

'Maisie, has Runner Bean –?' Charlie began.

'As far as I know, nothing has come out of that cellar,' said Maisie. 'Your *other* grandma could maybe tell you if she's seen anything.'

'Boys, your capes,' barked Grandma Bone.

Billy backed into the hall and Charlie followed, just managing to stop himself from saying something rude. Hanging their blue capes on the hall-stand, the boys rushed upstairs, dumped their bags in Charlie's room, and ran down to the kitchen.

'Lay the table, Charlie,' Grandma Bone ordered, rocking her chair back and forth. She seemed excited about something.

Charlie dutifully laid the table for five.

'Four,' said his grandmother. 'Your Uncle Paton's not here, thank goodness. Eating by candlelight gives me indigestion.'

Charlie removed a set of knives and forks, and they all sat down, while Maisie brought her lamb casserole to the table, and began to ladle it out. It was just as delicious as Charlie had hoped, but the meal was spoilt by Grandma Bone's looming presence; by the slurping noise she made, the rumbling of her stomach and the way she darted quick looks at everyone else's plate.

The meal was almost over when Charlie heard a large vehicle manoeuvring in the road outside. Through the gap in the curtains he could see that a white camper-van had parked in front of the kitchen window. He was surprised when Uncle Paton jumped out, quickly slammed the door and rushed towards the house, his black fedora pulled well down over his face. Charlie crossed his fingers and watched the street light. It didn't explode.

'Phew!' Charlie exclaimed as the front door banged.

'Can someone please turn out the lights,' Uncle Paton called from the hall.

Maisie obligingly lit the candles, while Charlie sprang for the light switch.

'Where on earth have you been all week?' Grandma Bone demanded as Paton came in.

Ignoring her question, Uncle Paton said, 'Something smells good.' He placed a well-worn briefcase beside the door and pulled a chair up to the table.

'I asked you a question,' said Grandma Bone.

'So you did, Grizelda.' Paton rubbed his hands together as Maisie put a steaming dish of lamb before him. 'And I see no reason to answer you. What I do is my business.' He turned to Charlie. 'Has the dog appeared yet, Charlie?'

Charlie shook his head. 'Runner's still stuck.'

'But I might be able to talk to him,' said Billy.

Paton frowned. 'Not you, Billy.' He began to tuck into his lamb.

'But perhaps . . .' Billy leaned forward eagerly.

'No,' said Uncle Paton firmly. 'We'll find another way. Though I confess, in my research I have yet to come across any mention of dogs caught in paintings.'

'Research! Research!' snarled his sister, leaving the table. 'Poking your nose into other people's affairs. Where d'you think that will get you?'

'Personally, nowhere, dear sister. Though what I unearth may be of great benefit to others.' Paton glanced at Billy Raven.

Charlie watched his grandmother march to the door. Here she hesitated, her right hand almost on the light switch. He could see that she was hugely tempted to turn on the lamp hanging above the table. If she did, Paton would be bound to shower himself and his meal with shattered glass. But she resisted and, with a resigned shrug, left the room.

'What exactly is your research, Mr Yewbeam?' asked Billy.

'Ah, my research.' Uncle Paton smiled, almost to himself. 'I am writing a history of our family, Billy. The Yewbeams. But digging and delving into the past has led me deep into the lives of others. There isn't another city in the country like this one, you know. It was built by a magician, for one thing, and a king at that. The magic, good and bad, is now part of the fabric of the place. It is like a seam that runs through the soil, the rock and clay, the marl and loam beneath our feet.'

Maisie uttered a soft 'Tch!' She shook her head and

said, 'Was it really necessary to buy a great van, Paton?'

'Our ancestors litter the country,' was Paton's reply. 'I've been travelling to graveyards, libraries, stately homes, council offices, you name it. At nightfall, I often found myself far from home. I could hardly go to a hotel, with all those lights. My only option would be to sleep on a park bench.'

'And get mugged,' said Billy.

'Mugged, indeed. Exactly, Billy.' Paton scooped up his last mouthful, declared it to be the best casserole he'd ever tasted, and sat back with a sigh of contentment.

'And have you found out anything interesting, Mr Yewbeam?' asked Billy.

Uncle Paton stared at Billy for a moment, as though he were deciding whether or not to confide in him. At length he replied, 'I have, Billy. I have, indeed. But at present the clues are a little foggy. In time I shall unravel some of the more puzzling details, and then . . .' he paused, 'and then, lives will be changed – dramatically.'

Charlie got the impression that his uncle's words were meant for Billy, alone, and that it was his life that would be changed so dramatically. Had Uncle Paton discovered something about Billy's parents?

Uncle Paton would say no more about his research. Changing the subject, he asked Maisie whether anything had happened to the painting while he'd been away.

'You don't think I've looked in the cellar, do you?' she retorted. 'After what happened to the poor dog.

Anyway, your sister keeps the door locked.'

'Just wondered, you know, if you'd heard a bark, or a whine . . . anything,' said Uncle Paton.

'No.' Maisie collected the dishes and carried them to the sink. 'But I have seen Benjamin Brown, gazing over here as if his heart would break.'

'What am I going to do?' cried Charlie, covering his face with his hands. 'I'll *have* to try and rescue Runner Bean, even without Claerwen.'

'You've lost the moth?' Uncle Paton looked concerned.

'I know where she is,' said Charlie, 'but I won't be able to get her back just yet.'

'And why not?' asked his uncle.

'It's too complicated to explain.'

Paton accepted this answer reluctantly. 'Don't so much as look in that cellar until you find her. That's an order.' He stood up and pushed in his chair. Bidding them all a good night's sleep, he tucked his briefcase under his arm, took a candle from the dresser and went up to his room.

When Maisie heard Paton's door close, she turned on the kitchen light, and held up a tea-towel. 'Right, boys. Who's going to dry?'

Billy chose to dry, Charlie to put away. Maisie was best at cleaning the pans.

Half an hour later, as Charlie and Billy were mounting the stairs, a cold draught swept through the hall. The coats on the stand swung in the breeze, two pictures swivelled sideways on the wall, the door mat lifted at one end, and

Uncle Paton's fedora flew up to the ceiling, turned over and dropped to the floor.

'What was that?' Billy clung to the banister.

'Dunno.' Charlie went to pick up his uncle's hat. He could hear no wind in the road outside, no doors rattled, no trees sighed. He looked down the passage leading to the cellar. He could guess where the evil wind was coming from, but decided not to tell Billy.

Could the shadow reach them, even here?

DESTRUCTION IN THE KETTLE SHOP

Piminy Street ran directly behind Ingledew's Bookshop. Its leaning, half-timbered buildings looked to be in danger of toppling into the street; their crooked doors were marked by arrow-heads and their slate roofs rippled like waves; yet the great fire of the eighteenth century had never touched these ancient houses. According to Miss Ingledew it was because, at that time, almost every house in the street had been occupied by a magician – of one sort or another.

Piminy Street, however, was home to Mrs Kettle, and there was nothing sinister about her. Unusual, perhaps, but not threatening. She had given Charlie a kettle that had been made by her ancestor, Feromel, five hundred years ago. It contained a dark liquid that could never be poured away. This timeless liquid was usually cool, but Mrs Kettle had warned Charlie that when the kettle felt hot to the touch, he would be in danger.

On Friday night Charlie hadn't been surprised to find the kettle so hot he could barely touch it. He felt it again

121

as soon as he woke next morning. It had cooled a little, but was still warm.

Billy knew about Feromel's kettle. 'Is it hot?' he asked.

'Not too hot.' Charlie pushed the kettle under his bed.

'We'll go and fetch Rembrandt from Mrs Kettle right after breakfast, shall we?' Billy swung his legs out of bed and put on his spectacles.

'Mm. Wish I could get hold of Tancred,' said Charlie.

Neither Charlie nor Billy owned a mobile phone. They weren't allowed in school, and Grandma Bone disapproved of them. Charlie didn't like the thought of speaking to Tancred from the phone in the hall, with Grandma Bone listening in.

The white camper-van had gone when the boys went down to breakfast.

'Your uncle must have left before dawn,' said Maisie, placing a large slice of bacon on each of their plates. 'He's on the scent of something – goodness knows what.'

After another slice of bacon and several pieces of toast and honey, Charlie and Billy set off for the Kettle Shop.

'You can always bring your rat here, Billy,' said Maisie, as she let them out of the front door. '*She'll* never know,' she added, glancing up the stairs, where Grandma Bone was having her morning gargle.

'Thanks, Mrs Jones.' Billy raced after Charlie.

Charlie was anxious to get away from number nine as fast as possible. He didn't want to see Benjamin again, before he had rescued Runner Bean.

As soon as they began to walk up Piminy Street, the sense of menace that Charlie often felt here seemed to be even stronger. He always imagined that someone was watching him from a dark window beneath the eaves.

The Kettle Shop lay beyond a curious fish shop where there were never any fish.

Before they reached the fish shop, however, they had to pass the Stone Shop. Of all the houses in Piminy Street, this was the most sinister. In the dark interior, carved stone figures brandished clubs and axes. There were stone soldiers, horses and dogs. But the mounted knight, which had once attacked the boys, was gone: broken in two by the Red Knight, and now lying, with his stone horse, at the bottom of the river.

'Let's keep going.' Billy plucked at Charlie's jacket. 'I hate that place.'

Charlie's nose was almost touching the window pane. He expected to see someone and, yes, there he was: Eric Shellhorn, Great Aunt Venetia's stepson. Charlie could just make out his face, peeping from behind a tall, robed figure; a Druid, perhaps.

'I knew he'd be in there,' Charlie muttered.

Billy tugged Charlie's sleeve. 'Let's go, Charlie. One of those things might start moving again.'

'I don't think Eric would do that in broad daylight,' said Charlie.

'He might. Come *on*. I want to see Rembrandt.'

Just before Charlie backed away from the window, he saw Eric dart across the back of the shop. 'What's he going to do next, I wonder?'

Billy was already speeding up the road and Charlie started to follow him, but then he found himself lingering outside the fish shop. The door to this peculiar place was always closed, always locked, and yet a strong smell of fish seeped from the building, as though the very bricks were made of cod or mackerel.

This was the home of Dagbert Endless; if you could call it a home. The window above the sign was dark and grimy. The curtains were threadbare, and all that could be seen of the shop beyond the window was an empty counter in a room with walls of cracked white tiles, and a floor of mildewed slate. Charlie wrinkled his nose and walked on. By the time he had reached the Kettle Shop, Billy was inside, making his way through the kettles displayed on stands and tables all round the room.

Charlie closed the shop door, which squeaked loudly on its somewhat rusty hinges; he followed Billy through an archway into yet another room filled with kettles. But here there were four chairs, grouped round an empty table, where customers could sit and examine the ancient kettles. On a stove behind the table, a copper kettle whistled merrily.

'I knew I'd see you today, m'dears.' The shop's owner lifted the whistling kettle and poured boiling water into a large brown teapot.

'Because of my rat,' said Billy, eyeing the plate of cookies that Mrs Kettle now placed on the table.

'Because of your rat, m'dear.' Mrs Kettle was a very large muscular person, with a crown of smooth copper-coloured hair. She wore a dark-blue boiler suit and thick leather boots, spotted with oil; for Mrs Kettle was a blacksmith first and foremost; kettle-selling was merely a hobby, a front for her secret profession.

'Where is he then?' Billy gazed round, hoping for a black rat to come bounding towards him.

'Guess!' said Mrs Kettle.

'I can't. I can't,' said Billy impatiently. 'There are too many places for him to hide.'

The blacksmith walked first one way, and then another, tapping kettles as she went. She hesitated, set off again, stopped and pondered, rubbing her chin. 'I do believe I've lost him,' she said.

'No-o-o!' cried Billy.

The lid of a huge iron kettle lifted slightly and then slid to the floor with a loud clang. They waited expectantly, but no black rat leaped out. Instead the head of a blue snake appeared. It swung from side to side, and the beautiful blue feathers adorning its head fluttered like silken banners in the wind.

'Oh, I forgot the boa was here.' Billy went towards the swaying head.

'He's a lovely fellow. I've got really attached to him,' said Mrs Kettle. 'I call him Solomon, he's so wise.'

On seeing Billy, the blue boa came slithering out of the kettle, slipped to the ground and began to coil itself round Billy's legs. But Billy lifted the creature and gently curled it round his shoulders, all the while hissing and humming to it. The boa replied with a soft chirruping sound, like a small bird.

'It's OK,' said Billy when the boa had settled. 'He won't make me invisible.'

'It's wonderful how you can do that, Billy, m'dear,' said Mrs Kettle. 'Solomon was very active before he took that little nap. Spiders, flies, beetles, even a mouse; he's been wrapping them up in his long blue coils and disappearing them all over the place.'

Charlie felt something on his foot. Before his very eyes the lace on his trainer began to disappear. 'Billy, I think I've found Rembrandt. He's eating my shoelace.' Charlie lifted his foot and kicked it towards Billy.

There was a loud squeak and Billy's white hair was suddenly tugged over his face. Billy put up his hands and clasped them round what appeared to be empty air. But Billy could feel whiskers and fur and a long skinny tail.

'Solomon's done it to Rembrandt,' said Billy, pleased to have found his rat, but worried by his invisibility.

'I expect you can soon put that right,' said Mrs Kettle. 'That boa would do anything for you.'

Billy put the unseen rat on the floor and began to twitter at the boa on his shoulders. But Rembrandt was obviously enjoying his invisibility. Charlie felt him run over his foot;

a table shook, a kettle fell to the floor. They all followed the tiny patterings and excited squeaks though the arch and into the shop. Mrs Kettle dropped to her knees and began to crawl round the kettle displays; the boys followed her example and the boa joined in, slithering across the floor with a purposeful look on his scaly face. Mrs Kettle began to laugh. Charlie couldn't stop himself from giggling, and now even Billy began to see the funny side of things, and he lay on the floor convulsed with laughter.

No one noticed the shop door opening just a fraction, not enough to make it squeak. No one heard soft footsteps crossing the floor, and no one saw Eric Shellhorn slip through the arch and run to the big metal door leading to Mrs Kettle's smithy.

It all happened in less than a minute, and then the blue boa was curling itself into a knot. There was a very loud squeal and a black rat jumped free of Solomon's shiny coils, and ran to Billy.

'Thanks, Solomon.' Billy picked up the trembling rat, gave him a stroke and slipped him into his pocket.

'A nice cup of tea is called for, m'dears,' said Mrs Kettle, getting to her feet, 'and maybe a cookie or two.'

The boys followed her back to the table, and Solomon slithered across the floor beside them. When Billy sat down the boa lifted his head and began to sway. Charlie sensed that it was anxious, even fearful. It looked up at Billy and hissed.

Billy answered the boa with a light hum. 'Solomon says

someone came into the shop,' he told the others.

'Well, there's no one here except us,' said Mrs Kettle. 'Did your snake say who it was?'

'I asked him, but he didn't know.'

Charlie watched the boa slide back to his home inside the big iron kettle. He felt uneasy. The boa had no reason to lie. It was wise and gentle, not a trickster. Something made Charlie ask. 'You've got the stone troll here, Mrs Kettle, haven't you?'

'You bet I have, Charlie,' Mrs Kettle assured him. 'It's been chained up in my smithy ever since it attacked that poor little girl and her father. That troll had a venom all its own once Eric had brought it to life.'

The stone troll used to stand outside Charlie's Great Aunt Venetia's house. On a day Charlie would never forget, the troll had attacked Venetia's new husband and his daughter, Miranda. The poor man had been bewitched into marriage, but once he'd come to his senses, he'd left the city and taken his daughter with him. Eric had remained with his stepmother. Venetia had her own unpleasant endowment: she could bewitch her victims by treating their clothes with poison. But she dreamed of using Eric's talent to further her craving for power.

'I think I met it,' Charlie said slowly, 'when it was real. It was called Oddthumb.'

'Met it, Charlie? The troll?' Mrs Kettle stopped stirring her tea and fixed her amber-coloured eyes on him. 'Would you mean – on your travels?'

'Yes,' Charlie replied, and he recounted his adventure in Badlock.

Mrs Kettle sat in rapt attention. Only once did she lift her teacup, very slowly, to take a sip of her rapidly cooling tea. And when Charlie had finished she could only shake her head for a while in mute dismay.

In the unfamiliar silence, Charlie felt a coldness pervade the shop. Was it his imagination or did the bright kettles suddenly lose some of their lustre?

'The shadow's trying to come back again,' Mrs Kettle spoke almost to herself. 'Lock your cellar door, Charlie, and throw away the key, before that painting captures you again.'

'But Runner Bean!' Billy protested.

'You'll forget him, Billy, if you're wise,' said Mrs Kettle.

She must know that we can't do that, thought Charlie. But Mrs Kettle looked so solemn, so weighed down with some secret trouble, he realised that her warning was in deadly earnest.

'The Stone Shop is occupied again,' Mrs Kettle said at last. 'For years it has been vacant; half-finished carvings in the yard, the statues in the shop covered in cobwebs. But two days ago I heard a hammering. Chink! Chink! Chink! Metal on stone. I left my smithy and walked down the alley behind the shops. I looked into the stone mason's yard and there he was: a fierce-looking man with a yellow moustache and a cowboy hat. Melmott, he said his name was. But that was all he'd tell me. I fear he's the first of many.'

'The first of many what?' asked Charlie.

'Magicians, m'dear, for want of a better word. Once the whole street was full of them, but by the time I'd inherited this place from my grandpa, they were all gone. And now . . .' Mrs Kettle collected the cups and took them to the sink beside the stove.

'And now what?' prompted Billy.

'And now the wickedness is coming back,' said Mrs Kettle. 'It's not just Eric, it's those children at Bloors: the drowner, the magnet, the poisoner, Manfred-the-hypnotist, and then there's that witch, Mrs Tilpin, the magnet's mother; they're all of them getting stronger, m'dears. And people like us have got to watch out for each other. I'm the only one left in this street, boys. The only one who can stop them, that is. And I've a strong feeling they're going to do something about it. Don't know what. But I'm on my guard.'

'Mrs Kettle, can I have a look at the troll?' asked Charlie.

'Now, do you really want to?' Mrs Kettle glanced at the metal door, reluctant to let Charlie into her smithy.

'I just want to make sure that Oddthumb's still in there.' Charlie's anxiety was growing.

Mrs Kettle sighed, wiped her wet hands on her boiler suit and opened the metal door. Charlie stepped into the smithy. It looked very much the same as the last time he'd been there. Bare brick walls, a dusty stone floor and an assortment of tools hanging from a beam. The anvil stood in the centre of the room, and the hum of flames could be heard behind a small iron door at the base of the chimney.

In a dark corner stood a squat stone figure. A double chain encircled its thick waist, the two ends fixed to large iron hoops in the wall. Charlie stared at the troll, his eyes gradually adjusting to the dark. Now he could see the wide fleshy nose, the thin scribble mouth and the small gimlet eyes.

'Satisfied, Charlie?' called Mrs Kettle.

'Yes.' Charlie was about to step back when he saw a glint in the troll's left eye. Was that a blink? Mesmerised by the blink, and terrified of what it might mean, Charlie felt behind him for the door.

He was too late. There was an ear-splitting crack as the troll broke free of the wall and came flying at Charlie. He ducked, with a scream, and Oddthumb sailed through the open door and into the shop.

His whole body shaking with terror, Charlie forced himself to follow the troll. He saw it making straight for Mrs Kettle. The blacksmith didn't stand a chance. Oddthumb slammed into her head, and she sank to the floor with a groan.

Not satisfied with this, the troll began to crash against the furniture, sending kettles tumbling to the floor.

Billy crawled under a table, his arms folded tight over

his bent head. 'No, no, no,' he moaned.

'Ssssh!' whispered Charlie, crawling towards Billy.

The silence that followed his whisper was so complete, Charlie could almost feel the troll thinking. What would he do next? Could he see them? Could a stone troll hear or smell? And where was he now? Charlie held his breath.

A violent crash gave away the troll's whereabouts. He had gone through the archway into the shop, and now he proceeded to crush, dent, break and shatter every kettle in the place. The sound of iron and copper, steel, enamel and even clay breaking apart was like nothing Charlie could ever have imagined. He wondered if the wounded blacksmith could hear the terrible destruction of her beloved kettles, and if her breaking heart might be a part of the dreadful and tragic noise.

When he's broken everything he can see, he'll come back for us, thought Charlie. He quickly crawled beneath the table where Billy was hiding. 'Our only chance is to get to the smithy and lock ourselves in,' he whispered. 'But we'll have to take Mrs Kettle with us. Quick, Billy! We'd better move now, while he's still busy in the shop.'

But Billy wouldn't move. He remained in his tightly curled huddle. Not a sound escaped him.

'Billy!' Charlie shook a clenched arm.

'Mmmm!' moaned Billy.

'Billy, we must –'

Charlie never finished his sentence. Above the troll's noise, he distinctly heard the loud squeak of the shop door. Someone was coming in.

There was a heavy thump, as though the troll had landed from a great height. And then silence.

PURR SPELLS

The noise made by the troll could be heard from one end of Piminy Street to the other. Yet none of the residents had appeared at their doors. Weren't they curious? Tancred wondered. As he approached the Kettle Shop the noise increased. He looked through the window and saw a grey, lumpen thing slamming ferociously into piles of ancient kettles. The speed of the creature's lethal work filled Tancred with an overpowering rage. He marched into the shop and the troll whizzed round to face him.

From the corner of his eye Tancred saw a movement in the room beyond the arch, but his gaze remained fixed on the troll. A burst of fury from the creature almost took Tancred's breath away. Using his own rage, he summoned up the wind that was always at his fingertips. Thunder rolled across the roof and a streak of lightning lit the troll's ugly features. And then came the wind. The strength of Tancred's power surprised him. It seemed to come from deep within him, a power that coursed through his body, almost as though it were drawn towards the vile creature before him. The troll's hatred was palpable, its desire for his destruction intense, for it knew that it had met a strength equal to its own.

Tancred's storm swept round the troll, sending broken kettles flying to the back of the shop. Not content, the storm-boy stepped up the force of his tempest, until the troll became the only thing that he could see between the curtains of his hair, caught in the wind that howled about them. And in this narrow frame the stone figure began to change. Its breast-plate took on the look of dull metal, its trousers a straw colour, its face an unhealthy sepia and its eyes a gleaming steel grey. As Tancred fought to keep his gaze on this terrifying transformation, the image of a helmet appeared on the troll's bald head, and its hand, with a huge deformed thumb, reached for the knife wedged into its belt.

Tancred filled the wind with bolts of ice, and the hand stopped where it was. Seconds passed. The boy and the troll were locked in an invisible battle. When Tancred felt the troll's strength weakening, he seized his chance and aimed a rod of energy, hard as iron, straight at the troll's heart.

The troll rocked, its grey eyes flashed and it fell to the floor. For a moment nothing moved. The storm died to a light breeze and a curious silence filled the Kettle Shop. After the uproar it was almost painful. Tancred moved cautiously towards the fallen troll. It appeared to be lifeless, drained of colour.

'Tancred!' Charlie peered through the archway. 'You've finished him off!'

'Can't be sure.' Tancred stepped over the broken kettles. And then he saw Mrs Kettle lying in the shadows. 'Oh no! Is she dead?'

'No, I can hear her breathing,' Charlie said quickly.

As Tancred reached the archway, a sound made him turn. Charlie, following his gaze, saw the troll rock back on to its feet and shoot straight through the window. It was only then that they became aware of the small boy creeping along beside the wall.

'Hey!' shouted Tancred.

Eric Shellhorn darted him a look of smug satisfaction, reached for the door and ran out.

'He'll go to The Stone Shop,' said Charlie.

'Better wait for reinforcements before we go there,' muttered Tancred. He went and knelt beside Mrs Kettle. 'I'll phone for an ambulance.'

'Mrs Kettle was afraid that something would happen to her,' said Charlie. 'It made me think of the stone troll. But I never saw Eric come in.'

Tancred owned more than his fair share of mobile phones. Today he had brought the latest edition. It was sleek and silver with a turquoise keyboard. He was just beginning to dial a number when his hand was caught in an iron grip and his mobile snatched away.

'NO!' commanded the blacksmith.

'Mrs Kettle! You're . . . you're . . .' Charlie dropped to his knees beside her.

'Conscious,' she said. 'Just.'

'I'm sorry. I seem to have made a horrible mess.' Tancred looked at the wreckage surrounding them. 'I was trying to blast that awful thing out of existence.'

'You saved the day, Tancred Torsson.' Mrs Kettle patted his hand. 'It could have been a lot worse.'

'You need to see a doctor.' Tancred reached for his mobile. 'Please, Mrs Kettle, let me phone someone.'

'No.' She clutched the phone to her chest and sat up.

'That troll gave you an awful bash,' Charlie remarked, staring at her forehead.

Mrs Kettle tapped it with her fist. 'Ouch! I'll live. But look, no ambulance, no police.'

'But –' Charlie began.

'No arguments. How would I explain? A stone troll banged me on the head and wrecked my shop. The police couldn't deal with that sort of information, could they?'

Mrs Kettle had a point. But her shop was destroyed, her window broken and when she rose, unsteadily, to her feet, Charlie noticed that she had to support herself against a table. They couldn't possibly leave her in this state.

'We'll sort out the kettles for you; they're not all broken.' Charlie lifted a big iron kettle on to its stand.

'Don't you worry, Charlie. I'm not without friends. They'll be here soon, if I'm not mistaken.' She tapped some numbers on Tancred's mobile and handed it back to him. 'Put that away, storm-boy, and let's have no more talk of doctors and police. Now then.' She bent over, with a small grunt, and looked under the table. 'You can

137

come out now, Billy Raven. It's all over.'

Billy crawled out with Rembrandt's head peeping above his collar. 'I wanted to make sure it had gone.' He stood up and, pulling his rat out of his sweater, began to stroke his head. 'Rembrandt was more scared than me,' he said. 'Did you finish it off, Tanc? That stone thing?'

''Fraid not. It's on the loose somewhere, and Eric Shellhorn's not far behind it. Together they're lethal.'

Mrs Kettle insisted that the boys leave her to put the shop to rights. 'My friends will be here soon,' she said, 'but I'd like to know where that troll has got to. Don't put yourselves in danger, m'dears. Make sure Eric's not with it. Just let me know what you find out.'

'I'll update you tonight, Mrs K!' Tancred waved his mobile. 'What's your number?'

'I don't have one of those flashy things. Just pop by.' Mrs Kettle ushered them out and closed the door.

'The fish shop next,' Tancred announced, as they walked down the street.

'What d'you want to go there for?' asked Billy. 'I wish we could get out of this street.'

'I was coming to the fish shop when I heard the rumpus in Mrs Kettle's place,' said Tancred. 'I've decided to give Dagbert his sea urchin.'

'Swap it for Claerwen? Thanks, Tancred. But are you sure?' asked Charlie. 'What made you change your mind?'

Tancred shrugged. 'You need that moth, Charlie. And the sea urchin, well, we'll have to rely on our own talents to get the better of Dagbert.'

When they reached the fish shop Tancred tried the door. It was locked, as usual. He pressed a rusty bell-push and they heard a long mournful ring echo through the building. Tancred pressed again. Nothing. The bell appeared to have given its last ring.

'Dagbert!' Charlie called up to the window. 'Are you there?'

No reply.

They waited another five minutes before walking on. They passed a candle shop and a picture framer's, and then they were standing outside The Stone Shop.

Charlie's instinct was to run on. Billy did. He ran until he was at the end of the road, and there he waited, one hand resting on the rat in his pocket, the other nervously twisting his hair.

'What d'you think?' said Tancred, looking into the dark shop.

'What d'you mean, what do I think?' asked Charlie.

'I mean, shall we go in?'

'You're joking!' Charlie realised he sounded hysterical. He tried to calm down. 'I don't think it's a good idea right now, Tanc. If Eric's in there, he could set the whole lot off.'

Tancred stood away from the window. 'You're right. Hmm. We'll have to think this through.'

But where could they go to think things through? Their usual meeting place was closed, Grandma Bone would be on the prowl at number nine, and Tancred lived miles away in the hills.

'My judgement's a bit off,' Tancred murmured. 'I feel weird after all that stuff with the troll.'

'Sorry, Tanc!' Charlie fell into step beside Tancred as he walked down the street. 'How did you get here today?'

'Gabriel's mum. She dropped me off in the High Street. She and Gabriel have gone to see Mrs Onimous.'

'Hey, let's go to the Pets' Café, anyway,' Charlie suggested. 'Even if it's closed to customers, they might let us in. We're friends.'

Fifteen minutes later they were standing in Frog Street and looking into the Pets' Café. Chairs were piled on to tables, a white sheet covered the counter and not one light showed in the lanterns that usually made the café such a colourful and cosy place. It looked absolutely and utterly closed. Even the tails, whiskers, wings and claws that decorated the sign above the door didn't look as bouncy as they had before. In fact, the whole place seemed to be receding, back into the huge ancient wall behind it.

'Mrs Silk parked round the corner,' said Tancred. 'But I know she was coming here.'

Charlie rang the bell.

A light appeared behind the counter as a door was opened. Mrs Silk appeared. She hesitated, saw the boys outside the window, and came to open the door.

'How's Mrs Onimous?' asked Charlie in a reverentially hushed voice.

'Come and see!' Mrs Silk looked surprisingly cheerful. Her blue eyes were twinkling and she had tied back her brown curls in a festive-looking ribbon.

The boys followed Mrs Silk round the counter, through the bead curtain that hung in front of the doorway and into the cosy kitchen. Gabriel was cutting some bread for Mrs Onimous, who had her arm in a sling, and there, sitting in an armchair by the stove, was Mr Onimous.

Charlie could hardly believe it. Such intense relief flooded through him, he couldn't speak. Nor could anyone else. They just let themselves be taken over by the widest, longest, happiest of smiles.

A large white bandage covered Mr Onimous's furry head, there was a sticking plaster on his nose and he had a black eye, but his broad smile revealed more of his small sharp teeth than any of them had ever seen.

Charlie ran over to the little man. 'M-Mr . . . Mr Onimous,' he stuttered.

Mr Onimous took Charlie's hand in his claw-like fingers. 'There, there, Charlie. You look quite upset and, as you see, I'm right as rain.'

'We thought you were dead,' Billy blurted out. 'How did you get better, Mr Onimous?'

'Ah, how indeed? I had visitors, Billy.' Mr Onimous put his head on one side and chuckled.

'Visitors?' Billy was none the wiser. 'What sort of visitors?'

'Furry ones!' Mrs Onimous declared, in a voice that

said Billy should have known very well what sort of visitors had cured her husband.

Mr Onimous laughed out loud and from beneath his chair there appeared three sleepy-looking cats.

'The Flames!' Tancred exclaimed, sinking into a chair beside Mrs Onimous.

'The Flames!' Charlie dropped to his knees and began to stroke the three bright cats.

Billy hesitated before settling himself on the other side of Mrs Onimous. 'Rembrandt's had a bad experience,' he told her. 'He might not want to play with the Flames just yet.'

'Why, Billy, they wouldn't hurt him,' she said.

'All the same.' Billy gently touched his pocket and Rembrandt sighed in his sleep.

Gabriel poured tea for everyone and, while Mrs Silk drew trays of hot cakes from the oven, Mr Onimous proceeded to tell the story of his miraculous recovery.

'I was lying in this hospital ward, middle of the night, patients snuffling and sighing all around me. I didn't care. I thought I was done for. Almost gone. And worst of all was the feeling that someone wanted me gone. And then, through the grunts and groans and heavy breathings, I heard this sound. Patter, patter, light as fairy dust. Closer and closer, and then came the purrs – gentle, soft purrs, warm and lovely. And I began to think, I'm not gone. Not gone at all. In fact I'm very much and altogether here. And what's more, I've got a job to do. As soon as that thought entered my poor old head, I felt one of the cats leap on to my bed, then another, and another. And then Aries brings his copper-coloured face right up close to mine, and he purrs. And orange Leo rubs his cheek against my arm and purrs, and Sagittarius nips my toes and kneads my feet and purrs.

'I tell you those purrs went deep into my heart, boys. When the Flames heard my merry heartbeat and saw my eager open eyes, they jumped from the bed and walked away, as quiet and graceful as they'd come. And no one saw them, not a soul. I asked the night nurse in the morning. "Cats, Mr Onimous?" she said. "There were no cats in this hospital, I can tell you. You were dreaming," she said, "and now you've made a miraculous recovery."' Mr Onimous smiled round at everyone. 'What d'you think of that?'

Charlie wasn't really surprised. He'd seen the Flames bring someone back to life before. He'd also seen them nearly kill someone.

'Mr Onimous, I think it's great,' said Tancred. 'But we need to find out who did this to you.'

'And we need to get your café open again,' Gabriel said forcibly.

Without lifting his hand from Leo's orange coat, Charlie said, 'We've got something to tell you, too, Mr Onimous.'

Tancred said quickly, 'Maybe not today.'

Mr Onimous looked offended. 'If there's something I

should know, it had better be now,' he said. 'So, come on, Charlie, spill the beans.'

Mrs Silk insisted they all have a snack first. 'I've cooked so much,' she said, handing out some plates. 'Most of it's for the animals. What with everything that's been happening, I forgot the café was closed. It's all good stuff, though, anyone can eat it.'

'Which is best for rats?' asked Billy.

Mrs Silk pointed to some thin, pinkish sticks, and Billy took a handful.

Charlie sat at the table and took three cookies with not a hint of pink about them. Tancred chose a flat nutty-looking cake, only to be told that Mrs Silk had made it especially for Shetland ponies.

Tancred neighed and said, 'Haven't you seen my hooves?'

Everyone laughed, but when the laughter had died, there was a long silence, the sort of silence that suggests it should be filled with a story. Charlie began with the troll in the Kettle Shop, and Tancred took over, telling it from his point of view.

Gabriel and the Onimouses remained perfectly quiet, but Mrs Silk became so agitated she couldn't keep still. She scraped the baking trays, washed the mixing bowls, put away the flour and then started wiping the table. She had to give up when Tancred really got going, though. Because as he spoke, things started blowing about: wooden spoons, paper bags, cake-cutters, nuts, oats, currants and dried maggots, salt and pepper, sugar and spices all lifted into the air, collided and sank. They drifted on to heads and shoulders, tables, chairs and every other surface. So tidying and sweeping became a rather pointless exercise.

As soon as Tancred's tale had ended, Mr Onimous blew out his cheeks and said, 'Well, that was an epic battle. What a monster!'

'His name is Oddthumb,' Charlie said quietly. 'I've met him.'

Obviously another story was called for, so Charlie described his visit to Badlock. 'And now Runner Bean's stuck,' he finished, 'and I can't seem to get back to rescue him.'

'Don't go near that painting, Charlie,' Mr Onimous warned. 'You say it *sucked* you in? I don't like the sound of it at all.'

'Not at all,' echoed his wife. 'Have nothing to do with it. Lock the cellar door and throw away the key.'

'That's just what Mrs Kettle said. But what about Runner Bean?' Billy said accusingly. 'I thought you loved animals, Mrs Onimous.'

'So I do, Billy Raven, so I do,' Mrs Onimous rose to her full six feet. 'But I love you, too. And it would break my heart if you were dragged into Badlock and never came back again.'

For a moment, Billy looked quite dumbfounded. 'I didn't know,' he murmured.

After another round of snacks, Mrs Silk suggested they

all leave the café, so that Mr and Mrs Onimous could have a little nap. Tomorrow, she herself would start a campaign to get the café opened again.

Gabriel was the last one to step outside. As he closed the café door behind him, he said thoughtfully, 'Suppose the person who got the café shut down was the same person who caused the Onimouses' accident?'

'Gabriel, I won't have you saying such things,' said Mrs Silk, frowning at her son.

'Gabriel's got a point,' Tancred ventured.

'Councillor Loom closed the café because of complaints,' argued Mrs Silk. 'Who on earth would want to harm those two dear people?'

'Norton Cross rides a motorbike,' said Charlie.

Their footsteps faltered, then stopped. They had reached the High Street. Everyone looked at Charlie.

'It's just a thought,' he said.

'Don't be ridiculous!' Mrs Silk turned right and began to stride up the High Street, calling, 'Gabriel, Tancred, you'd better hurry if you want a lift.'

'Why's your mum so cross?' asked Charlie.

'She gets angry when she's scared,' Gabriel explained. 'See you on Monday, guys.' He grabbed Tancred's arm and together they ran after Mrs Silk.

Charlie and Billy made their way back to Filbert Street.

When Uncle Paton still had not returned by nightfall, Maisie told the boys he was probably asleep in his camper-van, hundreds of miles away. 'In the Highlands probably,' she said cheerfully. 'Like a dog with a bone he is, when he's on the trail of something. But at least it's only us three for supper. Grandma Bone says she won't be back till late.'

Before he went to bed Charlie made sure the cellar door was locked. He went to see if Grandma Bone had returned the key to the blue jug. She had. But Charlie wasn't going to throw it away. He had to go back into Badlock, whatever the consequences.

When Claerwen is with me, I'll try again, Charlie told himself. He wasn't only thinking of the dog, he was thinking of his promise to Otus Yewbeam.

The boys soon fell asleep, exhausted by the day's events. But a little before dawn Billy woke up. He lay in the dark, believing he had heard a sound in the house. What was it? The creak of a stair tread? The click of a door closing?

Billy sat up. He found that he wasn't afraid. Something momentous had happened. A few hours ago Mrs Onimous had said she loved him. No one had ever told him that before. Not even the aunt he had lived with after his parents had died. It was such a new sensation Billy didn't know how he felt about it. And then, gradually, it crept up on him: a profound, comforting happiness.

And then came another sound. This time there was no mistaking it. Billy would have known Runner Bean's voice anywhere.

'*Billy! Help me! Billy! Where are you?*'

Without turning on the bedside light, Billy reached for his spectacles. The street lamp outside cast a thin beam of light under the curtains. Billy quietly slipped out of bed and went to the door. Runner Bean continued to call him, and yet he suddenly felt reluctant to open the door. He looked at Charlie, sleeping peacefully. Couldn't he hear the barking? Was it only meant for Billy?

Mrs Onimous said she loved me. Why did he feel that if he went through the door he would be throwing this wonderful gift away? For minutes he stayed where he was, his hand on the doorknob, and then the dog's call became so insistent, so desperate, Billy couldn't ignore it.

As he crept downstairs, a cold breeze whipped around his feet. He reached the hall. The cellar door key was in a jug on the dresser. Billy knew exactly which one. He was about to go into the kitchen when he noticed that the cellar door was wide open. A tide of sound washed towards him: the moan of the wind, and a deep melancholy howl.

'B . . . I . . . L . . . L . . . Y!'

Billy had no choice. He must reach the voice. Dog or human? Whatever it was, it drew him towards the cellar and down the steps until his bare feet began to turn blue on the cold stone floor. From the painting, Runner Bean gazed out at him. Howling and howling.

'I'm coming,' said Billy.

The wind screamed into his ear, spun him round and dragged him to the painting, closer and closer, until his cheek was pressed against the canvas, his fingers and toes already in Badlock.

A moment later, when the wind had died, someone quietly closed the cellar door and locked it.

MR BITTERMOUSE

Charlie woke up to the sound of barking. At first he couldn't tell where it came from. He looked at Billy's bed. It appeared to be empty. Charlie got up and looked closer. Yes, Billy was definitely not in bed. Putting that fact together with the barking gave Charlie a surge of hope. Had Billy found a way to rescue Runner Bean?

Charlie stuffed his feet into his slippers and ran down to the cellar. The door wouldn't open. Strange. Had Billy locked himself in?

'Billy?' he called. 'Are you there?'

The barking increased. Claws pattered up the wooden steps and scratched the cellar door.

'Runner!' cried Charlie. 'It is you, isn't it? You're out.'

He was answered by a series of joyful barks.

'What's going on?' said a voice from the stairs.

Charlie looked up to see Grandma Bone in her purple dressing gown and pink hairnet.

'Runner Bean's got out of that painting.' Charlie couldn't disguise his excitement. 'I don't know how it happened, unless Billy did it, but the cellar door's still locked so . . .'

'Better unlock it, then.' Grandma Bone tightened her dressing-gown belt and went upstairs again. 'And get that dog out of the house,' she called. 'It's Sunday morning and it'll wake the whole street.'

Charlie ran to the kitchen. A chair had been placed beside the dresser. That was odd. He was certain he had pushed it back to the table after he'd replaced the key in the jug. Billy must have got it out, unlocked the cellar door and then locked himself in. In which case the key would be in the cellar, not the jug. Charlie climbed on to the chair and took down the jug. The key was still there.

Thoroughly mystified, Charlie took the key and hurried back to the cellar. As soon as he opened the door, Runner Bean leapt out, knocked him down and covered his face with wet kisses.

'OK! OK!' Charlie grabbed the big dog round the neck and pulled himself back on to his feet. 'Quiet!' he commanded. 'Sit!'

Runner Bean was an obedient dog. In spite of his excitement he did as he was told.

Charlie called into the cellar. 'Billy! Billy, are you there?'

There was no reply.

Charlie went down to take a better look. The painting hadn't moved but, now, not a breath of wind escaped it. Badlock appeared dull and bleak, a place of fiction, not somewhere just a step away.

'Billy!' Charlie searched every corner, beneath old mattresses, behind wood-wormed cupboards, old doors and suitcases, and bags of rubbish. There was no sign of Billy. Obviously, Runner Bean's escape had nothing to do with Billy. But, in that case, where had Billy gone?

First things first. Benjamin must have his dog.

While Runner Bean waited patiently, Charlie ran upstairs, dressed hurriedly and took the big dog across the road to number twelve.

In all his life Charlie had never seen anyone as happy as Benjamin when he set eyes on Runner Bean. The noise from both of them was enough to wake the dead, let alone every household in Filbert Street. The squeals and barks of joy brought Mr and Mrs Brown tumbling out of bed and down the stairs.

A breakfast of sausages, beans and broccoli was quickly served up, and Runner Bean was given a bone almost as big as his own leg.

Charlie was hungry but before he was halfway through the meal he suddenly stood up. 'The thing is,' he explained, 'Billy Raven's gone missing, and I ought to go and look for him.'

'Missing?' Mr and Mrs Brown laid down their knives and forks. Missing persons were right up their street. Not one of their cases of missing persons had remained unsolved.

'If you can't find Billy, come straight back to us,' said Mrs Brown.

'Will do. Thanks, Mrs Brown.' Charlie ran back to number nine.

Maisie was up, and another fine breakfast awaited Charlie: sausages, beans and mushrooms.

'I'm sorry, Maisie. I don't think I can eat much.' Charlie explained what had happened.

'I thought I heard barking,' Maisie exclaimed. 'Oh, Charlie, what wonderful news.'

'Except that Billy has disappeared,' said Charlie.

Maisie's face fell. 'Charlie, are you sure? He must be in the house somewhere. Or he could have run up the road for something. Check his clothes.'

Charlie went up to his bedroom. Billy's clothes were piled neatly on a chair, exactly where he had left them. His shoes were under the chair, his slippers by his bed. So he can't have gone far, Charlie said to himself. And, once again, he tried to dismiss the thought that had persisted in entering his head ever since he had searched the cellar. Billy was in Badlock.

No. A wave of nausea made Charlie sit down, quickly, on his bed. He was far more frightened for Billy than he had been for himself. What chance did Billy have, with his white hair and poor eyesight? The shadow's army was bound to catch him. But what possible reason could the Count have for taking Billy and letting Runner Bean go?

Unless it had been the shadow's plan all along? He had known that Billy could never resist a cry for help from a dog. Charlie remembered Manfred's insistence that Billy should come back to number nine, where the painting of Badlock waited, like a trap.

Charlie tore downstairs. 'He has gone, Maisie. And I know where. He's in that painting.'

'I can't believe it, Charlie,' said Maisie. 'If he's gone I'm going to ring the police, there's no two ways about it.' She went into the hall and began to dial.

Knowing it would be useless to try and stop her, Charlie waited in the kitchen. He listened to Maisie's voice insisting that a child called Billy Raven was missing, and then her angry response at something she'd been told. 'Bloor's Academy. Mr Ezekiel Bloor, or perhaps the headmaster, Dr Bloor. But the boy disappeared from here, not there.'

There was a pause while Maisie sighed heavily and tapped her foot. 'Thank you. And will you let me know? . . . I'll ring *you*, then. Goodbye.' She slammed down the phone and came back to the kitchen, looking flushed and cross.

'They can't proceed until they're authorised to do so by the child's guardian,' said Maisie. 'I suppose it must be Dr Bloor, Billy being an orphan. What a palaver!'

Charlie said nothing. He was now utterly convinced that Billy had been captured by the painting. How pleased Grandma Bone had been when she saw Billy arrive. It was obviously she who had locked the cellar door after Billy had 'gone in'.

Charlie sat by the kitchen window, waiting for Uncle Paton to arrive in the white camper-van. He saw Benjamin and Runner Bean walk down to the park. He saw Mrs

Brown go to the post-box; she was wearing a skirt and high-heeled shoes, for a change. It was no use telling Mrs Brown that Billy was still missing.

Maisie brought Charlie a mug of hot cocoa. 'Your uncle might not come back till next week. Don't look so forlorn, Charlie. I'm sure little Billy will turn up.'

'He won't,' muttered Charlie.

He discovered that the cellar door key was still in his pocket. When he'd finished his cocoa he went down into the cellar and stared at the painting of Badlock. He scrutinised every inch of it, looking for a way in. He didn't care if he was caught again, if only he could find Billy. But the shadow had no use for Charlie Bone at present. It was Billy he wanted.

'Why have you taken him?' Charlie shouted at the painting. 'Have you made a bargain? Billy for your freedom to travel back into the world? Well, you won't do it, Count Harken. Not now. The Mirror of Amoret was broken, *so there's no way back. Ever!*'

A blast of wind hurled Charlie against the opposite wall.

'You heard me, then!' he cried.

Dust, laden with splinters, flew into his face and he covered his eyes, just in time. His nostrils were filled with grit: it even crept between his teeth. Choking and sneezing, Charlie crawled across the cellar floor. He stumbled up the steps and fell into the hall. As he lay there, rubbing his eyes and spitting dust, he became aware of a tall figure looming over him.

'Foolish boy,' said Grandma Bone. 'What did you hope to achieve?'

Charlie sat up and glared at her. 'You did it, didn't you? You opened the cellar door and then locked it behind Billy. I know he's in Badlock, and somehow I'm going to get him out.'

'Don't meddle with the shadow,' she said grimly.

Charlie watched his grandmother walk to the front door. She was wearing her Sunday best: shiny black shoes, a Persian lamb coat and a purple velvet hat. The back of her bony shoulders expressed utter contempt.

There was roast beef for lunch, accompanied by Yorkshire pudding, roast potatoes, crispy sprouts and rich gravy. It was Charlie's favourite meal, and he tried to do it justice, but the food kept sticking in his throat and he had to lay down his knife and fork. 'I'm sorry, Maisie, it just won't go down,' he said.

'Tell you what, I'll give the police another ring,' Maisie said. 'Let's see if they've made any progress.'

Charlie didn't expect to hear good news, but he was totally unprepared for what Maisie had to tell him. She came running back from the phone crying, 'They've found him, Charlie!'

Charlie stood up, his fork clattering to the floor. 'Found him?' he said in disbelief.

'He went back to Bloor's, that's what the police said. They rang the school and Dr Bloor said that Billy had turned up very early this morning. He was feeling homesick, the headmaster said.'

'But, Maisie, he left his clothes, even his slippers. He can't have walked all that way in bare feet and pyjamas.'

'Then they're lying, Charlie, and I don't know what I can do about that.' Maisie went to the sink. She ran the tap and water splashed loudly on to the dirty plates and pans. 'I wish your parents were here,' she muttered. 'Your father understands these things better than I do.'

'Well, he isn't here,' said Charlie, adding bitterly, 'he's never here.'

Maisie turned to face Charlie. She didn't reprove him for what he'd said. Instead a look of pity crossed her face. 'I'm sorry, Charlie,' she said gently. 'These things that happen to you and your friends, they're beyond my comprehension. I just can't deal with them.'

'I'll go to the bookshop,' said Charlie, leaving the kitchen. 'The others may be there.'

'Don't go alone, Charlie, please,' called Maisie. 'I know something's not right in this city, even if I can't understand it. I believe in your flying trolls and magic kettles and . . . and evil paintings, you know I do. I just get so upset sometimes.'

Charlie's mind was made up. But, as luck would have it, he didn't have to go out alone. The doorbell rang and, when Charlie opened the door, there stood Benjamin and Runner Bean.

'Want to come over to my place?' said Benjamin.

When Charlie explained that he was on his way to the

bookshop Benjamin agreed to go with him.

On their way to Ingledew's, Charlie brought Benjamin up to date. Runner Bean bounded along in front of them, as though he were trying to escape from his own tail. His eyes still had a wary look and he was easily spooked. Flying litter, swinging gates and hooting cars all had him leaping sideways with a loud yelp.

'I can't believe a headmaster would lie,' Benjamin panted as they ran to catch up with the yellow dog.

'Well, he did,' said Charlie. 'I know that Billy's in Badlock. What I can't work out is why the shadow wants him.'

They were now in the older part of the city, where the great cathedral towered above the surrounding shops and houses. Runner Bean had dropped behind them for some reason. Every now and again he would give a low whine, and sniff anxiously round a doorstep or a lamp post. All at once, the dog's whining became a full-blooded yelp of terror.

Charlie and Benjamin turned to see a huge and hideous creature approaching. The thing had to be a dog, but its legs were like concrete pipes and its body showed not a trace of hair. Its head was a grotesque mockery of a hound with a broad snout and dead stony eyes. The 'thing' had teeth, however. Oh, yes, it had teeth; longer and sharper than any earthly dog should have.

Runner Bean growled and, with incredible courage, moved forwards; his ears were back, his body low and his tail touching the ground. He was afraid, but determined to defend the boys.

Benjamin grabbed Charlie's arm so tightly it hurt. 'That thing will kill him, Charlie.'

Charlie was thinking fast. Eric had to be near. It was Eric they had to deal with, not the hound. Charlie scanned the doorways and saw a crouching form, tucked behind a narrow porch.

'Ben, get Runner to attack the boy,' cried Charlie. 'See! There! Quickly!'

The two dogs were getting closer to each other. The stone hound's feet pounded the cobbled street like a slow, heavy machine. Thump! Thump! Thump! And then it made a sound, hollow and unearthly; it stopped Runner Bean in his tracks, but he didn't retreat.

Benjamin spotted the crouching form. 'Runner!' he yelled. 'There! There! Get him!'

Runner Bean looked back. He seemed confused.

'There!' Benjamin pointed. 'There, Runner. Get him! Now!'

Runner Bean ran so fast the stone hound had no time even to put out a paw. But as Benjamin's dog leapt on to Eric Shellhorn, the boy emitted a hissing chant and the stone hound turned and flung itself at the yellow dog.

There was an explosion of sound and a cloud of dust filled the street. One side of the porch had fallen in, and its narrow tiled roof hung at a dangerous angle. The front door had vanished, so had the hound. It was now inside the house.

Runner Bean limped towards Benjamin, holding up a paw. There was no sign of Eric. Hidden by the dust cloud, he must have raced back to Piminy Street.

'Now what?' said Charlie. 'Why is Eric doing this? Does he want to kill me, or is it Runner Bean he's after?'

'Look, the owner,' whispered Benjamin.

An elderly had man emerged through the broken doorway. He stared at the boys with a dazed expression. He was very thin, with strands of crinkly white hair, deep-set eyes and the sort of skin that appears never to have seen the sun. His black suit was shiny with age, and his high collared shirt was a dirty parchment yellow.

'Did you see that?' The man's frail voice hardly reached them.

Realising he couldn't deny it, Charlie walked towards the man, saying, 'Yes, we did, sir.'

'There's a ruddy great stone thing in my hall,' the man said tremulously, 'all broken up. Looks like a stone dog.'

'It is, sir,' said Charlie, peering into the old man's hall. 'At least it was'. The hound's head had separated from its body; the rest lay about the floor, covered in bricks.

'I am a retired solicitor,' the old man told Charlie. 'Mr Hector Bittermouse. You may have heard of me.' He didn't wait for Charlie to reply. 'Look! I haven't done any harm for sixty years, so why would anyone do that?' He pointed to the rubble in his hall. 'Who was it?'

Charlie struggled to reply. He could hardly tell Mr Bittermouse that a six-year-old boy was responsible for demolishing his door. It was too incredible. 'It was . . . it was . . .' Charlie was aware that Benjamin and Runner Bean were now standing just behind him. Benjamin also found it impossible to provide Mr Bittermouse with an answer.

'No!' Mr Bittermouse suddenly cried out. 'It was one of them, wasn't it?'

'One of who?' asked Charlie.

'One of those people from Piminy Street. I should have moved years ago, but I thought they'd all gone, and moving is such an upheaval.' The old man began to wring his hands. 'Oh dear, oh dear. What am I to do?'

Mr Bittermouse was clearly not up to the task confronting him, so the boys helped to clear the rubble into the street and prop up the broken door. And then Charlie had a bright idea. Norton Cross, the large Pets' Café doorman, would probably be looking for work.

'If you send a letter to Mr Norton Cross, the Pets' Café, Frog Street, I think he'll be able to help you, Mr Bittermouse,' said Charlie. 'He's very strong, and nothing frightens him.'

'Write it down for me, young man.' Mr Bittermouse beckoned them into a dark study, where a huge mahogany desk filled almost an entire wall. The old man pulled down a flap as big as a table and, taking out a pen and a notepad, handed them to Charlie. Charlie wrote down Norton's name and the Pets' Café address.

'And what would your name be, young man?' asked Mr Bittermouse.

'Charlie Bone, sir.'

'Bone,' said the old man thoughtfully. 'My older brother knew a Bone – Lyell Bone.'

'He's my father,' said Charlie.

'They were friends,' went on Mr Bittermouse, 'good friends. Their relationship wasn't just professional.'

Charlie had no way of knowing that his next question would have far-reaching consequences. He merely wanted to know how and why his father had become friends with a man who must be very old. 'Who is your brother, Mr Bittermouse?' asked Charlie.

'He's a lawyer like me, *was* a lawyer, I should say. Though he still does a bit of work, now and again, for special friends. Barnaby Bittermouse is his name. He's over ninety but his memory is a lot sharper than mine. Lives all by himself in Tigerfield Street. Number ten.'

Charlie filed all this away in his mind. But how could he forget names like Tigerfield and Bittermouse? And how could he forget the number ten?

TANCRED'S NOTE

Charlie and Benjamin left Mr Bittermouse without meeting his wife. She must be very deaf, thought Charlie, not to have heard her porch falling down. Nobody else had heard either, for that matter. Or if they had, they were keeping well away. The street was deserted. But then most people would be huddled round a fire or the TV on a cold Sunday afternoon.

Ingledew's bookshop was not far from Mr Bittermouse's house. Had Miss Ingledew heard the noise?

Yes, she had. 'Charlie, Benjamin, how good to see you,' said Miss Ingledew as she opened the door to them. 'You didn't happen to see what caused that awful crash just now, did you?'

'Yes, we did,' said Charlie.

Olivia, who had been packing books behind the counter, suddenly popped up like a jack-in-a-box, causing Runner Bean to leap in the air with a yelp.

'So what was it?' asked Olivia.

'I'll tell you about the crash first,' said Charlie, 'but really I've come to ask Miss Ingledew's advice.

Something awful has happened to Billy Raven.'

Olivia pulled aside the curtain behind the counter and called, 'Bad news, Em!'

'Oh, no!' said Emma in a suitably tragic voice.

They all joined her in the back room, where Miss Ingledew had a good fire burning. A pile of roast chestnuts by the grate reminded Charlie of Christmas. There was even a jug of hot blackberry juice just inside the fender.

Tucked into a corner of the sofa, with hot chestnuts in his hands and a mug of blackberry juice on the table beside him, Charlie recounted his extraordinary weekend. There were interruptions, of course, most of them from Olivia, but Benjamin and Runner Bean, lying together on a rug before the fire, fell fast asleep. The others looked quite exhausted by the time Charlie had finished, but at least they'd stayed awake.

Charlie was disappointed with Miss Ingledew's reaction. 'Your uncle will know what to do,' she said. Her face was a picture of worry.

'But he's not here,' said Charlie, peeling his last chestnut.

'Where is he, Charlie? Where's he gone? He was away all last week. What are we going to do without him?' Miss Ingledew seemed to have reversed their roles. Now *she* was asking Charlie for *his* advice.

'I was hoping you would know,' Charlie replied.

'Oh!' Miss Ingledew, who was sitting at her desk, nervously flipped over a page on her calendar, picked up a pen and put it down again. Was it possible that she was missing Uncle Paton?

Wedged in beside Charlie, Olivia was frowning with concentration. Emma, at the other end of the sofa, was staring into the fire, with her chin resting on her hands. All at once, Olivia made a loud huffing sound and cried, 'I know. We'll go and see the headmaster. Perhaps Billy did go back to school, but if he's not there, we'll ask Dr Bloor where he is. He'll have to tell us.'

'He won't tell us the truth,' Emma said gloomily. 'He could easily say he's sent Billy away, or something.'

Miss Ingledew stood up and began to pace about. 'It's the Piminy Street business that worries me,' she said. 'Poor Mrs Kettle. I must pay her a visit. And Mr Bittermouse! That creature could have killed him. Something should be done about Eric.'

Benjamin had woken up. Rubbing his eyes and yawning, he grumbled that Runner Bean had never hurt anyone, so why had a stone dog been sent to kill him?

'Perhaps it wasn't,' Olivia said brightly. 'Do you want to know what I think?'

'Tell us, Olivia.' Miss Ingledew sat down again and put on an earnest expression.

'I think the stone hound was *meant* to break down Mr Bittermouse's door,' Olivia said triumphantly. 'Runner Bean just happened to be in the way. Remember, Charlie? You said Mr Bittermouse said, "I haven't done any harm for sixty years." Which means he did once, and someone's getting back at him, at last.'

Nobody argued. It made perfect sense. Except, as Miss Ingledew pointed out, the someone who put Eric up to his nasty tricks must be quite old, by now, if Mr Bittermouse had harmed them such a very long time ago.

'It could be a family feud,' Benjamin suggested.

'Yes, yes, Benjamin, I think you're right.' Miss Ingledew sat down again. 'Their descendants are returning to settle old scores, to continue the feuds that began centuries ago.' She frowned. 'But why now? And who has summoned them?'

'The shadow,' said Charlie.

Olivia shook her head. 'It can't be the shadow. Why do you keep coming back to him, Charlie? The shadow was banished. He's gone. If he hadn't, he'd be seen in the streets, causing trouble, appearing at Bloor's. He was an enchanter, for goodness' sake; he'd be creating mayhem, after what happened to him.'

'Then he's reaching those Piminy Street people through someone else,' Charlie claimed. 'Mrs Tilpin. She still has the Mirror of Amoret. Even though it's broken, perhaps she can still talk to the shadow.'

'Let's hope no one can mend the mirror,' said Emma.

Miss Ingledew gave a little shiver, as though she were trying to shrug off something unpleasant. 'I must get back to work. I've a lot to do before the shop opens tomorrow. Stay as long as you like, boys, and finish those chestnuts while they're warm.'

When Miss Ingledew had gone, no one spoke for a while, and then Olivia said, 'Shall we go and see Dr Bloor tomorrow, then, Charlie?'

He didn't like the idea at all; he knew that Billy was in Badlock, but Olivia had boxed him into a corner. 'I'll go alone, if you don't mind,' he said. 'Billy was staying with me, so it's my responsibility.'

'OK. But just let me know if you want me to come.' Olivia peeled another chestnut. 'I think I'll dye my hair green tonight.'

'Good,' said Charlie, for want of a better word.

So much had happened over the weekend Charlie couldn't be blamed for overlooking a very important detail. It was Benjamin who brought it up as he and Charlie were walking home.

'Was Rembrandt with Billy when he disappeared?' asked Benjamin.

Charlie stopped dead. 'I don't know,' he said slowly. 'He wasn't in my bedroom. I'd have seen him.'

'Well, if you find him in the cellar, it means that Billy was definitely there, doesn't it?' Benjamin looked rather pleased with himself.

'Certainly does, Ben.' Charlie felt much more optimistic. At least there was something he could do to prove that Billy had gone into the cellar.

'Good luck, then, Charlie!' Benjamin sprinted across the road to number twelve, with Runner Bean bounding beside him.

When he reached his own front door, the yellow dog looked back at Charlie, as if to say, 'Rather you than me.'

Rembrandt was not in the cellar. Charlie turned over every mattress, bag, box, moth-eaten blanket, pillow and suitcase. He even forced himself to look behind the sinister painting, still propped against the wall.

'Charlie, whatever are you doing?' Maisie called softly from the hall.

'I'm looking for Rembrandt,' Charlie shouted, not caring who heard.

'Rembrandt? Didn't Billy take him, then?'

'Yes, he probably did,' Charlie said angrily, as he climbed the cellar steps. 'Only *you* think he took him to Bloor's, and *I* think he took him to Badlock.'

Maisie said sadly, 'I wish your uncle would come back.'

But Uncle Paton didn't come back. And next morning there was no sign of a white camper-van outside the house, and no answer when Charlie knocked on his uncle's door.

There was, however, a postcard.

'Look! Look!' cried Maisie, running into the kitchen. 'Your mum and dad have written. I'm so glad it arrived before you left for school.'

Charlie looked at the picture on the front of the card. A cold shiver ran down his spine. He picked up the card and stared at it.

'Charlie, whatever is the matter?' said Maisie. 'Turn it over and read the message.'

But Charlie couldn't tear his gaze from the image

on the front: a small sailing boat, riding the waves of an endless grey sea. It was the boat Charlie had seen in his nightmares, in the moments when he had fought off Manfred's hypnotising stare, and glimpsed the thoughts behind those cruel black eyes.

Unable to bear the suspense, Maisie snatched the card away and read:

'This is such fun, Charlie, we have decided to stay away a little longer than we had planned. A letter to Maisie will explain. I'm giving this to the captain of a passing yacht. He'll reach dry land long before we do.

We think of you every day. All our love, Mum and Dad xxx'

'Well, that's not so bad, Charlie. We'll manage, won't we? Don't look so upset.'

'It's the boat.' Charlie's throat was dry with fear.

'What about it?' Maisie turned the postcard over. 'It's a nice little boat. I expect they've got someone to sail it for them. They wouldn't go out alone.'

'It's going to sink,' Charlie said with conviction.

'I've never heard such rubbish. They might not even be on this boat.' Maisie jabbed a finger at the postcard. 'It's just a picture, Charlie. Whatever's the matter with you? Anyone would think you begrudged your poor parents a little bit of time together.'

Charlie felt too wretched to reply. He walked out of the kitchen, went to fetch his bags, and left the house without even saying goodbye.

News of the 'wicked weekend', as Olivia was calling it, had reached everyone who mattered in Bloor's Academy before the first break. Unfortunately, it had also reached a lot of people who didn't matter. Although Joshua, Dorcas, Dagbert and the twins probably did matter, in so far as they made Charlie feel even worse with their sidelong smirks and snide remarks.

It all came to a head as they were filing down the Corridor of Portraits for lunch. Joshua sidled up to Charlie and whispered, 'Where's your friend, the little white rat, Charlie? Has he been adopted by a nice mummy rat?'

Charlie shoved Joshua backwards, grunting, 'Shut up, you moron!'

Joshua had legs like pins. He lost his balance at the slightest shove. Charlie's small push sent him flying into the portrait of a rather disagreeable-looking woman. The very same woman whom Dagbert had so tactlessly insulted.

This time Manfred's great-great-great-grandmother, Donatella Da Vinci, came tumbling off the wall. There was a scream of pain as the portrait landed on the already prostrate Joshua Tilpin.

'What's going on?'

Silent children parted like waves as the Talents Master came storming down the corridor. When he saw the portrait

170

of his ancestor lying across Joshua Tilpin, Manfred's mouth fell open in horror. He uttered a strangled cry and then, turning in fury, bellowed, 'Who did this?' It was clear that he was more concerned with the fallen portrait than the boy underneath.

'Charlie Bone, sir.' Dorcas Loom tried not to smile, but the effort was too great.

'Do you think this is funny, Dorcas Loom?' Manfred demanded.

'No, sir,' answered Dorcas, instantly losing her smile.

'Someone help me!' Manfred lifted one side of the portrait.

Bragger Braine stepped forward and took the other side. A moment later, Donatella was back in place but, horror of horrors, there was a small hole above her right eyebrow. It had not been noticed while she lay on Joshua, probably because of the long wrinkle on her unforgiving forehead.

There was a chorus of gasps. Charlie caught Donatella's eye. She was cursing him in the most unpleasant language. He hoped, desperately, that he wouldn't find himself in her century.

Manfred was turning from white to red, and back again to white, all in the space of thirty seconds. Charlie didn't dare to move. He wanted to close his eyes, but forced himself to keep them open while he awaited his fate.

The Talents Master uttered a crescendo of growls that ended in a very long roar. In one breath he screamed,

'Charlie Bone go to the headmaster this minute and tell him what you've done!'

'Yes, sir.' Charlie was glad of the opportunity to escape Donatella's curses, but he would have preferred to visit the headmaster in different circumstances. He began to make his way back down the corridor, which was difficult because of the press of children who were trying to get to the canteens.

Fidelio, squeezing himself closer to Charlie, whispered, 'Good luck.' He pressed a note into Charlie's hand. 'Tancred . . .'

Someone pushed Fidelio aside and Charlie failed to hear the rest of his friend's sentence. He quickly put the note into his pocket as Fidelio was swept away.

'I'm still going to ask him about Billy,' Charlie said to himself as he walked to the door leading to the west wing. When Charlie opened the door a small white caterpillar, hidden in a crack in the old wood, fell on to his shoulder. Slowly it began to crawl down the back of his blue cape. By the time Charlie had reached Dr Bloor's study, the caterpillar had tucked itself into the sleeve of his shirt.

Before he knocked on the door, Charlie glanced down the thickly carpeted corridor. There was not one empty space between the rows of doors on either side. Every inch was filled with shelves of books, glass cases holding skulls and ancient artefacts, upright leather trunks, carved chests, grandfather clocks, gilt-framed mirrors and oddly dressed wax figures.

As if all this were not enough, the ceiling was hung with stuffed birds, dried plants and mechanical toys, all moving slowly in a draught from the distant staircase; their tinny, rustling, creaking sounds competing with the melancholy ticking of the grandfather clocks.

Charlie wondered what went on in the many rooms behind the shiny oak-panelled doors. He decided that he would rather not know. Squaring his shoulders, he took a deep breath and knocked on Dr Bloor's door.

'I'm coming,' said an irritated voice.

This was not what Charlie had expected. He knocked again.

'For goodness' sake, what's the hurry? Will the soup get cold if I'm a minute late?'

Plucking up courage, Charlie said loudly. 'It's Charlie Bone, sir.'

'What the dickens?' Quick strides could be heard approaching the door. The next moment it was flung open and Dr Bloor stood glowering at Charlie. 'What's the meaning of this?' he demanded. 'I don't see miscreants at this hour. It's lunchtime.'

'I know, sir.' Charlie swallowed the unwelcome lump that had arrived in his throat. 'But the Talents Master sent me.'

'For Pete's sake, why?'

Charlie ran his sleeve beneath his nose and sniffed.

'Don't *do* that!' bellowed Dr Bloor.

'Sorry, sir. I'm here because I knocked Joshua Tilpin

over and, somehow, he banged into a portrait and . . . and . . . and . . .' Charlie was finding it difficult to describe the hole in Donatella's forehead.

'AND?' shouted Dr Bloor.

'And Donatella Bloor, née Da Vinci, I believe, now has a hole,' Charlie placed a finger above his right eyebrow, 'just here.'

For what seemed like a very long time, Dr Bloor could not speak. He just stared at Charlie, his grey lips working away beneath his neat moustache. At last, in a low, menacing voice, he said, 'You stupid, insufferable, loathsome, detestable child. I knew it would come to this.'

Charlie was going to ask what Dr Bloor meant by 'this' but just then, Weedon emerged from a door further down the corridor.

'Your lunch is served, Headmaster,' the porter announced, in a tone that suggested a feast had been prepared.

Dr Bloor grunted, 'In a moment. Weedon, take this boy to the Grey Room.'

Charlie would never know where he got the courage to say what he did next. With Weedon thumping towards him, he knew he didn't have much time, so he just came out with it, all in a rush.

'Dr Bloor, Billy Raven didn't come back here on Saturday, did he? I know he didn't, so why did you tell the police he did? I mean if he *is* here, then where –'

Charlie watched Dr Bloor's face go through an

amazing transformation. At first he looked astonished, as though he couldn't believe that Charlie had the temerity to ask such a question, and then his features hardened into a cold, forbidding mask. 'Get him away from me,' he shouted at Weedon.

Weedon had already grabbed Charlie's collar, and now he heaved him half-choking down the corridor.

'I know he's not here,' Charlie spluttered doggedly. 'I know . . . I know . . .'

Weedon suddenly opened a door and thrust Charlie inside. There was a loud click. Charlie didn't have to try the door to know that it was locked. He found himself in a cold, grey room. There was nothing in it. Not one thing. The floorboards were rough and unpolished, the walls plain grey stone. There was no heating of any kind. At one end of the room a small, round window showed four quarters of a sky the colour of lead. Charlie had no way of reaching the window. It was far too high, and there was nothing to stand on. But Charlie wasn't easily disheartened. He pulled his hood over his head, wrapped his cape tightly around himself, sat in a corner with his knees up, and prepare himself for what was obviously going to be a long wait.

In such a position the slightest movement in any part of the room would have alerted Charlie, so when the caterpillar appeared on the floor beside him, he was immediately interested. He watched the tiny creature make its way across the floor and then begin to climb the stone wall. When it was a few inches above the level of Charlie's head, it began to twist and turn, releasing a thread of glistening silk. Round it went, up and down, the silk covering its body in a shining cocoon.

While the caterpillar was occupied in this way, Charlie suddenly remembered the note Fidelio had given him. Charlie pulled the crumpled paper from his pocket and unfolded it. The note read:

You'll have your moth by tonight, Charlie. I'm meeting Dagbert in the Sculpture Room before supper.
Tancred.

'You're a star, Tanc!' Charlie quickly pushed the note back into his pocket. And then, for no reason that he could think of, he had a pang of misgiving.

What was wrong with him? He stared at the silk cocoon, its radiance increasing every minute, until the grey walls were bathed in a comforting glow. With a sudden explosion of light, the cocoon burst apart, and a white moth flew out in a shower of stars.

'Claerwen!' breathed Charlie.

The moth settled on to his knee and spread her damp wings. But even as those white wings began to dry and shine with a greater brilliance than ever, Charlie was thinking of his friend.

If Claerwen was here, then what was in store for

Tancred when he descended into the Sculpture Room, where Dagbert-the-Drowner was waiting?

A DROWNING

'Hide!' Charlie whispered.

The white moth allowed her wings to fade until they were the same colour as the dull stones in the wall, and then she crawled into the pocket of Charlie's cape.

When the moth was safely hidden, Charlie began to bang on the door. 'Hey!' he called. 'When are you going to let me out? I'm sorry, OK? I didn't mean to spoil the portrait.'

He was answered by the half-hour chimes of five grandfather clocks. Charlie looked at his watch. Only half past three. Perhaps they would release him at tea time.

But no one came at four o'clock. Or five. At half past five, hungry and thirsty, Charlie began to bang on the door again. He had to see Tancred before he returned the golden sea urchin. Who knew what Dagbert could do once he had all the sea-gold charms again?

At twenty minutes to six, hoarse from shouting and overcome by a terrible weariness, Charlie slumped to the floor and fell asleep. He had no way of knowing that a battle was about to begin.

In winter, the hours between the end of lessons and supper were considered free-time for the students of Bloor's Academy. Some were busy with rehearsals, of course, but Tancred and Dagbert were not gifted in music or drama, so half past five seemed a good time to meet.

Only Fidelio and Lysander were aware of Tancred's plan, but Fidelio had to rehearse with the school orchestra, and Lysander was playing table-tennis in the gym.

The Sculpture Room could only be reached by opening a trapdoor in the Art Room and descending a steep spiral staircase. At the end of the school day, the trapdoor was always closed.

Emma was surprised to see Dagbert Endless lifting the trapdoor at half past five. She had never seen him in the Art Room before. There was such a forest of easels in the room, Dagbert didn't notice Emma working behind her canvas in a far corner. Tancred didn't see her either. Emma watched him descend into the Sculpture Room, only moments after Dagbert.

Everything Tancred did mattered to Emma, and when she saw him following Dagbert down to a room where an old tap dripped constantly into a stone trough as big as a bath, she was instantly alarmed.

For a few minutes Emma continued to add colour to the group of birds in her painting, but she found it difficult to concentrate. She decided she must know what was happening in the room below. But if Tancred saw her looking in, he would regard her as an interfering girl, a nosy-parker or, even worse, a spy.

There was another way. Emma could use her endowment. It was something she did very seldom. While some used their unusual talents almost every day, Emma preferred to keep hers for emergencies. Was this an emergency? Decidedly yes, she thought, remembering the dripping tap and the tomb-like trough.

Putting down her paintbrush, Emma stepped away from her easel, took off her cape and closed her eyes. She thought of a bird, very small, like a wren; a tiny, brown speckled bird that would never be noticed, perched, in shadow, at the back of a wrought-iron step.

While Emma imagined her bird, she began to dwindle; smaller, smaller and smaller, until she was the size of a fledgling wren. Her arms became brown speckled wings and her legs black and needle-thin beneath the downy feathers that covered her body; and then came the head with its bright black eyes and sharp yellow beak.

The brown bird hopped across to the open trapdoor and dropped on to the top step.

White sheets covered the undefined shapes standing about the Sculpture Room like ghosts. Tancred had his back to a wood-carving; a seven-foot gryphon. Dagbert sat on the edge of the stone trough. Behind him, the old tap dripped. The trough appeared to be half full.

'I like the carving,' Dagbert said. 'Is it yours?'

'Lysander's,' Tancred replied. 'It's a gryphon. Have you brought the moth?'

'Have you got my sea-gold creature?'

'Of course. Where's the moth?'

Dagbert smiled. 'Here.' He drew a small glass jar from his pocket. At the bottom lay something white. Tancred couldn't see what it was. He had to step closer.

'The sea urchin!' Dagbert demanded.

Tancred peered into the jar. It certainly looked like Charlie's moth lying at the bottom. How could he know that Dorcas Loom had made an excellent replica? She had even painted the wing-tips a luminous, glowing silver.

Tancred put his hand inside his cape and withdrew the sea urchin. As Dagbert made to grab it, Tancred snatched the jar. Now both boys had what they wanted, their meeting should have ended but Tancred stared uncertainly at the motionless object lying at the bottom of the jar.

'You've tricked me!' Tancred suddenly cried, filling the room with a wind that blew the covers off every sculpture and carving. 'This isn't Charlie's moth!'

White sheets flapped in the turbulent air; tools, brushes, pots and tins rolled about the floor, and Emma huddled down on her step as the wind swept through her feathers.

The full force of the wind struck Dagbert in the face. He closed his eyes and with one hand clutched his seaweedy hair as though it might be torn from his head. 'I'm stronger than you, Tancred Torsson!' he screamed.

The dripping tap spun off the wall and water gushed out in a torrent. In a second the stone trough had overflowed and a bubbling stream rushed across the floor. Staggering against the current, Tancred slipped and crashed against the stone trough.

Emma heard a thump as Tancred's head hit the side of the trough. He lay unconscious, face down in the water. The wind died and, hopping forward, Emma saw Dagbert standing over Tancred.

'You'll never get my sea-gold charm again,' cried Dagbert. 'Never, never, never.'

Emma held back the shriek that she wanted to utter. If she were to help Tancred, she must stay alive, stay hidden.

Clutching his golden sea urchin, Dagbert leapt up the stairs. He never noticed the tiny bird sitting like a dried leaf in the corner of the top step.

With a juddering bang, the trapdoor closed, and Emma heard Dagbert's footsteps thundering above. There was no time to wonder if the trapdoor had been locked. Emma flew down to Tancred. Perching on his head, she began to peck frantically at the blond hair, but the storm-boy didn't move. She would have to roll him over, Emma realised, so that his nose and mouth were not beneath the water. For a tiny bird this was impossible. She would have to change.

'Hurry! Hurry! Hurry!' Emma urged herself as the feathers melted and her body grew. A girl at last, she rolled Tancred on his back, put her hands under his arms and dragged him upright.

Tancred gave an enormous spluttering cough and sat up. 'Aw, my head,' he groaned. 'Em, what happened? What are you doing here?'

'Dagbert,' was all she said, before whirling up the steps.

It was as she had feared – the trapdoor was locked. It would be useless to scream; no one would hear them. The whole school would be in the dining hall by now. Emma tore down the staircase and ran to the trough. Plunging her hand into the water, she found the tap and tried to jam it into the wall, where water still gushed from an open pipe.

It was impossible. Time and again the tap dropped out. The trough was overflowing and there was now at least fifteen centimetres of water in the room. Soon it would be a metre, two metres, three. This was no ordinary flow. It was a torrent, brought on by Dagbert and his set of golden charms, complete now that he had the sea urchin. Water was seeping under the door into the next room, where first-formers took their drawing lessons.

There were no windows in these basement rooms. Strips of halogen lighting ran across the ceiling and two small vents let in the air. Emma dragged a chair to the wall, jumped up on it and tugged at the grille covering one of the vents. It fell into the water with a loud splash, and Emma looked into a dark cavity, where fresh air swirled from an opening high above. I must go in there, thought Emma, there is no other way.

Tancred had closed his eyes. Emma ran to him and shook his shoulder. He slipped sideways and fell into the water. Pulling him upright, Emma cried, 'Tancred, you must sit up. You *must*. I have to get help, but if you fall into the water and I'm not here . . .'

Tancred opened his eyes. 'Yes, Em,' he mumbled. 'My . . . legs . . . are . . . under . . . water.'

'Yes, but you must keep your head above. Can you walk?'

'Think so.' His voice was little more than a croak.

Emma helped him to stumble across to the chair beneath the vent. The water splashed against their shins in a vicious tide. Tancred dropped on to the chair and clung to the sides, but it was obvious that he found it hard to stay upright. Emma looked round the room. The gryphon would be too heavy to move, she decided, but there were two plaster tigers that might serve her purpose.

Emma pushed the tigers either side of Tancred. Their heads came just above his elbows. 'Who made these?' she asked as she hastily began to change shape again.

'I did.' Tancred smiled sleepily. 'My tigers.' Resting his arms on their wide, painted heads, he looked down at the small bird skimming the water close to his knees. 'They'll keep me safe, Em.'

Would they? Suppose they couldn't? Emma thought as she flew into the vent. Above her the darkness was complete. It wasn't easy, even for a tiny bird, to fly blind, up and up, through a narrow pipe. Time and again her wing-tips brushed against the sides, tilting her backwards and making her head spin. But at last she reached a bend in the pipe and found that she could stand. Ahead of her a tiny patch of light showed the way out. She hopped to the end of the pipe. Now she had to make a quick decision. The whole school would be in the underground dining hall. No one would hear her if she knocked on the great oak doors. And if she rang the bell, who would open the door? Weedon, the porter, who had not an ounce of sympathy for any endowed child.

There was only one place she could go; only one man strong enough to demand entry to Bloor's Academy and rescue Tancred. Emma flew towards the Heights, a distant hill crowned by a thick forest of pines.

The Thunder House stood in a forest glade; visitors to the place were few, for the surrounding air was always turbulent. Thunder growled above the trees and an incessant north wind carried hailstones, even in the summer.

Small birds became as helpless as toys when they drew near the Torssons' home. Tossed between clouds and deafened by thunderclaps, they could do little more than close their eyes and hope to keep airborne.

But hope was not good enough for Emma. In the whole world, no bird was as fiercely determined. She *would* reach Tancred's father, and he would save Tancred.

As Emma approached the mysterious house with its three pointed roofs, the wind increased its grip. She could hardly breathe as the current's iron fist tightened about her. With a soundless cry of fear she gave in to the wind and allowed it to hurl her at the Thunder House.

The bruised little bird ruffled her feathers and stretched

her needle-thin legs. 'Haste! Haste!' she cried, and before she was fully changed, she began to rap on the Thunder House door with a fist that still had not lost all its feathers.

When the door was opened, it would be difficult to say who was the most startled; the half-bird-half-girl on the step, or the seven-foot man with his moon-yellow hair and electrified beard.

They had met once before and Emma knew Mr Torsson was a kind man beneath his stormy exterior. 'It's Emma,' she said. 'I'm sorry I'm still not quite me.' Then, reaching her full, featherless height, 'Ah, here I am.'

'Emma Tolly?' boomed Mr Torsson.

'Yes,' Emma shrieked through a thunderclap and, without pausing for another breath, she cried out her news. Every word she uttered increased the tempest that erupted from the thunder-man, and before she had finished her hand was seized in long icy fingers.

'We'll ride the storm,' roared Mr Torsson, whirling Emma off her feet.

Afterwards, Emma could never find the words to describe her journey through the air. She was flying and yet she was not a bird. The storm lifted her, cradled her, swung her feet into its arms and rushed her through the sky. The storm had moon-yellow hair and bolts of lightning grew from his beard. Beneath him, the hooves of an invisible horse thundered over the clouds.

It was over in less than two minutes. They landed in the courtyard of Bloor's Academy and, before Emma could gather her thoughts, Mr Torsson had mounted the worn stone steps. One blow from his icy fist sent the great doors crashing apart, their long iron bolts scudding over the flagstones.

'Where's my son?' roared the thunder-man, striding into the hall.

'This way,' cried Emma, running to the staircase.

The ancient wood groaned in distress as Mr Torsson mounted the stairs. The banisters rattled and the carpets sighed as hailstones bruised their thick pile.

'This way! This way!' called Emma, running down the passage that led to the Art Room.

Voices could now be heard in the hall. 'Who's there? What's going on?'

Easels clattered to the floor as Mr Torsson marched through the Art Room. He reached the trapdoor and Emma pointed to the bolt that held it shut. She could hear the water gurgling beneath them. How high would it be, now?

In almost one movement, the thunder-man had pulled open the trapdoor and whirled down the spiralling steps. Emma, following, saw to her horror that the water was now level with the tigers' eyes. Tancred had gone.

'Don't touch the water!' Mr Torsson commanded as he waded through the flood.

Shafts of electricity lit the water and the room was bathed in the reflected blue-white glow. The thunder-man bent down and with a dreadful sucking splash lifted his son out of the water. Tancred's face was a deathly grey.

'NO!' With tears streaming down her face, Emma scuttled back up to the Art Room. Thundering footsteps and the steady stream pouring from Tancred's clothes followed her up the steps and through the tangle of fallen easels.

Squelch! Squelch! Squelch! Mr Torsson's wet boots punched damp holes into the floorboards as they hurried down unlit passages, until they came to the landing above the hall.

Dr Bloor stood looking up at them. Behind him, some of the staff had gathered. They stared at Mr Torsson, their mouths agape, like dying fish.

'You'll pay for this!' bellowed Mr Torsson, raising the boy he carried.

Hissing blue water streamed down the polished staircase and spilled on to the flagstones. Fearing electrocution, the crowd moved back with exclamations of alarm. But old Mr Ezekiel, in his rubber-wheeled chair, moved to the foot of the dripping stairs and croaked, 'Why should we pay? Your son has evidently made a mess; must have left the tap running and slipped in the water.'

'LIAR!' boomed the thunder-man.

Hailstones the size of oranges rained down on the terrified staff. Most ran, howling childishly, into the nearest passage; a few, including Dr Saltweather, raised their hands protectively above their heads and waited to see what would happen next.

They didn't have to wait long. The next minute a bolt of lightning whizzed round the panelled walls. Flames began to eat at the wooden signs above the cloakroom doors, and then all the lights went out. When Mr Torsson thumped down the staircase, the whole building shuddered. Distant bangs and crashes could be heard as paintings fell off walls, furniture toppled over and cupboards flew open, disgorging their contents over anything and anyone in their way.

Down in the dining hall, children clutched their plates while knives and forks flew in every direction.

'Do not impale yourselves,' Mrs Marlowe, Drama, called theatrically through the darkness. 'It's just a thunderstorm. Stay calm.'

'A typhoon more like,' said Bragger Braine.

'A typhoon, definitely,' echoed Rupe Small.

Crouching on the landing, Emma watched Mr Torsson's huge silhouette move across the hall. In the dangerous flicker from tiny fires all round the room, she could just make out the retreating figures of Dr Bloor and Mr Ezekiel, in his wheelchair.

With a final, deafening crack of thunder, Mr Torsson stepped between the open main doors and down into the courtyard. Emma longed to follow him, but she didn't dare to move. She stayed where she was while the staff rushed about, shining torches and setting things to rights. And then she crept up to her dormitory and waited to tell Olivia the unbelievable, heartbreaking news.

Charlie sat huddled in a corner of the Grey Room. He guessed that the violent thunderstorm must have had something to do with Tancred. But what had happened? He longed to know.

When the storm had passed, a profound silence settled into the passage outside. It was as though the grandfather clocks and mechanical toys were holding their breath. A minute later they started up again, even louder and faster than before.

Charlie looked at his watch. Nine o'clock. Had they forgotten his existence? Did they intend to starve him? He was too hungry and too cold to sleep.

At half past nine the door opened. Charlie leapt up. A powerful light was beamed at his face, and he covered his eyes with his hand.

'Can I go now?' asked Charlie. 'And . . . and could I have something to eat?'

'Oh, yes, Charlie Bone, you can go!' It was Weedon's gloomy voice. 'You've been excluded.'

'Excluded?' uttered Charlie.

'I'm taking you back to your home, where you can cool your heels for a while.'

'But –'

'No buts. Follow me.'

Charlie had no choice. He was led down to the hall, where there was a strong smell of burning.

'I suppose the storm knocked the lights out,' said Charlie.

There was no reply.

'Can I get my bag?' asked Charlie.

'No bag. No fraternising,' growled Weedon as he fiddled with the main doors.

'The bolts are broken,' Charlie observed. 'Was that the storm, too?'

'Shut up!' said Weedon.

Charlie followed the burly figure across the courtyard and down into the square. The street lights still gave out their bright glow, and Charlie saw a black car parked beside the school steps.

'Get in,' Weedon ordered.

Charlie obeyed. He was a little frightened and very confused. This had never happened before. Why hadn't he been given detention, or some other punishment?

Weedon swung himself into the driver's seat and turned on the engine.

'Why is this happening?' cried Charlie. 'What's going on? Can't you tell me, please, Mr Weedon?'

'I can tell you one thing, Charlie Bone.' An ugly smile crossed Weedon's face. 'Your friend, the weather-boy, was drowned tonight.'

CHARLIE IS EXCLUDED

I don't believe you. The words were on Charlie's tongue but he couldn't utter them. A sickening, deadly chill settled over him and he knew it must be true. Dagbert-the-Drowner had won. And Tancred had lost.

Charlie held his face in a rigid mask. He would not let the man beside him see the tears that had filled his eyes. But Weedon did not even glance at Charlie. The porter was staring at the road ahead. Raindrops the size of pebbles began to lash the windscreen and intermittent thunder rolled above the city.

'Who does he think he is?' growled Weedon. 'The thunder man.'

The thunder man! So Tancred's father knew what had happened. Had he tried to save his son? Charlie wondered. He didn't want to speak to Weedon but suddenly found himself asking, 'Did Mr Torsson come to the school?'

'Huh!' Weedon grunted. 'Don't know how he knew, but he was there all right. Nearly set fire to the place.'

'But he couldn't save Tancred?'

'No.' Weedon put on a silly, spiteful voice. 'He couldn't

save his little boy.'

Charlie gritted his teeth. There were no more questions to ask.

'Soon there won't be any of you left, will there, Charlie Bone? Now little Billy's gone too.' Weedon gave a hoarse cackle. 'You might as well give up and use your talent for something useful. Give old Mr Ezekiel a hand.'

Never, thought Charlie.

'I hope you haven't forgotten your mummy and daddy, all alone on the big wild sea.' Weedon's tone had changed. He sounded in deadly earnest.

Charlie didn't have to answer. They had arrived outside number nine, Filbert Street.

'Get out,' said Weedon.

As soon as Charlie had climbed out of the car, Weedon leaned over and slammed the passenger door. The car sped off, showering Charlie with a muddy spray.

Charlie imagined that Maisie would answer the door. He began to prepare an explanation for his sudden arrival. But he needn't have bothered. It was Grandma Bone who stood on the threshold when the door opened. She had obviously been waiting for Charlie.

'They've told me everything,' Grandma Bone said grimly as Charlie stepped into the hall. 'Upstairs.'

'Could I have –?'

'Nothing,' she said. 'That's what you can have. Nothing.'

'But I'm so hungry.' Charlie clutched his stomach. 'I haven't eaten since –'

'Didn't you hear me?' his grandmother raised her voice. 'Upstairs.'

Maisie's frightened face appeared round the kitchen door. 'What's going on?' she asked. 'Charlie? You're soaked, love. What's happened?'

'None of your business,' said Grandma Bone.

Annoyed by her tone, Maisie walked assertively into the hall. 'It certainly is my business. Charlie's soaked. Come into the kitchen, love.'

'I haven't eaten since breakfast,' Charlie said with desperation. 'I'm *so* hungry, Maisie.'

'He has been excluded from school,' said Grandma Bone. 'He is being punished for outrageous behaviour.'

'You surely wouldn't begrudge him a sandwich, Grizelda.' Maisie felt Charlie's damp cape. 'Take that off, love. You'd die of pneumonia *and* starvation if some people had their way.' She threw a defiant look at Grandma Bone and pulled off Charlie's wet cape.

'One sandwich,' said Grandma Bone, reluctantly. 'Then bed.' She went upstairs and slammed her door.

Maisie drew Charlie to the stove and sat him down in the rocker. 'Tell me everything, Charlie. What's been going on?' She went to the fridge and brought out an armful of food. 'You'll soon have the biggest sandwich I can manage. So come on, love. Tell all.'

Maisie's kindness was too much for Charlie. A sob rose up from his chest and threatened to choke him. 'Oh,

Maisie,' he cried. 'Tancred's dead.'

'What?' Maisie stared at him aghast.

The tears that Charlie had been holding back now streamed down his face and splashed on to his hands as he vainly tried to wipe them away.

'Charlie! Charlie, tell me what happened!' begged Maisie, using her hanky to dab Charlie's cheeks.

'I don't know, Maisie. I don't know. I was locked up.' And Charlie told Maisie everything that had happened until the moment Claerwen had emerged from her shining cocoon. 'I knew Tancred had been tricked, then.' Charlie gave a shuddering sigh and wiped his eyes. 'But I never thought Dagbert would . . . would really drown him.'

'So it's come to this.' Maisie put a plate of huge sandwiches on Charlie's lap. 'I'm glad you've been excluded, Charlie. I don't think you should ever go back to that awful place.'

'But I've got to, Maisie. There's only three of them now. Well, four, if you count Olivia, I suppose. They *need* me there.'

'No, they don't. Your parents need you. I need you. And there's an end to it.' Maisie pulled up a chair and sat opposite Charlie, watching him eat.

It would be useless to try and explain, Charlie realised. He could hardly explain it to himself, this instinctive need to be with the others: Gabriel, Emma, Olivia and Lysander. Because only if they were together could they stop the shadow from returning to the city and . . . And what? Charlie didn't even dare to think about that.

'Claerwen!' he cried. 'She's in my pocket.'

Maisie caught the plate that would have rolled off Charlie's knees as he leapt up and ran into the hall. The white moth had climbed out of his pocket and now sat on top of the coat hooks, sending tiny rays of light across the dark hall. She immediately flew on to Charlie's arm and he carried her into the kitchen.

Maisie watched Charlie settle back into the rocker and handed him his plate. 'Don't think you can go travelling again,' she said, eyeing the moth. 'Grandma Bone's taken the key to the cellar door. So you can't get into that painting, Charlie, with or without your little moth.'

'Oh?' Charlie gave Maisie a sideways look. 'Billy *is* in Badlock, Maisie. He wasn't at school.'

'Whatever you say, Charlie.' Maisie folded her arms across her chest. 'Now you eat up that sandwich and go to bed, or your other grandma will be down here telling me to pack my bags or else.'

Charlie didn't want that to happen. If Maisie went, number nine wouldn't be a home at all. So he wolfed down the very delicious sandwich and dutifully took himself up to his room.

In a last long, mournful rumble, the thunder rolled away, and the storm's heavy tears became a thin drizzle. The troubled citizens turned their pillows, closed their eyes and fell asleep at last. But if any of them had been watching the Heights, they would have seen three bright lights, red, orange and yellow, moving swiftly up the hill towards the Thunder House.

When the great cathedral clock chimed two Charlie was still wide awake. How could he have slept after such a dreadful day? He put his hand under his bed and touched the iron kettle. He had expected it to be hot, but it was barely warm.

Claerwen appeared to be asleep. She lay with folded wings at the end of Charlie's bed. A few hours ago Charlie had been more afraid than at any other time in his life. And yet here, in his room, the danger seemed to have receded. The city was quiet, except for a sound, quite close: a light, rhythmic beat.

Charlie went to the window and looked out. Was that a horse trotting down the street? He must be mistaken. But when a white horse moved into the circle of light thrown out by the street lamp, Charlie saw the rider; he saw the red feathers lifting in the breeze like a halo around the silver helmet. And he saw the jewelled scabbard at the knight's side, and the glint of the Red King's sword-hilt.

Charlie watched the red knight and his horse move slowly down the street. He watched until they had disappeared from sight, then he lay on his bed and fell fast asleep.

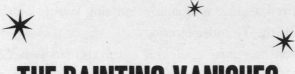

THE PAINTING VANISHES

Bloor's Academy was in shock. Something had happened to Tancred Torsson, that much was certain. But very few people knew what it was. The Children of the Red King knew, and they weren't telling.

There had been a thunderstorm. The Sculpture Room was flooded, the school had been in darkness for twenty-four hours. The cloakroom signs were scorched and a strong smell of burning lingered in the hall.

Rumours abounded. Some said that Tancred had drowned. Children kept their distance from Dagbert Endless. The staff carried out their duties, but most of them seemed distracted. They lost their lesson notes, forgot their books and, on occasion, even went to the wrong classroom.

Lysander Sage was in danger of exploding into violence. His mind was in a turmoil, his thoughts full of vengeance for his lost friend. Such passion was bound to wake his spirit ancestors, and the sound of their drumbeats followed Lysander wherever he went. Dr Bloor knew better than to rebuke the African, aware that it would probably make things worse.

Only Mrs Tilpin, in her flooded rooms, threatened to 'do something' about Lysander Sage. With water underfoot and drumming overhead, she complained to Manfred that she was losing her mind. 'And then where would you be?' she snarled.

Manfred told her to bide her time.

Dr Saltweather spent more and more time in the blue canteen. He was frequently seen in Cook's company. They both looked worn out with talking.

Two days after the thunderstorm Gabriel and Fidelio reached the blue canteen five minutes before lunchtime. As they had hoped, Cook and Dr Saltweather were sitting at a table in the corner. They were deep in conversation and didn't notice the two boys enter the canteen. Cook had her back to them.

Fidelio gave a slight cough as he approached the corner table. He didn't want to give Cook a fright.

Dr Saltweather looked up and said, 'What do you boys want? You're five minutes early.'

'We wanted to ask you something, sir.' Gabriel looked over his shoulder to make sure no one had followed them.

Cook swung round quickly and smiled with relief. 'I'm glad it's you two,' she said.

'We know what happened to Tancred,' Fidelio said solemnly. 'Emma told us. And that's bad enough –'

'It's about the worst thing that's ever happened.' Gabriel brushed his floppy hair out of his eyes. 'And I still can't really believe it. There are so many rumours flying about. But what we can't figure out is –'

'What's happened to Charlie, sir?' Fidelio said in a rush. 'He was here on Monday, then he was sent to the headmaster, and we haven't seen him since.'

'He's been excluded.' Dr Saltweather gave a wry smile. 'For damaging a valuable painting. But he'll be back next week.'

'Don't worry, boys. Dagbert hasn't got to him yet.' Cook suddenly grabbed Gabriel's arm. 'Perhaps I can ask you something now. Do you know what's happened to my little Billy Raven?'

Gabriel looked at Fidelio before saying, 'Yes. Emma told us. Charlie thinks Billy is in Badlock.'

'What?' Cook jumped up and looked hard at Gabriel. 'That can't be true. Billy's not a traveller. And how could Charlie possibly know?'

'There's a painting in Charlie's cellar,' Gabriel told her. 'His great-aunt put it there. It's a picture of Badlock, Charlie says, where the shadow lives. Billy went into the cellar . . . and never came out.'

Cook and Dr Saltweather looked so shocked, Fidelio added quickly, 'Dr Bloor says Billy came back here, but we haven't seen him.'

'And nor have I.' Cook spoke so quietly they could hardly hear her. 'Nor have I.'

'What shall we do, sir?' Gabriel asked Dr Saltweather.

The large Music teacher stood up. 'Keep me posted,' he said. 'That's all I can suggest. Let me know everything you think I *should* know, and I'll do my best to find out what's going on.'

Dr Saltweather marched out of the canteen, just as a crowd of Music students came rushing in. They began to queue beside the counter, and Cook hurried into the kitchen.

Fidelio and Gabriel went to the back of the queue. Neither of them wanted to stand directly behind Dagbert Endless. Fidelio allowed a gap to form until he was several paces away from Dagbert.

'What's the matter?' Dagbert turned and gave Fidelio one of his icy blue-green stares. 'What have I done?'

'You tell me,' said Fidelio, bravely closing the gap.

Dagbert shrugged and moved on.

No one wanted to sit with Dagbert. But he didn't seem to care. He took his plate of spaghetti to a far corner and tucked in. He didn't look up, once, during the whole meal. And he walked out after his first course, even though it was treacle tart for pudding. He'd been summoned by the Talents Master. But Dagbert didn't want anyone else to know that. He was going to be late, but he didn't see why he should go without a bit of spaghetti to keep up his strength.

Manfred was in his study, eating, when Dagbert knocked on the door.

'You're late,' called Manfred. 'Come in, then, Dagbert.'

'Sorry, sir.' Dagbert pressed the knot of wood and the door swung inwards.

'I told you to come before lunch,' said Manfred, without looking up from his plate.

'I'd have missed the spaghetti.' Dagbert eyed the slice of tart on Manfred's plate. 'I went without my treacle tart, anyway.'

'Don't think you can have mine.' Manfred gave Dagbert a spiteful glance. 'Going without lunch was supposed to be part of your punishment.'

'*Punishment?*' Dagbert looked extremely offended. 'What have I done?'

'Now you're being stupid.' Manfred pushed the last of his tart into his mouth and washed it down with a glass of water.

Dagbert waited, inwardly fuming, but not confident enough to show it.

'The flood,' Manfred said at last. 'You didn't have to go that far. Fairy Tilpin's furious. The water seeped into all her rooms. Now she's demanding to be relocated.'

Dagbert's arctic eyes roved round Manfred's study. 'It's a big house,' he said. 'I'm sure you could squeeze her into a room in the west wing.'

'Not enough bathrooms,' said Manfred. 'Dad and I don't like sharing.'

'She'd only need a basin and a –'

'Stop talking about bathrooms.' Manfred's fist came down hard on his desk. 'I'm disappointed in you, Dagbert. I thought we had an understanding. I'm afraid you're getting detention. The headmaster has ordered it.

No going home on Saturday.'

Dagbert smiled. He hated his temporary home in the fish shop, where an elderly carer cooked unappetising food, washed his clothes, snored in bed and never spoke to him.

'And you can stop smiling,' said Manfred. 'You've drowned someone. You weren't supposed to do that. You were only meant to scare them. What possessed you?'

Dagbert let his gaze drift down to his feet. He wasn't afraid of Manfred, but he knew the Talents Master could probably hypnotise him if he wanted to. 'I couldn't stop myself. I suppose I was trying to prove I was as strong as my father.'

'Ah, the family curse.' Manfred lifted an eyebrow. 'Do you believe it, then?'

Dagbert shuffled his feet. 'I have to. It's written in the annals of the North, and they have never lied. When the Lord Grimwald's first son is in his thirteenth year, he attains full power, and either he or his father dies. In eight hundred years the prophesy has never failed. My mother gave me the sea-gold charms to help me overcome my father.' Dagbert lifted his head and his eyes flashed defiantly. 'But Tancred Torsson got under my skin, he taunted me, he stole a sea-gold creature . . . he . . . he . . . had to be stopped.'

The Talents Master listened to Dagbert and a thin smile softened his gaunt features. 'You shouldn't have done it, though. You'll have to make amends to Fairy Tilpin.'

Dagbert shrugged. 'I'll clean out a room for her; carry her stuff upstairs, if you like.'

'Good idea. I dare say we can find somewhere in the attics. She seems to like the dark.' Manfred smiled again, this time to himself. 'You can go now.' He waved his hand.

'Thank you, sir.' Dagbert walked over to the door and turning to Manfred added, 'I always try to do what you want – always.'

'I know you do,' said the Talents Master. 'And very soon you'll be called upon to perform the hardest task of your life. Until that time comes, you must keep an eye on Charlie Bone.'

'A picture-traveller?' Dagbert snorted. 'What can he do?'

'Don't underestimate him.' A look of hatred crossed Manfred's face. 'The blood of a Welsh wizard runs in Charlie Bone's veins. And something tells me that he has reclaimed his wand.'

Charlie had been confined to the house for almost a week. He longed to talk to his friends and he worried about the schoolwork he was missing. How would he catch up when he returned to Bloor's? He'd have to work all day and all night if he didn't want to get detention.

On Friday morning Grandma Bone carried a pile of books up to Charlie's room. Attached to the books were several lengthy notes from his teachers.

'You're to do all this work before Monday,' she said, plonking the books on Charlie's table.

Charlie looked at the notes and sighed. They were from Mr Carp, English; Mr Pope, History; Madame Tessier, French and Mrs Fortescue, Biology. 'All of it? It's much more than I usually have in a whole week. I can't do it.'

'Can,' said Grandma Bone, and strode out.

Charlie sat at his table and began with History. There were so many dates to memorise. He would need help.

'Claerwen!' Charlie called softly.

The white moth flew down from the curtain and settled on Charlie's wrist.

'Helpu fi,' said Charlie, using the language his Welsh moth preferred. 'Help me.'

Claerwen crawled quickly up Charlie's arm and came to rest on his shoulder, just beneath his right ear. Charlie read the dates aloud once, twice, three times, then he closed his eyes and let Claerwen's gentle presence seep into his mind. Opening his eyes, he covered half a page with his hand, so that only the questions were visible. He found that he could remember every single date.

'Thank you, Claerwen.' Charlie closed his book with a smile. Not for the first time, he wondered about his Welsh ancestor, the magician who had made a wand of ash wood, a wand so cunning it could transform and survive all attempts to destroy it.

The front door slammed and Charlie looked out of the window. Grandma Bone was walking briskly up Filbert Street. She wore her grey shopping hat and wheeled a large black basket.

'I think it's time for you and me to go and find Billy,' Charlie said to the white moth.

Maisie was in the kitchen with the volume turned up high on the television. It would be difficult to convince her that he must try, just once more, to rescue Billy. Charlie would have to distract her, somehow, so that he could get the cellar key. And then his heart sank, for he remembered that Grandma Bone had taken the key away. He was about to open the kitchen door when Claerwen suddenly left his arm and flew down the passage towards the cellar.

'What is it?' Charlie followed the moth.

The cellar door appeared to be open, just a fraction. An invitation, perhaps, for Charlie to enter the painting again, and be trapped forever. Or did Grandma Bone know that the shadow would block any attempt to reach Billy, and therefore locking the cellar was an unnecessary precaution?

Charlie stood at the top of the cellar steps, pondering. He descended one, two, three steps, and peered down into the dimness of the dank-smelling room. It had changed in some way. He descended another three steps until he could see the whole cellar.

The painting had gone.

'No!' Charlie rushed up the steps and along the passage, crying, 'Maisie, Maisie, it's gone. Where did it go?'

He burst into the kitchen, where Maisie was sitting in her favourite armchair, enthralled by a weepy movie.

'What's gone?' she muttered, wiping a tear from her eye.

'The painting!' Charlie shouted. 'The one in the cellar! Where is it, Maisie?'

'How should I know?' she said, still held by the drama on the screen.

'But I can't get into Badlock!' cried Charlie.

'If you ask me,' said Maisie with a sigh, 'it's all for the best.'

THE SHADOW'S PALACE

Billy's journey into Badlock had been swift. One minute he had been putting out his hand to touch the painted Runner Bean, and the next something had seized his arm and dragged him forward, past the howling dog and into a mist that fell about him like the softest rain. On and on, through a forest of silver trees and shining lakes. Sometimes he flew and sometimes he gently trod a path that whispered like silk beneath his bare feet.

And now, here he was, standing before a door as tall as a lamp post, an iron door with small sharp spikes protruding from it; they ran down each side, across the top and all along the bottom. There was no handle and no lock, which suggested that the door must be operated either by some heat-sensitive device – or by magic.

As soon as Billy realised that he wasn't dead, or even hurt, that he could breathe just as easily as he had before the painting had kidnapped him, he forgot to be frightened, and curiosity took over. He stepped back to get a better look at the building that spread into the mist on either side of the iron door. It was like a fortress but the walls appeared to be made of marble, smooth, glossy black marble whose surface had an oily gleam in the moist air. Halfway up the walls, iron brackets had been set into the marble. There must have been at least twenty of them, and in every one a tarry fire blazed.

Badlock was not how Charlie had described it. There was a wind, true enough, Billy could hear it moaning and howling in the distance, but it did not touch him in any way. His smooth white hair remained unruffled, his face and hands merely warmed by the flames above him.

Billy turned around and found that, if he had taken just one step more, he would have fallen to his death, for he was standing at the very edge of a steep cliff. Below him a vast plain stretched to the horizon, where strange narrow towers pointed at the sky. On either side of the plain, barren grey mountains rose endlessly into the purple clouds that rushed in every direction above the bleak and seemingly deserted land.

A voice, slippery as satin, said, 'Well now, Billy Raven!'

Billy swung round with a gasp. The iron door had opened soundlessly, and there stood a man Billy had seen only once before, but whose image had burned in his memory every since.

Count Harken, the shadow, was of average height, but he gave the impression of being very much taller. His shining, gold-flecked hair rose high from his forehead; his eyes were brown one moment, the next a deep olive green. He had prominent cheekbones and a high-bridged imperious nose. He was dressed entirely in emerald-green velvet.

Billy opened his mouth, and closed it uselessly.

'Enter.' The count stood back and made a mocking bow. 'Welcome to my palace.'

Billy stood frozen to the ground. Beyond the count he could see a long hallway carpeted with furs. Rushlights flared from the black marble walls and, worst of all, to Billy, the ceiling was hung with the heads of many animals, their glassy eyes still reflecting the terror of their capture.

'What ails you, boy? Come.' Count Harken seized Billy by the arm and dragged him inside. The iron door closed silently behind him.

'Follow,' commanded the count.

Billy had no choice. Stepping as lightly as he could over the soft pelts of bears and tigers, he followed his host down the long, death-filled corridor, half-closing his eyes so that he should not see the distant heads that he would have to walk beneath. And it was then that Rembrandt chose to speak.

'*Billy, where are we? What's up?*' the rat squeaked.

The count whirled round. 'What is that?'

Billy had completely forgotten that Rembrandt was sleeping in his deep pyjama pocket. Without thinking, he answered, 'My rat, sir.'

'What *is* that?' the count demanded.

'I told you, sir, my rat,' said Billy.

'WHAT IS THAT?' bellowed the count.

210

It dawned on Billy that the count did not actually know what a rat was, or had somehow forgotten. He gently lifted Rembrandt from his pocket and held him out.

'*Oops!*' squeaked Rembrandt. '*This is bad news, Billy.*'

'I had forgot,' grunted the count. 'We do not have rats here. My soldiers ate every one of them, long, long ago. Give it to me.'

'No.' Billy clasped Rembrandt to his chest. 'I can't. I can't live without Rembrandt. I won't!'

The count looked surprised. 'You have spirit, boy. Very well, you can keep the odd-named thing, if it occupies you. It spoke. Don't deny it. I know you understand its language. What did it say?'

Billy wondered if the question was a trick. Perhaps the count could speak the language of animals. Billy decided to chance a lie. 'He said we are in a fine place, sir.'

The count eyed Billy quizzically. 'Did it say that? Hm. I shall have to trust you – for now.' He turned and strode on, his long pointed shoes hissing softly over the thick furs. And Billy followed, feeling almost guilty that such a carpet should be so warm and comforting to his bare toes.

It took a considerable time to reach the end of the corridor, but at last they were there, and another iron door slid back soundlessly to reveal a vast chamber. Suspended from the roof by iron chains were three circles, set one upon the other at intervals of twelve inches or so, the smallest at the top, the widest at the bottom. At least fifty candles had been set into each circle, and every one burned with a fierce white flame. Billy was so taken with this amazing chandelier it took him several seconds to notice the three figures seated before a huge fire at one end of the chamber.

'My family!' the count announced. He dragged Billy forward. 'And this is *it*!'

'The boy!' cried a girl, leaping up from a mound of cushions. 'You have brought it.' As if Billy were a thing.

She came bounding towards Billy, over a sea of rugs, a small, bright-faced girl with black curls and round brown eyes. She wore a long yellow dress, patterned with golden flowers, and her wide smile immediately put Billy at ease. When she saw Rembrandt, however, she stopped abruptly and, pointing at the rat, cried, 'What is that?'

'A rat, child,' the count told her, 'from your grandmother's land. It won't harm you. The boy holds it fast in his power.' He turned to Billy. 'Matilda is my granddaughter. Over there,' he pointed to the fireplace, 'you see my grandson, Edgar, and my wife, Lilith.'

Billy nodded wordlessly. The boy, in dark green jacket and breeches, did not look up from the book on his lap. The woman, however, turned to stare at Billy from the large chair where she reclined. Her head rested on the chair's tall carved back, her hands lay on the thick wooden arms. When Billy met her black-eyed gaze he felt a chill run through him, and Rembrandt whispered, *'This is a mistake.'*

'It made a noise,' cried Matilda. 'Your rat, sir.'

212

'I am not a sir,' Billy said quietly. 'I am just Billy.'

At this the boy did look up. He was older than his sister by at least four years, and he was not a bit like her. His blond hair was neatly cut, and his eyes a startling green.

Matilda came up to Billy, still watching Rembrandt anxiously, but Billy hastily slipped the black rat into his pocket, and this brought the smile back into her face. 'I like your mask, sir, but it is glass, and I can see right through it.' She touched the arm of Billy's spectacles. 'It is something from the future, perhaps.'

'Er – yes,' said Billy.

'Oh, and your eyes are the colour of berries,' she went on. 'How enchanting. And your dress, too, is most interesting. But you have no shoes.'

'I didn't have time to put them on,' said Billy, glancing at the count.

'Our grandfather told us that he would bring a boy from the future for our amusement.' Matilda gently drew Billy towards the great marble fireplace. 'And he said it would be our duty to care for you. Isn't that right, my lord?'

'Make sure he is ready to dine.' The count threw these words at Matilda as he walked back to the iron door which, obediently, opened for him, and closed after he had gone.

Billy stood before the roaring fire. On his right, Edgar had returned to his book; on his left, Lilith continued to stare at him. Billy felt intensely uncomfortable. Her gaze was so hostile all attempts at conversation drained away from him. Luckily, Matilda was a chatterer.

'I shall take you to the room we have prepared for you,' she said. 'I think you'll like it, Billy. And there are new clothes for you – and even shoes. And you shall have a servant, of course, to –'

'I think I should be getting back now,' Billy said.

Matilda looked baffled. 'Back where?' she asked.

'Back to my home.' Billy found he was trembling. 'I don't belong here. I want to go. Why can't I go home?' He turned to the stony-faced Lilith. 'Why am I here?'

'You don't have a home,' said the woman.

For a moment Billy was too shocked to speak, and then he said, 'I do, I do. I live with Charlie Bone.'

'That's a lie,' she said. 'They house you out of pity. But they do not want you.'

At these words a numbing coldness settled on Billy. He barely felt Matilda's touch on his arm, but followed her blindly across to the door, which slid open before they had even reached it.

Matilda led Billy a few paces down the corridor of furs, and then turned and climbed a narrow marble stairway. At the top there was a long passage where a single rushlight burned at the far end. Matilda walked towards the light and stopped before a door that had a real latch. She lifted the latch and Billy followed her into the room that was to be his – for how long? He dared not think.

It wasn't so bad. A fire burned in an iron grate and the walls were a soft green marble. The bed was a high four-poster, hung with ivory-coloured curtains. There was a fur rug, of course, a chair and a large oak chest. A set of clothes lay on the bed: a blue velvet jacket, braided in gold at the collar and cuffs, and blue and gold trousers. The shoes had been placed at the foot of the bed. They had long pointed toes and gold decorations.

'The enchanter says we are very fortunate.' Matilda lifted the blue jacket. 'In other lands they have rough clothing; boys have to wear coarse woollen stockings and scratchy tunics. Here, in Badlock, we are very advanced.'

'Really?' Billy walked over to the fire and held his hands before its blaze. The chill that had descended on him wouldn't shift. He had no home but this.

Matilda hitched herself up on to the bed and swung her legs. 'You can be happy here, Billy, can't you? I am so lonely sometimes. Edgar will never be a friend, so I have none.' She paused. 'And I am afraid of the enchanter and his wife.'

She spoke as though they were barely related, Billy thought. And yet, weren't they her grandparents, the enchanter and his wife?

'Where's your mum?' asked Billy.

'My mother? She is dead, of a weakness of the heart. My father, too. He was a brave knight. His name was Gervaise de Roussillon, and he was killed in an unfair fight.' Matilda lowered her voice. 'My old nurse said the enchanter had a hand in my father's murder. But I cannot tell for sure.' She glanced nervously round the room.

'What is it?' said Billy. 'Are you afraid of something?'

'You will soon see,' she replied. 'I can hear his footsteps.'

And Billy did see, for a moment later a patch on one of the marbled walls began to move, like worms squirming in mud; a fuzzy cloud appeared, as though the marble were steaming, and through the cloud stepped Edgar.

'You could have used the door,' said Matilda.

'I chose not to,' retorted her brother. 'You are required to dine, immediately.' He threw a look of contempt at Billy. 'Why are you not dressed correctly?'

Billy gazed helplessly at Matilda.

'He has not had the time,' she said, jumping from the bed. 'I will —'

'Leave him,' said Edgar. 'The servant will do it.' Without another word, Edgar shuffled backwards and, with an awkward twist of his shoulders and an ungainly swing of his right foot, he allowed the wall to swallow him up.

Matilda grinned at Billy. 'Luckily, Edgar is not careful with his talent. I can always hear him coming, and his exits and entrances are very rude and clumsy. Listen, you can hear him even now.'

Billy could, indeed, hear stumbling footsteps retreating down the passage.

Matilda crossed the room and opened the door. 'You can come in, now,' she called. 'I'll see you in the dining hall,' she told Billy.

He was alone for only a second before a squat figure darted into the room and began tearing at his pyjamas.

'NO!' cried Billy.

The small being looked up at him, aghast. Billy couldn't tell if it was male or female. A woollen cap covered its head and, presumably, its hair; its face was without eyebrows and its body was so wide and lumpish, it was difficult to tell where its waist might have been, or where its legs began.

'You can wait outside,' said Billy.

To his surprise, the being shuffled out and gently closed the door.

Billy took off his pyjamas and put on the blue velvet suit. Next came the shoes. These were a worry. They didn't fit very well and the long toes made a slapping noise when he walked. It was like wearing flippers. Billy felt silly, but then bare feet would look even sillier, he realised. To his dismay he found there were no pockets in his jacket or trousers. He couldn't possibly leave Rembrandt behind. What would he eat?

'Er, excuse me,' called Billy, not knowing how to address the being outside. 'You can come in now.'

The thing opened the door a fraction and peeped in. Its eyes were the grey-brown colour of bark, but there was kindness in them.

'Please, can you help me?' said Billy. 'I need a . . . a pocket, or a bag, or . . . or something.'

The creature came in and stood before Billy. 'Dorgo,' it said in a masculine voice. 'Name Dorgo, me. What for you want pocket?'

Dorgo hadn't noticed the rat sitting on Billy's bed, cleaning himself.

'For him.' Billy pointed at Rembrandt.

Dorgo gave an earsplitting scream and clutched Billy round the waist. 'What? What? What?' he cried.

'He's only a rat,' said Billy.

'*And what's he?*' squeaked Rembrandt, staring at the trembling Dorgo.

'A person,' whispered Billy. He gently pushed the terrified Dorgo away, saying, 'He really won't hurt you, but I need to put him in something, so that I can carry him with me.'

Dorgo nodded. Without raising his eyes from the floor, he walked over to the oak chest and lifted the lid. He proceeded to rummage in the chest like a burrowing rabbit, sending shoes and clothing flying out in all directions. After a few seconds he reached the bottom and pulled out a leather belt with a gold-braided pouch attached to it. He held them out, still with his eyes lowered.

'Perfect. Thank you,' said Billy, fixing the belt round his waist. He grabbed Rembrandt and popped him into the pouch.

'*Now what?*' squeaked Rembrandt.

'Food,' Billy squeaked back. 'I hope.'

Dorgo had closed his eyes. Billy touched him on the shoulder. 'I believe the people here eat rats,' he said, 'so please don't tell anyone else about it.'

'Never, never, never,' said Dorgo. He opened his eyes,

rushed to the chest, flung back its contents and closed the lid. 'Follow, please. Master dine now,' he said.

To be called master was rather satisfying. It made Billy feel instantly taller and more confident. 'Lead the way,' he said, more pompously than he intended.

'*Oh dear!*' came a muffled remark from the gold pouch.

Dorgo shuddered and scuttled out of the room. He led Billy down the marble stairway, along the corridor of heads and furs and into the most astonishing room Billy had ever seen. Although to call it a room would hardly be accurate. It was a vast black marble hall, with a high vaulted ceiling of glittering stars. The walls were hung with weapons and precious objects: spears, shining swords, shields decorated with mythical creatures, tiger skins, painted masks, a golden wheel, horns of ivory, gilt-framed mirrors, tapestries embroidered with pearls, diamonds and emeralds, and things that Billy had never seen but could only assume were used in warfare. He stood in the doorway with his mouth agape.

The count was sitting at the far end of a glass-topped table, at least twenty feet long. 'Be seated, Billy Raven,' he called, and his voice echoed up to the glittering ceiling, increasing the light from the golden stars.

Lilith had her back to the door, Edgar and Matilda sat facing each other, halfway down the table. Billy was relieved to see an empty place-setting beside Matilda's. As he made his way towards her, Dorgo followed, pulled out Billy's chair and pushed it in when he was seated.

Matilda gave Billy a reassuring smile.

Billy noticed that they all had a version of Dorgo standing behind them. And there were other servants, standing at intervals around the room. They each held a golden tray. Almost everything on the table was made of gold: the candelabra, the plates, bowls, cups, knives and spoons. There was so much shine, Billy had to remove his spectacles and rub his eyes.

'Have you ever had an enchanted supper, Billy Raven?' boomed the count from the end of the table.

Billy shook his head.

'You are about to,' said the count. 'What do you wish to eat?'

'Erm, spaghetti, please,' said Billy.

'Spaghetti,' said the count to a tall servant, dressed rather more grandly than the others.

There was a long silence while the tall servant stared at his empty tray. Then he cleared his throat and, lifting his head, sang out, 'Not known.'

'Not known! Not known! Not known!' repeated the other servants.

Billy was embarrassed.

'Another,' the count commanded.

Billy tried to think of something that everyone, throughout the ages, must have eaten. 'Bread,' he said.

'Bread,' boomed the count.

The tall servant's tray instantly filled with black loaves. Dorgo grabbed Billy's plate, rushed over to the man with the tray of loaves, put them all on Billy's plate and brought it back to him.

'Countess?' This time the count's voice filled the hall. It had to, in order to reach his wife.

Lilith recited a list of peculiar names. The count repeated them, and the tall servant's tray filled with peculiar-looking fruits – or were they vegetables? Lilith's servant rushed to receive them and delivered them to his mistress.

Edgar chose raggots, maggots, cabbage and cheesum, which looked disgusting. Matilda chose cordioni soup, which smelled delicious, and the count went for the same sort of stuff as his wife.

Billy felt very self-conscious with his plate of black bread. He had no idea how to eat it.

'*Supper?*' Rembrandt squeaked hopefully.

Before Rembrandt's squeaks became too loud, Billy attacked a loaf. Tearing it apart with his bare hands, he managed to get a sizeable chunk into the pouch on his lap.

When Rembrandt squeaked his thanks, Matilda giggled. Edgar glared at his sister and said, 'The boy is giving food to a creature. That is rude and wasteful.'

Count Harken waved his hand dismissively. 'No matter, Edgar. It occupies our guest.'

Edgar sullenly pushed a spoonful of food into his mouth. But from the other end of the table, the countess continued to stare at Billy, even while she ate her unpronounceable meal. Her look was so heartless Billy wished he were a thousand miles away, back in Charlie Bone's house, even if he wasn't wanted there.

The second course was much better than the first. Matilda advised Billy to ask for pears sweetened in wine. They were delicious, just as she had promised.

After supper Dorgo led Billy back to his room. The little servant turned down the bedclothes and left Billy with a single candle, burning in a metal saucer on the chest. Billy changed into his pyjamas and got into bed. He watched the candle flame burn lower and lower, and wondered if he would ever sleep. He was very tired but his mind continued to wander through the glittering rooms below. Charlie will come and fetch me, he thought, because Charlie can travel.

Outside, the distant wind moaned across the plain. And then, above the wind, came the sound of heavy feet, dragging themselves across the ground. They were accompanied by a scuffling and shuffling and the rattle of chains.

Billy jumped out of bed and looked into the passage. Dorgo was sitting beside the door. His head lolled forward, but he was not asleep.

'What, master?' asked Dorgo.

'I heard something,' said Billy. 'Footsteps.'

'The giant, master.'

'Giant?' said Billy.

'They bring him to dungeon. He bad. Punished he must be.'

'What did he do?'

Dorgo sighed. 'He hide boy-from-future, like you.'

Charlie, thought Billy. Charlie's ancestor was a giant.

'Sleep now, master,' said Dorgo.

Billy stepped back into his room and closed the door.

THE SPY

It was Saturday morning. Charlie sat in his room feeling impatient and helpless. His thoughts kept returning to Tancred. How could someone with such a powerful endowment have been overcome? Charlie could not bring himself to believe that he would never again see Tancred's cheerful face with its shock of blond, spiky hair or the billowing green cape as Tancred's volatile nature brought on the wind and the rain. And then there was Billy.

If only the painting of Badlock could be found, Charlie was sure that his moth could help him to re-enter that shadowy, sinister world. He had no idea how he would find Billy, if he ever got to Badlock. He supposed he would discover what to do when he got there.

Charlie wondered if Grandma Bone had hidden the painting in her bedroom. It was unlikely, but there was just a chance. If she had, she would probably have locked her door. But . . .

Nothing ventured nothing gained, Charlie said to himself as he left his room.

He could hardly believe his luck. His grandmother's door was not locked. Charlie slipped into her room. It was extremely untidy and reeked of stale perfume. Bits of clothing overflowed every drawer. Black stockings hung from the bedpost, a hat sat on the pillow and underwear was scattered over the quilt. The dressing table was covered in messy bottles and the mirror was hung with beads and bracelets.

Where to look? The painting was large and would not be easy to hide. Charlie looked under the bed. He counted ten pairs of shoes, but there was no painting. He looked in the wardrobe: more shoes, ancient dresses, two fur coats smelling of moth balls, and more skirts than Charlie could count. He was about to close the door when something caught his eye: Grandma Bone's second-best handbag lay on top of a pair of suede boots.

Charlie pulled the bag into the light. It was made of patchworked leather and stuffed with scarves, gloves and handkerchiefs. There was also a bottle of pills, a lipstick and a white card with the day before's date at the top. Printed below were the words:

Meeting of sympathisers to our cause.
The Old Chapel, Piminy Street.
Saturday. 8.00 p.m.
T.T.
Bring card.

'T.T.' Charlie murmured. T is for Tilpin, and didn't someone say that Mrs Tilpin's first name was Titania? He quickly memorised the message on the card, replaced it and put the bag back into the wardrobe.

Running to his room, Charlie jotted down the words he'd memorised in exactly the same order as he'd seen them. 'About postcard size,' he muttered, 'and the print is like a newspaper.' He realised that he would never be able to attend the meeting himself. He needed an accomplice. An adult. No child would be able to get into the meeting.

Charlie knew exactly who to ask. He decided to wait until Benjamin came home from school. Mr and Mrs Brown would be working until then. In the meantime there was more homework to do.

At precisely four o'clock, Charlie looked out of his window and saw Benjamin ambling down the street with his backpack slung across his shoulder. Charlie banged on the windowpane and waved violently. Benjamin looked up and waved back. He pointed at Charlie and then to number twelve. Charlie nodded and stuck up his thumb.

Two minutes later, Charlie walked downstairs and took his jacket from the peg in the hall. 'I'm going to see Ben,' he called out.

'You are not,' said a voice from the kitchen. Grandma Bone appeared in the doorway. 'You are not going anywhere until you've finished your homework.'

'I have finished it,' said Charlie.

Grandma Bone stared at him through narrowed eyes. 'I suppose you cheated.'

'How could I cheat?' said Charlie. 'It was all memorising stuff. You can test me if you like.'

His grandmother's eyes became tiny slits. Her lips pursed into a wrinkled bud. She did not want to test Charlie because her favourite programme, 'Health Affairs', was coming up on the radio.

'So I'm going, OK?' Charlie gave her a forced sort of grin.

The wrinkled bud of his grandmother's mouth relaxed and she said, 'Kippers for supper.'

'Great!' Charlie made for the door. Kippers were his least favourite food and Grandma Bone knew it. She must have bought them specially to punish him. But he had far more important things to worry about.

Benjamin and Runner Bean gave him a great welcome and, as luck would have it, Mr and Mrs Brown had just returned from a very satisfactory bit of detective work. Flushed with success, they were now celebrating with a champagne tea in the kitchen.

While occasionally chewing a tasty snack, Charlie told the Browns everything that had happened at Bloor's Academy before he'd been excluded. He kept his voice very steady, while they gasped and exclaimed and paced about, because he knew that if he stopped talking his eyes would fill with tears, and before that happened he wanted to get to the real reason for his visit: the vanished painting and tonight's meeting in Piminy Street.

'Murder!' shouted Mr Brown when Charlie had come to the end of his shocking account. 'We can't let them get away with it.'

'I feel like going to see that disgraceful excuse for a headmaster right now,' said his wife.

Charlie shook his head. 'They'll say it was an accident. No one will be able to prove that Tancred was drowned on purpose.'

Mrs Brown patted her husband's hand. 'Charlie's right. The police will never believe this Dagbert Endless boy has a . . . a drowning power.'

Charlie pulled the hastily scribbled note from his pocked and spread it out on the table. 'This is the message I found in Grandma Bone's handbag. I thought if we copied it, someone could take it to the meeting and find out what's going on.'

Mr and Mrs Brown studied the note.

'Sympathisers?' muttered Mr Brown, stroking the stubble he'd had to grow on his chin for his last case. 'Sympathisers with what?'

'The cause,' said Benjamin. 'You know, Dad. All the bad stuff that's been going on.'

'Ah.' Mr Brown scratched his stubble even more fiercely. 'And you think we might learn something of their future plans, Charlie? Get one step ahead, as it were.'

'That's part of it,' said Charlie. 'But, actually, I thought you might find out where they've put the painting.'

'Ah, yes. I could take a recorder. Get proof of the drowning. I've an excellent little instrument that fits into the arm of a pair of spectacles.'

Something about this device worried Charlie. There were people in Piminy Street who were gifted in ways that he could only begin to imagine. There might well be a clairvoyant among them, or someone with super-human powers of detection. He explained this to the Browns, who reluctantly agreed that it would be safer to leave the recorder behind.

'Obviously I can't go as myself,' said Mr Brown. 'I would be instantly recognised as a non-sympathiser.'

'I don't think you should go at all,' said his wife. 'Even in a disguise you would be recognised by people like *that*. It's your height and the way you move.'

After a brief argument, which Mr Brown lost, Mrs Brown went upstairs and returned, fifteen minutes later, looking nothing whatsoever like her old self. Three inches had been added to her height, not with high-heeled shoes, but with ingeniously built-up boots. Her fair hair was tucked into a severe grey wig and her face given a dusting of dark pink powder, which made her look hot-tempered and irritable. Her eyebrows were thick and black, her chest had expanded and her lips were reduced to thin, greyish lines.

For a moment Charlie actually believed that some evil-looking woman had broken into the house. When he realised who it was, he joined in with Benjamin's applause.

Mrs Brown's transformation was truly amazing.

'Trish, you've surpassed yourself,' Mr Brown congratulated her. 'You've even fooled the dog.'

Runner Bean had rushed out of the room and was now howling dismally in the corridor. It took a good long sniff of Mrs Brown's hand to convince him that the grim-looking stranger was none other than Benjamin's mother.

It was decided that Mr and Mrs Brown (as herself) should drive to a quiet avenue, not too far from Piminy Street. Once there, Mrs Brown would change into her disguise and, making sure that no one was watching, she would leave the car and make her way to Piminy Street. Mr Brown would drive around for a bit, and then return to the same quiet avenue and wait for Mrs Brown to leave the meeting.

'I'll remove my disguise in the car,' said Mrs Brown, who was getting quite excited, 'and we'll drive back to Filbert Street, just like an ordinary couple who've been to the movies.'

'Maybe Ben could sleep over at my house,' Charlie suggested.

'Excellent,' said Mr Brown. 'We'll leave Runner Bean to guard the house.'

Runner Bean pricked up his ears, but didn't appear to object.

Mr Brown printed out an exact replica of the invitation card Charlie had described and, at half past five, Charlie and Benjamin wished Mrs Brown good luck, and walked over to number nine.

Charlie was given a key at weekends so that he could let himself into the house without disturbing his grandmothers. Maisie was alone in the kitchen when the boys walked in. She was pleased to see Benjamin and only too happy to let him stay the night.

Not so Grandma Bone. A few minutes after the boys had arrived she marched in and demanded to know why there was an overnight bag sitting in the middle of the kitchen, ready to trip someone up.

'Ben's staying the night,' Charlie told her.

'Oh, is he? And who says?' asked Grandma Bone.

'He won't be any trouble, Grizelda,' said Maisie.

'That's as may be.' Grandma Bone kicked Benjamin's bag aside. 'But I like to be asked. What I don't like is irresponsible parents dumping their offspring willy-nilly on long-suffering neighbours.'

Benjamin scowled and Maisie said, '*Really*, Grizelda! You take the biscuit.'

Ignoring her, Grandma Bone demanded, 'So what's the excuse this time?'

Making a super-human effort to keep calm, Charlie said, 'Sorry, Grandma, but Ben's parents were given tickets for this great movie, just half an hour ago, and Ben can't go because it's for over-sixteens, so I thought he could come here for the night.'

Grandma Bone glared at Charlie for several seconds

before saying, 'Kippers for both of you,' and sweeping out.

Maisie said quietly, 'You don't have to have kippers, boys. Grandma Bone won't be here. She's going out for the evening. I'll give the fish to next door's cat.'

Charlie and Benjamin were upstairs when Great Aunt Eustacia's car came snorting and squealing down Filbert Street. Peeping furtively over the windowsill, the boys saw Grandma Bone, dressed all in purple, climb into the passenger seat. The back of the car appeared to be rather full, and when it bumped off the kerb and screeched down the road again, they saw a small, pale face staring out of the rear window.

'They must be taking Eric to the meeting,' said Charlie.

'Poor thing,' said Benjamin.

After a very good supper of scrambled eggs and beans, and an hour watching television, the boys returned to Charlie's room, just in time to observe Mr and Mrs Brown leaving number twelve. Mrs Brown gave them a cheery wave and swung herself into the car. Mr Brown grinned at the boys in the window and then drove off, rather more expertly than Great Aunt Eustacia.

'I hope Mum'll be all right,' Benjamin said anxiously.

'Course she will,' Charlie reassured him. 'Your mum's the best private eye in the country.'

Which was probably true.

Mr Brown had chosen Argos Avenue, where gardens and houses were hidden from the road by tall evergreen hedges. He parked beside the broad trunk of a plane tree and watched the road with an expertise that only the most skilled detectives possess. Meanwhile, Mrs Brown swiftly applied her make-up, pulled on her wig and exchanged her everyday winter coat for a moth-eaten and rather smelly fur coat. A plastic bag containing a rag soaked in chloroform was pushed into one pocket, in the other she had a pair of very sharp scissors, and a bottle of smelling salts. The smelling salts were to help her recover from any fainting that might overcome her, after too much excitement.

The intrepid detective squeezed her feet into her built-up boots, gave her husband a kiss and jumped out of the car.

How do I look? Mrs Brown mouthed through the windscreen at Mr Brown.

Mr Brown lifted his thumb. Reluctant to lose sight of his wife, he drove very slowly behind her as she walked down the avenue. She was approaching the turn into Piminy Street when a group of three stepped out of a side street and hid Mrs Brown from her husband's view. Mr Brown was worried. The three people following his wife were all extremely wide, and walked with a clumsy, uneven stride.

Mr Brown stopped the car at the top of Piminy Street. He dared not drive any further, for fear of drawing attention to himself and thus arousing their suspicions. 'Good luck, brave Trish!' he whispered.

Other groups now began to emerge from the houses in Piminy Street. They slid from behind trees, wafted through gates and out of doorways: silent, undefined figures, muffled in furs and hoods, all moving towards the Old Chapel.

Mrs Brown was aware of the strangers accompanying her down Piminy Street. She had a momentary flutter of panic, and then sternly told herself that, even if her true identity were discovered, no one would dare to harm her, unlike poor Tancred and little Billy.

People were now moving into the dimly lit porch of the chapel. Mrs Brown joined the throng and held out her card. It was grabbed by a tall man with elephants printed on his jacket. Mrs Brown was convinced she had seen the man before, but couldn't place him. He gave her an odd look and she quickly moved on. Finding a seat at the end of a row, quite close to the back, she sat down, breathing rather fast. Beside her sat a woman with lank, red ringlets and over-rouged cheeks. She looked about ninety.

The sympathisers were unusually quiet people. They moved to their seats in wordless shufflings, only acknowledging each other with soft grunts and mumbles.

The Old Chapel was no longer used for worship. It had been standing derelict for as long as Mrs Brown could remember. The windows had been boarded up and the altar removed. In its place green velvet curtains hung from a long brass pole. The chancel was now a stage.

The two wooden railings that had once separated the altar from the congregation were still in place and today they gleamed with polish. Deep green ivy twined its way along both rails and fell in long strands down each side of the steps, on to the cracked slate floor. At the top of the steps, slightly to one side, a stone gargoyle squatted. It was a hideous thing with bulging eyes, long pointed ears and a wide toothless mouth. Mrs Brown tried not to look at it.

When every seat had been taken, the man in the elephant jacket closed the door. There was a moment's silence before footsteps could be heard, tapping down the side of the hall. A woman emerged at the front. She climbed the five steps to the stage and turned to face her audience.

Mrs Brown saw a woman whose age could only be guessed at. She could have been anywhere between forty and eighty. Her hair fell in thin, grey strands to her shoulders and a string of ivy encircled her head. There were dark shadows beneath her eyes, her nose was a pale mauve and her gaunt face ash-grey. She was wearing a sparkling black cloak and a long dress that glimmered as she moved.

'Welcome!' said the woman in the sparkling cloak. 'How gratifying to see that so many of you answered my call. For those of you who do not know me, I am Titania Tilpin. Like you, I am a direct descendant of the Shadow of Badlock, Harken the Enchanter.'

A murmur of approval rippled through the audience. Mrs Brown joined in. 'Ah,' she said.

'As you know,' Titania continued, 'the shadow managed to return, very briefly, last year. He might have stayed with us if it had not been for the interference of a wayward boy called Charlie Bone. Charlie and his infernal uncle discovered a spell that sent our beloved ancestor tumbling back to Badlock; and now he cannot enter our world again, because the mirror that assisted his entrance was broken by that same Charlie Bone.'

A rumble of dismay broke out in the hall and, once again, Mrs Brown joined in with a disgruntled, 'Huh!' This time she felt the woman beside her turn and frown in her direction. Mrs Brown hoped she had not overdone things.

'Don't lose heart, my friends,' Titania sang out. 'I want to show you something.' She walked to the side of the stage where a large painting stood facing the wall. Seizing the painting Titania pulled it to the centre of the stage. The dark towers and barren mountains of Badlock drew a gasp of admiration from the crowd. Mrs Brown remained silent.

A curious sound came from the painting. Mrs Brown could hardly believe her ears. It was wind. Several people in the front row actually clutched their hats as a cold breeze whistled across the stage.

'Behold Badlock!' Titania said proudly. 'The shadow painted it himself, and it has an awful power. It can draw into itself any living thing.' Before anyone could gasp again, she held up her hand for silence. 'And, would you believe, *there is a boy in there*,' she tapped the painting, '*right now*. A boy the shadow is holding for some friends.

And in return these friends have agreed to help me in my quest, our quest,' she threw her arms out to the audience, 'to mend the Mirror of Amoret, so that the shadow may come back to guide and protect us, to rid us of our enemies and to rule this land as it should be ruled.'

Vigorous applause broke out. A few gruff voices said, 'Hear, hear!' Mrs Brown glanced at her neighbour and clapped politely. The woman with red ringlets appeared not to notice. She was staring at the stage, where Titania Tilpin had been joined by a tall woman with black hair and a bright scarlet coat. She was holding the hand of a small, fragile-looking boy in a blue jacket. Mrs Brown instantly recognised Charlie's great-aunt, Venetia Shellhorn.

Venetia told the audience that she was there on behalf of the Bloor family, who had agreed to assist Titania in her mission to bring back the shadow. 'And now I want to introduce my little treasure,' she said, pushing Eric to the front of the stage. 'This is Eric, my stepson. He has a truly remarkable talent. It has already been put to use by Mr Melnett, the stone mason, whose father was ruined by the solicitor Bittermouse.' She paused while a gruff voice from the front emitted a kind of growl. 'Mr Bittermouse has been well and truly punished I would say, wouldn't you?' She smiled at the growler, and continued. 'If any of you have a family score to settle, or a grievance unavenged, Eric and Mr Melnett make a fine team, and they would be glad to help. In return we would welcome your assistance in mending the Mirror of Amoret. I know there are wizards among you,' her black eyes darted over the faces in front of her, 'magicians, scare-mongers, poisoners, shape-shifters, heart-stoppers.'

Some members of the audience shifted in their seats, coughed and blew their noses.

'Perhaps your power has lain dormant for too long,' Venetia suggested. 'Perhaps you are afraid to use it in the present day. But look what Eric can do for you.' She grabbed the small boy and pulled him back to stand in front of her. 'Eric – the gargoyle.'

All eyes turned to the hideous creature crouching at the front of the stage. Eric stared at it. His small face contorted and a low hum came from him. The gargoyle lifted itself on thin stone legs, lurched down the steps and stopped at the bottom.

This time the applause was slightly restrained. It would never do to let a small boy's admittedly impressive talent go to his head.

Venetia smiled forgivingly. 'I'm sure many of you have equally formidable talents. But if you need Eric, you can contact me at number thirteen, Darkly Wynd. Now . . .' she spoke the last word with an expressive sigh, 'Titania will treat you to something rather special.'

Venetia and Eric stepped aside and Titania Tilpin strode to the centre of the stage. You could tell by the excited glitter in her eyes that she had saved the best part of her presentation until the end. She treated her audience to a broad smile, unhappily revealing several missing teeth. And then, from the folds of her cloak, she withdrew a mirror. Holding it up with a dramatic flourish, she cried, 'The Mirror of Amoret!'

It was an astonishingly beautiful object. The jewel-encrusted frame sparkled with a thousand colours, and the glass itself, though cracked, had an unearthly radiance. Holding the handle in her right hand, Titania gently laid the mirror across her left palm and gazed into the glass. 'We cannot have the count among us yet,' she said in a harsh whisper, 'but, friends,' she looked out at the audience, 'I *can* reach him.'

A profound silence settled on the audience.

Titania's gaze returned to the mirror. 'Count Harken,' she called in a floaty voice, 'I beseech you – favour your humble descendants.'

Like everyone else, Mrs Brown stared at the mirror. What she saw there shook her to the very roots of her being. A green mist seeped from the mirror. As it drifted upwards it swelled into a thick, evil-smelling cloud. Titania waved the mirror several times until the cloud parted. She smiled into the glass and held it out to face the audience. The head and shoulders of a man began to form in the glass; he wore a green jacket and his thick brown hair was touched with gold. His face was so cruel and arrogant, Mrs Brown couldn't hold back a tiny gasp. The shadow seemed to be looking directly at her; she was sure he could see her.

Mrs Brown began to feel faint. She put her hand in

her pocket and drew out the bag of chloroform. Having almost anaesthetised herself, she suddenly realised her mistake, pushed back the chloroform and thrust the smelling salts under her nose. Her neighbour jabbed Mrs Brown's arm, and the smelling salts fell to the floor.

'SPY!' shouted the woman with red ringlets. 'FRAUD! IMPOSTOR! ENEMY!'

Mrs Brown leapt out of her seat and rushed to the door. Several burly figures stood up.

'Stop her!' screamed Titania.

The man in the elephant jacket grabbed Mrs Brown's arm, just as she reached for the door handle. She stuck the scissors into his thigh with one hand, and shoved the chloroform over his mouth and nose with the other. The big fellow staggered back with a groan, and Mrs Brown wrenched open the door.

By now, some of the larger members of the audience were close on her heels. Mrs Brown bounded out of the chapel and raced down the street. Even in built-up boots she was as swift as a hare. Her flying feet had rescued her from many a sticky situation but, too late, she realised that she was running away from Argos Avenue, rather than towards it. All was not lost, however, for Piminy Street curved sharply in the middle and Mrs Brown saw that, if she could draw ahead sufficiently, she might be round the bend before her pursuers could see her duck behind a wall or a hedge.

But, oh dear, there were no walls and no hedges. Apart

from a few small porches, most of the doors opened directly on to the pavement. Mrs Brown could hear shouting behind her. The voices grew louder. They were angry, deep, murderous voices and their owners were gaining on her.

All at once, before she had time to draw breath, Mrs Brown was seized round the middle and carried into a darkened house. She screamed.

The door slammed and a quiet female voice said, 'Hush, m'dear. I'm rescuing you, not murdering you.'

TRAVELLING WITH THE BOA

Benjamin woke up very early. He could hear Runner Bean barking. Something was wrong. It was still dark and Charlie was sound asleep. Benjamin found his clothes and dressed quickly. He was about to open the door when Charlie woke up.

'Ben, is that you?' Charlie said sleepily.

'I'm going home,' Benjamin whispered. 'Runner's barking. I want to see if Mum's OK.'

Wide awake now, Charlie leapt out of bed and put on the light. 'Don't go without me, Ben. I want to know what happened.'

When Charlie had pulled on his clothes, the boys crept downstairs and left the house. Filbert Street was deserted and silent. Runner Bean had stopped barking, but there was a light in the hall at number twelve.

In all the excitement of the previous night, Benjamin had forgotten his front door key. He rang the bell and Runner Bean started barking again. A few moments later, Mr Brown opened the door with the chain still on. He looked out through a ten-centimetre gap and said, 'Who's there?' in a loud, challenging voice.

'It's only us, Dad.' Benjamin shoved his face into the gap. 'Let us in, please.'

'Who's us?' demanded his father.

'Charlie and me. We want to know if Mum's OK.'

'It's me, Mr Brown.' Charlie stood on tiptoe and looked over Benjamin's head.

'I see. All right.' Mr Brown took off the chain and opened the door. 'Quick as you can. Come on. They might be on to us.'

'Who?' asked Charlie, as he followed Benjamin and Mr Brown into the kitchen.

'Them,' said Mr Brown. 'I can't say any more than that.'

Mrs Brown was sitting at the kitchen table. She was dressed in her usual skirt and sweater but she hadn't removed her make-up very well. Her forehead was covered in grey swirls and one cheek was striped pink and white. 'It's only five o'clock,' she said with a yawn. 'What are you doing over here, boys?'

'Runner woke me up,' said Benjamin. 'And we wanted to know what happened to you, Mum.'

The kettle boiled and Mr Brown filled the teapot, saying, 'It's a long story, boys. Your mum was rumbled, Ben. She had to spend half the night with a blacksmith called Mrs Kettle.'

'Mrs Kettle?' Charlie exclaimed. 'She's a friend.'

'She is indeed, Charlie,' said Mrs Brown. 'I wouldn't

be here now if she hadn't rescued me.'

Mr Brown handed everyone a mug of tea and while she sipped and stirred, Mrs Brown began to talk about her terrifying adventure. At last, Charlie learned where the painting had gone, and how, dressed in Mrs Kettle's boiler suit and cloth cap, Mrs Brown had eventually managed to evade the gruesome sympathisers and reach her husband, who was waiting, in an agony of suspense, for her return.

'I don't know who those people were,' said Mrs Brown, draining her cup, 'but I can tell you they were a mighty sinister bunch. Mrs Kettle believes they have been lying low in Piminy Street for years. Biding their time, waiting for someone like Mrs Tilpin to stir them into action.'

'They are certainly stirred up now,' said Mr Brown.

'So the painting is in the Old Chapel,' Charlie said thoughtfully.

'Charlie, you can't go there,' Mrs Brown declared, 'it isn't safe.'

'But I have to,' argued Charlie. 'I've got to rescue Billy from the painting.'

Mrs Brown threw up her hands and looked at her husband.

'We'll think of another way, Charlie,' said Mr Brown. 'We'll talk it through and come up with a solution for you. We always find a solution when we put our mind to things, don't we, Trish?'

'Of course we do.' Mrs Brown beamed at Charlie. 'The

best thing you can do, Charlie, is to go back home and get some more sleep. You can come and see us later, when we've all had a bit more time to think.' She closed her eyes and gave a long yawn.

Charlie took the hint. 'OK.' He stood up and Benjamin saw him to the front door.

'Don't do anything without me, will you, Charlie?' Benjamin begged.

'Not if I can help it,' Charlie said.

Number nine was still in darkness. Charlie let himself in and tiptoed up to his room. He lay on his bed, fully dressed, knowing he wouldn't get to sleep again until the following night. His mind was made up. He had to get into the painting before it was moved again. But how could he walk up Piminy Street without all those menacing sympathisers watching him? And that was the least of his problems. The Old Chapel would be locked, no doubt, and even if Charlie managed to break in through a window, there was no certainty of his actually getting into the painting again.

'But I know that I can,' Charlie whispered into the darkness, 'because you're going to help me, Claerwen.'

A soft light moved through the air above him and landed on his arm. Was she merely answering to her name, or was she telling Charlie that she could help?

'I've got an idea,' Charlie told the moth. He slid off the bed and, turning on his light, wrote a short note to Maisie. The note said:

Me and Benjamin have gone to the bookshop.
See you later, Maisie.
Love, Charlie.

Charlie didn't like lying to Maisie, but she would only worry if she thought he was alone. He just hoped that Benjamin wouldn't come looking for him after breakfast.

Charlie left the note on the kitchen table, where Maisie was bound to see it. She was always up before Grandma Bone.

Dawn was slowly approaching. There was a thin light on the horizon but the streets were still dark, and the air was bitterly cold. Charlie began to run. Before he reached the bookshop he would have to pass the end of Piminy Street and he dreaded it. He was nearing the turn to Cathedral Close when he sensed that something was following him. He stopped and turned, very slowly. And there they were: Aries, Leo and Sagittarius, their big paws pounding the cobbles, their heads up and their tails erect, their fiery colours brightening the morning.

'Hi there, Flames!' Charlie called softly. 'Thanks for the escort.' He passed the turn to Piminy Street with confidence and pressed on to the bookshop.

The cathedral clock chimed seven just as Charlie emerged into the square. Ingledew's didn't open until nine o'clock. Charlie began to feel foolish. But when he peered into the darkened shop, he was sure he could hear voices. He rang the bell.

The Flames padded across the cobbled square and looked back at Charlie from a distance. Miss Ingledew, wearing a red dressing gown, came into the shop and stood behind the counter. She stared at Charlie through the window, not recognising him.

'It's me, Charlie,' called Charlie.

Miss Ingledew crossed to the door and unlocked it. 'Whatever are you doing here at this time of the morning?' she asked, not unkindly.

The Flames, satisfied that Charlie was safe, went about their business.

Charlie bounded down the steps into the shop. 'It'll take me a while to explain,' he said.

'You'd better come and have some breakfast.' Miss Ingledew led him through her sitting room and into the small kitchen at the back of the house. Charlie was surprised to see Olivia and Emma eating boiled eggs. Or rather, Olivia was eating. Emma hadn't touched her egg.

'Wow! You're having breakfast early for a Saturday,' Charlie remarked.

'And you're having a walk early for a Saturday,' said Olivia.

Emma lifted a wan face and said, 'I can't sleep, and that makes it difficult for anyone else to sleep. Do you want an egg, Charlie?'

Charlie was so shaken by Emma's mournful expression he didn't know what to say. 'No . . . er, yes . . . um, just toast,' he mumbled.

'Don't look so shocked, Charlie,' Olivia barked. 'How would you feel if someone you really cared for was . . . well, that you were never going to see them again?'

'I'd feel bad,' he said, taking the chair between them. 'I do feel bad,' he added. 'That's why I'm here.'

'It's about Billy, isn't it?' Emma might have been grief-stricken, but she was still aware of other people's troubles.

'It's just,' Charlie began awkwardly, 'that Billy still has a chance.'

'And Tancred hasn't,' said Emma.

'I don't mean that.' Charlie leaned sideways as Miss Ingledew put a rack of toast on the table. He suddenly realised that he couldn't speak about the sympathisers' meeting. If Miss Ingledew heard about Mrs Brown's hair-raising escape from Piminy Street, she was bound to stop Charlie from attempting to get into the Old Chapel.

'What *do* you mean?' asked Olivia, frowning at Charlie.

'Don't look at me like that,' begged Charlie. 'You probably think it was all my fault, Tancred's . . . drowning. But I didn't know he was going to meet Dagbert in the Sculpture Room. I was locked up. I couldn't do anything about it.'

'We don't blame you, Charlie,' Emma said gently. 'Have you tried to reach Billy again?'

Charlie hesitated. He couldn't mention the Old Chapel with Miss Ingledew hovering behind him. 'Not since I found Claerwen,' he said.

'You *found* her? Why didn't you say?' Olivia scolded.

'I forgot.' Charlie put his hand in his pocket and felt the moth's delicate feet touch his forefinger. 'Here she is.' He lifted her out and set her on the marmalade jar, where her silvery wings caught the light from the overhead lamp.

Both girls smiled at last. 'Awww!' they breathed.

'She really is beautiful,' said Miss Ingledew, sitting opposite Charlie. She swept back her long chestnut hair and asked, 'Is your uncle back, Charlie?'

'No. We don't know where he is.' Charlie shrugged. 'Maisie's tried to ring his mobile, but there's never an answer. We think he's hundreds of miles away, where there isn't a signal. Actually, I wish he would come back.'

'So do I.' Miss Ingledew stared at the moth in a dreamy way for a moment, and then she stood up and said brusquely, 'I must get dressed. I've work to do.'

As soon as her aunt had left the room, Emma whispered, 'I think she misses your uncle more than she's letting on.'

'Definitely,' Olivia agreed. 'Why don't they get married?'

Charlie didn't know the answer to this. 'I think I'd better be going now,' he said. 'I'll leave by the back door if that's OK.'

'Why do you want to go that way?' asked Emma.

'Why did you come here in the first place?' said Olivia. 'What for? Just to show us the moth?'

'I'm going to the Old Chapel in Piminy Street,' said Charlie in a low voice. 'I want to go the back way so that no one sees me. The painting's there.'

Olivia raised her eyebrows. 'I suppose that'll have to do for now.'

The girls followed him to the back door at the far end of the kitchen.

'You can lock it again after I've gone,' said Charlie, stepping into the small yard behind the shop.

'Won't you be coming back this way?' asked Emma.

'Um. Don't know. I'll knock if I do.' Charlie made his way past empty book boxes, to the gate in the wall. The gate was rusty from lack of use and made a loud screech when Charlie opened and closed it.

He was now in the narrow alley that ran between the back yards of Piminy Street and Cathedral Close. The girls could hear him picking his way over the slippery, uneven cobbles long after the dark morning had swallowed him up.

Emma whispered, 'I don't like it, Liv. It isn't light yet and the Piminy Street people are . . .'

'Dangerous,' said Olivia. 'I think we ought to contact the others.'

'Who? Fidelio will be at a concert somewhere, Gabriel's running round the city with his petition, Tancred's . . .' Emma gave a little sigh '. . . out of it, and Lysander . . . ah, Lysander!'

'Definitely,' said Olivia.

'Yes, of course, Lysander.' Emma followed Olivia back into the kitchen, feeling a little less anxious.

Charlie was passing the yard behind the Kettle Shop

when blue flame suddenly lit the window of the smithy. Mrs Kettle obviously started work early. It was comforting to know that she was close by. Charlie wondered why he hadn't thought of Mrs Kettle before. He went up to the smithy window and looked in.

The blacksmith, in her boiler suit and visor, appeared to be welding a handle on to a large iron kettle. When she saw Charlie she gave a little start, then put down her welding iron and came to the back door.

'What the dickens are you doing here, Charlie Bone?' she asked, pulling up her visor.

Charlie looked furtively over his shoulder and whispered, 'I was on my way to the Old Chapel.'

'I can guess why,' said Mrs Kettle. 'Mrs Brown spilled the beans. Come in for a minute, Charlie.'

Charlie stepped into the warm smithy. It was here that Mrs Kettle had forged the invincible sword the Red Knight now carried at his side. There were other swords hanging on her walls, Charlie noted with satisfaction, and large tools that could, no doubt, do serious damage.

Mrs Kettle gathered some of her smaller implements together and put them in a canvas tool-bag. 'You'd given no thought to the method of entering that chapel now, had you, Charlie?'

'I had, but I didn't come to a definite conclusion,' Charlie admitted.

'No, you were going to wait till you got there, and then be caught, most probably while you were just standing about thinking. Well, you'll need these for a start.' She held up a formidable-looking pair of pliers.

Charlie was impressed. Not only had Mrs Kettle made no attempt to dissuade him from entering the chapel, she was actually going to help him. He couldn't stop himself from smiling.

'This is a serious business, Charlie,' Mrs Kettle warned him. 'We'll have to be very, very careful.'

'Yes, Mrs Kettle.'

'There's something else. Wait here.' She went through the heavy door into her shop and returned, a moment later, carrying a large lidded basket. 'Solomon,' she said. 'You'll need him.'

'The boa?' Charlie stepped back a pace. 'Why?'

'Why d'you think? Invisibility would be a great advantage in a place like Badlock, would it not?'

'Of course,' Charlie agreed. 'Yes, it would. But I can't talk to Solomon. Only Billy can do that.'

'Use your moth. They understand each other. Both are ancient, both have known the Red King.'

Mrs Kettle looked so grave and resolute, Charlie found himself taking the basket without another word. They left the safety of the smithy and made their way, cautiously, along the alley. The houses on either side loomed against a sky that was already lighter. It cast a grey wash over the cobbles beyond reach of the single street lamp. Here and there a light could be seen in one of the windows; the Cathedral Close citizens were waking up, but if the inhabitants of Piminy Street were awake they showed no sign of it.

'Here we are, m'dear,' whispered Mrs Kettle.

They had reached an ivy-covered wall, where a wooden door stood half open on to the alley.

'Well, I'm blessed; they haven't even bothered to close it,' the blacksmith remarked in a low voice. 'I won't need the pliers after all. Come on, Charlie.'

There were only a few metres between the wall and the back of the chapel. Charlie couldn't see a door. High above him, an arched window had been boarded with several sturdy planks. He wondered how they would reach it.

'Round the side.' Mrs Kettle plucked Charlie's sleeve and he followed her round the side of the building.

Treading softly down the gravelled path, they came to a freshly painted green door. A large padlock hung beneath the door handle.

'This is going to be easier than I thought,' said Mrs Kettle. Kneeling beside the door, she took from her tool-bag a metal ring holding several slim iron rods. Inserting one of the rods into the padlock she twisted it once, twice, three times. A sparkling blue mist flew out and, with a gentle click, the padlock sprang open.

'Now for the next one.' Mrs Kettle tapped the keyhole beside the door handle. This called for a slightly larger rod. The blacksmith turned it twice in the lock. This time the dust was pink and the opening click more of a groan. Mrs Kettle stood up and turned the handle. The door swung inwards and Charlie found himself standing on the threshold of an ivy-clad stage.

'There!' Mrs Kettle pointed to a large canvas standing against the far wall of the stage.

Charlie found he couldn't move.

'Go on, Charlie,' urged his friend. 'You haven't much time. It's getting light.'

'I can't,' he muttered hoarsely. 'There's something in there. Something stopping me.'

'Wickedness,' said Mrs Kettle in a matter-of-fact voice. 'People like that are bound to leave their thoughts about, so folks like us can't breathe the air that they have used. But you can do it, Charlie. You've got Mathonwy's wand. She'll see you through.'

The moth was already out of Charlie's pocket and fluttering round his head, as though she knew that the time for her help had come.

Charlie walked slowly across the stage. He put down the basket and turned the painting round to face him. Once again he experienced the dizzying effect of looking upon such a dreadful world.

'The boa, Charlie!' Mrs Kettle called softly. Her large figure, almost filling the doorway, gave Charlie an immediate surge of courage and he opened the basket. The blue boa slid out and waved its feathery head in the air.

'Claerwen, tell the boa I want to be invisible,' said Charlie. 'Anweledig,' he added, remembering to use the

254

Welsh. 'And you'd better tell him to become invisible himself. Boa anweledig.'

The moth settled among the boa's feathers. It was an odd sight. Was she talking to him in her own magical language? It seemed to have worked, for the snake regarded Charlie in a questioning way and then ducked its head and started to coil itself round his feet. Bit by bit, Charlie's feet, in their grey trainers, began to disappear.

'Goodbye, Mrs Kettle!' Charlie called.

'Good luck, Charlie,' she replied, in a voice that was already sounding distant.

It was an odd sensation, seeing himself disappear, and yet not unpleasant. The snake's embrace was cool and firm, and Charlie thought of it as a kind of friendly hug. When he felt himself to be completely invisible he gazed at the painting, waiting for the wind that had previously come howling out of it.

Nothing happened. Not a whisper. Not a breath. Charlie was not wanted in Badlock. Was the shadow even aware of him, standing there at the very edge of his own time?

'Claerwen, let us enter,' Charlie whispered. Then, using the Welsh, ''dwi isie mynd mewn.'

The white moth flew across the painting. She flew over the towers and mountains, over rock and scrub and stony plain. She flew across the lowering sky and her wings moved so fast Charlie lost sight of her shape; all he could see was a blur of glittering silver, and he had to rub his eyes against the brightness. He could feel the boa, heavy on his shoulders, and something sliding beneath his feet.

When he opened his eyes, he was travelling very fast through a forest of naked trees, their branches burdened with frozen snow. And then came the wind.

A TIGER WITHOUT
A HEART

It was only at night that Billy heard the giant. He had
questioned Dorgo, but the servant would only shake his
head, regretfully, and say, 'Giant prisoner long time. He
here now for punishment. But he make no noise.' The
little man placed his hands over his woollen hat, where
Billy guessed his ears might be, and added, 'I not hear.'

Billy asked Matilda about the giant. She looked
puzzled. 'I've heard of a giant,' she said, 'but he lives in a
tower across the plain. He is not a true giant; he is just a
very tall man.'

'Dorgo knows that he was brought to the palace,' said
Billy. 'Can't you hear him, Matilda? His voice is so low
and sad.'

'No.' Matilda stared at Billy for a moment. 'Perhaps you
can hear him because he is from your world, or perhaps
. . .' she frowned thoughtfully, 'perhaps it is because of
your power, Billy. If you can hear and understand the
voices of tiny creatures, you can hear words that cannot
reach people like me.'

'Do you think the enchanter can hear him?' Billy asked.

'Without a doubt,' she said.

They were in Billy's room, playing with some of the toys the enchanter had devised for them: miniature knights with miniature horses that moved at the press of a button, set into a small wooden box. The horses had tiny silver shoes nailed to their ivory hooves, and the sound of their galloping on the wooden floor always made Matilda laugh.

The two children now went everywhere together. Billy had never liked anyone as much as Matilda except, perhaps, Charlie. But Charlie hadn't come to rescue him. Matilda was kind and generous. When she listened to Billy's stories of life in Bloor's Academy, she always wore an anxious frown, and at the end of the stories she would say, 'You have no home in the future, Billy. This is your home for always now.'

And Billy would agree. It was only when he heard the giant's melancholy voice drifting up through the darkened building that Billy would have a moment of doubt. He didn't belong here, in this palace of enchanted food and magical toys, out of time.

On the fourth night, the giant's voice was so insistent Billy got out of bed and tiptoed to the door. He looked into the passage. Dorgo appeared to be fast asleep. He was snoring loudly. Leaving the door ajar, Billy crept past the slumped figure and ran to the stairway. Nothing stirred; the giant's voice was the only sound. Billy padded softly down the smooth twisting stairs. When he reached the bottom he listened intently, trying to guess where the voice was coming from. And now the giant's words reached him clearly. 'Amoret! Amoret!' He was calling to his wife.

Something caused Billy to turn. The fires were out in the corridor of furs. But in the cool light of false stars, pinned to the ceiling, he could make out the dreadful heads with their glistening eyes. There was a sudden bright flash, and Billy leapt with terror.

The enchanter stood at the far end of the corridor. He was dressed in such glittering magnificence Billy could hardly bear to look at him. He wore a golden cloak embroidered with silver, and his long green robe was encrusted with diamonds. A brilliant sunburst sat atop his gold-flecked hair and the head of his ebony wand was a star of mirrored glass.

Billy might try to look away from the shining figure, but he couldn't avoid the gaze of the ivy-green eyes. They willed Billy forward, over the carpet of furs, closer and closer to the enchanter.

Without a word the enchanter suddenly turned in to an open doorway. Billy followed, but the bright figure had vanished, and Billy found that he was alone in a forest. 'In a palace?' he asked himself. 'A forest in a palace?' He followed a path through trees with unusual, rubbery leaves, and then he was in a moonlit glade. If the moon beaming down at him was false, then it was artfully made, for Billy could see the rifts and valleys of the same moon that he saw from windows in the real world.

A bear walked into the glade: a black bear, on all fours. 'A bear?' Billy whispered. 'But there are no animals in Badlock.' And then, before he knew it, a tiger brushed past him, so close he could feel its warm breath. The glade was suddenly full of sound and, looking up into the trees, Billy could see monkeys playing in the branches, bright birds flying through the leaves and a gleaming snake coiled around the trunks.

A herd of deer wandered into the glade. They began to crop the grass quite close to where the bear sat idly licking his paws. The tiger crouched beside Billy. Very slowly he put out his hand and touched the striped head. The tiger began to purr. It was a warm, comforting sound and reminded Billy of the three Flames. He spoke to the tiger, using a language he hoped the animal would understand. The tiger didn't reply. It continued to purr, but its purr made no sense.

Billy tried to talk to the bear, but the animal didn't respond. He spoke to the deer, the monkeys, the snake and even the birds. They didn't understand him. Had he lost his endowment? Had the enchanter stolen it away?

'*They have no hearts*', said a voice. '*They'll never speak to you.*' Rembrandt was peeping out of Billy's pocket. '*I'll admit he's done a fine job,*' said the rat, '*but it's quite obvious that they're just enchantments.*'

'Really?' Billy wondered if the enchanter could see

him. 'But they're warm and the tiger purrs, and the birds sing so beautifully.'

'*Don't be disappointed,*' said Rembrandt. '*At least they won't eat you.*'

Billy walked further into the glade. A gorilla lumbered out of the bushes, scratched itself and plunged back into the undergrowth. Billy followed it and saw an elephant moving through the distant trees.

'I've always wanted to see an elephant,' breathed Billy.

'*It isn't real. Let's go to bed,*' said Rembrandt.

Billy yawned. He felt very tired. But when he turned to leave the forest, he couldn't see the path that had brought him to the enchanted glade. As he stared at the undergrowth, a line of bushes began to sway, as though a large creature were moving through them. Suddenly, Dorgo's head popped up through the sea of leaves.

'Master lost,' said the little servant. 'Bed this way.'

Leaping towards Dorgo, Billy found that the path was still there, under the thick springy leaves. He was now so tired all he could think of was his warm, comfy bed.

When they climbed the marble stairway, the giant's voice was lost in the patter of their feet and, by the time Billy fell asleep, he had forgotten all about it.

The next morning, Billy could think of nothing but the forest of enchanted animals. He wanted Matilda to see them, and hoped that another spell wouldn't cause them to disappear. He needn't have worried.

Matilda was delighted. She danced about among

the animals, stroking their heads and listening to their chattering, singing and purring. 'How clever he is,' she cried. 'Oh Billy, the enchanter never did anything like this for me, or Edgar. My brother is already jealous of you. Wait till he sees this forest.'

'Perhaps it wasn't meant for me,' said Billy. 'Perhaps it was meant for all of us.'

'No, no. The count wanted to please you especially. He wants to keep you here.'

Two days ago this would have worried Billy. Now he felt almost pleased. He wished that Lilith and Edgar wouldn't look at him with such resentment, though. 'Why is your brother jealous of me?' he asked.

Matilda blushed. 'I said that I liked your white hair and berry-coloured eyes, and the count told me I had excellent taste. Edgar was listening and he walked away, looking sulky.'

It was a new sensation for Billy, being admired for his albino colouring. He grinned with pleasure.

Edgar refused to visit the enchanted glade. At supper he complained that animals were 'dirty and dangerous'.

'Not these animals, Edgar,' said the count. 'These are special. How do you like them, Billy?'

Billy answered that he liked them very much. Lilith threw him a pitying look and Edgar scowled.

Matilda had advised Billy what sort of food to ask for, and he now looked forward to every meal. At the end of one of the lavish dinners, Billy made a puzzling discovery.

The candles on the table were burning low and, as everyone rose to leave the room, their long shadows moved across the walls. The count was washing his hands in a bowl held by the tall servant. The servant's lofty shadow could clearly be seen on the tapestry behind the count, but where the count's shadow should have been, there was nothing. No shadow shook its fingers and wiped its hands, even though the bowl of water and the shadow droplets were visible on the lush colours of the tapestry.

It is part of his enchantment, Billy told himself.

Every day Billy and Matilda would play in the forest, and Billy would listen to the false songs of the multicoloured birds; he would enjoy stroking the tiger that purred but had no heart, and he would watch the monkeys playing in trees that had no names. At night he slept soundly and never heard the giant's voice. But Rembrandt, sitting alert at the foot of Billy's bed, would listen to the giant calling, 'Amoret, oh, Amoret.'

Rembrandt knew that Billy was falling under a spell: a spell that was all the stronger for being so delicately done. He tried to remind Billy of the other world, where they belonged. But Billy wouldn't listen. 'This is our home now,' he told the rat.

One day Matilda took Billy exploring. While everyone thought they were with the animals, she led him along an unfamiliar passage, down a flight of steps and on through rooms full of musical instruments, marvellous costumes and sumptuous oriental furnishings. Now and again, Matilda would look at the walls and the ceiling and whisper, 'I used to think that the count could see everything, but there are days when he is occupied with magic and not so vigilant. Today is one of those days.'

They came, at last, to a room full of paintings. There were rolls of cloth lying at one end of a long table; at the other end stood several boxes of coloured powder. Brushes of every size and shape were scattered in groups about the floor, and paintings stood against the walls. Most showed landscapes or marvellous cities with golden domes and pointed turrets, and then Billy saw a city he recognised and his heart gave a lurch.

'That's where I come from,' he said.

Matilda clapped her hands. 'I thought so.' She looked round the room and lowered her voice. 'My grandfather talks to it. One day I came down here and I heard voices. The count was standing close to that painting and listening. There was a woman's voice in the room, but I could see no one, so I knew her voice must be coming from your city. I believe she is the count's descendant.' Matilda grinned. 'Perhaps she is my descendant, also; if not mine, then Edgar's.'

Billy didn't find this funny. 'Her name's Mrs Tilpin, and she's a witch,' he said.

'Oh!' Matilda's smile vanished. She sat on a bench and drew Billy down beside her. 'I will tell you about the count,' she said. 'I know he is trying to get into your city; he makes no secret of it. There is a mirror that he can use for travel. He hid it in the grounds of the Red King's castle, and the woman now has it, but it is broken and she cannot help him to journey into the future.'

'He's already halfway there,' said Billy. 'He's a shadow in the Red King's portrait and my friend, Charlie, says that's how he got into our world before, through his shadow.'

'Ah, the shadow!' Matilda lowered her voice until it was almost a whisper. 'He is monstrously clever, my grandfather. He cut himself away from his shadow and now it can travel while he stays at home, growing old. His shadow will live forever, he says.'

Billy stared at her. 'The count has no shadow. Of course, I noticed it. I thought it was just part of his enchantment.'

'It is,' said Matilda.

They left the room of paintings and began to make their way back to the dining hall. As they passed the marble stairway, Billy stopped and looked up. He could hear footsteps coming down the stairs. But no one was there. The footsteps came closer.

'What is it?' asked Matilda.

'I don't –'

Before Billy could finish his sentence a feathered blue snake's head appeared in mid-air. It swayed towards Billy, bringing its long, scaly body behind it.

Matilda screamed and leapt away.

'Sorry,' said a voice.

'Charlie?' Billy gaped at the snake, which was lying several feet above the stairs.

'Yes, it's me,' said Charlie. 'I got Solomon to make me invisible. He was invisible too, but I suppose he was so pleased to see you, he forgot himself. I'll put him down.'

The boa rocked gently to the floor where it curled itself into a neat bundle. 'Hello, Billy,' it hissed.

'Hi!' Billy replied in a puzzled tone. 'Good to see you, Solomon.' He tried to focus on the space above the boa, where he imagined Charlie's face to be. 'I thought you'd come sooner. What kept you so long, Charlie?'

'You've no idea,' sighed Charlie. 'I tried, tried and tried. And then they took the painting away. It's a long story, but here I am, so are you ready?'

Billy gazed into space. 'I . . .'

Rembrandt poke his head out of Billy's golden pouch and politely asked after the boa's health.

'I'm doing well,' hissed the snake. 'How about you?'

'Could be better,' squeaked the rat.

Billy put his hands over his ears. 'I can't think, with all that chat going on.'

'Billy's not going back with you,' said Matilda, coming to Billy's side.

'Of course he is,' said Charlie, rather taken aback by the appearance of a pretty girl all in yellow. 'Who are you, anyway?'

'She's my friend, Charlie, and she's right. I'm sorry but I'm staying here.' Billy began to walk down the corridor of heads and furs, with Matilda several paces behind him.

'You must come,' Charlie called.

Matilda looked over her shoulder. 'Shh!' She put a finger to her lips. 'Come with us. It's not safe here.'

Charlie became aware of the animal heads hanging in the corridor. He was reluctant to walk beneath them, but felt he had little choice. Lifting the boa on to his shoulders he followed the two retreating figures. He caught up with them seconds later, in a forest of extraordinary trees.

'Where *are* we?' Charlie whispered.

'We're in a forest in the enchanter's palace,' Billy told him. 'He made the trees and animals especially for me.'

'Lucky you.' Charlie let the boa slither to his feet. 'It's odd, when I came here before I arrived outside a giant's tower.'

'Perhaps you naturally gravitate towards your ancestor,' Matilda said in a solemn voice.

'What?' Charlie regarded the girl who, all at once, looked infinitely wise. He turned to Billy. 'You can't stay here, Billy. You don't belong.'

'I don't belong in your city,' said Billy. 'I haven't got a home there. It's nice here. The food is good and everything is beautiful and,' he looked at Matilda, 'I've got a friend.'

'But I've came all this way,' said Charlie, shocked by Billy's words. 'You know you can stay with me any time you want.'

Matilda took Billy's hand. 'You'd best go home, Charlie Bone, and take your snake because . . .' she stared at a tree. 'Oh, dear! Here he comes.'

The next moment, Edgar came walking out of a tree. 'I heard a scream,' he said.

Matilda let go of Billy's hand and pointed at the blue boa. 'The Enchanter had made such an excellent snake, we thought it was real.'

The boa waved its head and hissed.

Edgar stepped back. 'Stupid girl,' he said. 'Snakes don't have feathers. You are late for dinner again. Come immediately.'

Charlie watched them all go. They didn't even turn in his direction. The boa made no attempt to follow Billy. He seemed to know it was his place to stay with Charlie. Or was it Claerwen's influence? The big snake had curled himself into an invisible coil.

Claerwen had emerged from Charlie's pocket and was now fluttering among the high branches, as though investigating the artificial forest. Charlie sat on the ground and put his head in his hands. He had been totally unprepared for Billy's rejection. Billy had been spellbound, he decided. But how he was to break the spell, Charlie had no idea.

'Help me, Claerwen,' said Charlie. 'Helpu fi.'

She came and settled on his arm, but although she gave him comfort, she couldn't provide an answer.

In the distance, Charlie could see animals moving through the trees. 'They're not real, are they?' he murmured to Claerwen. None of the animals came near him.

I'll wait until they've gone to bed,' Charlie told himself. I'll find where Billy's sleeping and, maybe, if he's alone, I can make him come with me.

An unreal moon was already beaming down into the forest. Charlie wondered if he would be able to tell when night fell in this palace of false light. I wouldn't want to live here, he thought, as he stretched himself on the ground. He rested his head on the boa's smooth coils and, before he knew it, he had fallen asleep.

Charlie woke up, with a start. A girl in a long white robe was standing in the trees. She held a lighted candle in a metal saucer.

'Are you there, Charlie Bone?' the girl asked, in a whisper.

Charlie sat up. 'I'm here. Where's Billy?'

'He didn't want to leave his room. I've come with a message.' Matilda ventured a little closer to Charlie. 'Billy won't come back with you, Charlie. I'm sorry that you've come all this way, through the years, and not without danger to yourself, I'm sure. But there is *someone* you might want to see before you return.'

Charlie rubbed his eyes and got to his feet. 'You mean my ancestor, the giant. Perhaps you can tell me how I can reach his tower, because I know it's miles away.'

'Not miles away, Charlie. He is here.'

'Here?' Charlie remembered Matilda's words. 'Is that what you meant about gravitating towards my ancestor?'

'Of course.' She gave him a wise smile.

'Where is he?' asked Charlie.

'In the dungeon. I will show you the entrance, but I dare not come with you.' She looked at her candle. 'I could give you a light, but it would be seen.'

'I don't need a light,' said Charlie.

'Come with me, then.'

Charlie followed Matilda's flickering candle along the silent passages. It must be dead of night, he thought, for the rush lights had died and the false stars had lost their shine. He supposed that even enchanters needed their sleep.

The passages became darker. The walls were now rock and stone, the ground a path of rubble. A deep, melancholy voice echoed down the passages and as they hastened ever deeper, Charlie could make out the word, 'Amoret!'

'My ancestor,' Charlie whispered.

'I can hear it now,' said Matilda. 'At first only Billy could hear the giant's voice. We are getting nearer.'

They came to a half circle of rusty iron railings and, lifting her candle, Matilda said, 'Down there!'

Charlie saw a stairway of rocky steps, twisting down into the darkness.

'I wish you well, Charlie Bone,' Matilda whispered.

'Thank you.' Charlie hoped they would meet again. She was just about the most beautiful girl he had ever seen. Who was she? Did she have a place in the long tangle of the Red King's descendants?

'Make haste!' Matilda looked at the ceiling where a

star was beginning to flicker into life. 'The enchanter is waking up.'

'Goodbye, Matilda!' Charlie touched her hand and she stared at it in wonderment.

'Goodbye, Charlie Bone!'

Charlie put his foot on to the first step and began to descend. It was the steepest, blackest set of steps he had ever come across and he was glad of Claerwen's bright light. He worried that his loud stumbling would wake the guard that must surely be watching the giant's cell.

At the bottom of the steps a sharp turn brought Charlie into a narrow space where a figure sat slumped beside a table. A pile of candles lay on the table, and one flickered in a brass candlestick. But it was Claerwen's light that showed Charlie the heavily barred cell beyond the guard and the giant's gaunt face peering out of it.

'Who is there?' whispered Otus.

Charlie looked at the sleeping figure. A bunch of keys lay on his lap. Which one opened the cell? Charlie would have to choose quickly. He tiptoed closer to the sleeping guard. And then he saw the huge, lumpy thumb. Snatching up the keys, Charlie tried to push the first one into the lock on the cell door. It didn't fit.

The giant watched the floating keys in astonishment. 'Who is it?' he asked again.

'Me, Charlie, your descendant,' Charlie whispered. 'I'm going to take you to your wife.'

'Amoret?' The giant shook his head. 'You lie. She is dead.'

The rattle of iron in the lock must have woken the troll for, all at once, he opened his eyes and stared at the keys in mid-air. Leaping up, he shouted, 'What is this, giant? Are you trying to use magic?'

The giant backed away, still shaking his head, and Oddthumb seized the keys. He stared at them suspiciously. Charlie made a grab for them, but Oddthumb lifted his great fist and brought it smashing into Charlie's stomach. He reeled back with a groan.

'There you are,' said the troll. 'You scoundrel. You won't get the better of Oddthumb with invisibility, I can tell you.'

What made the boa act then, Charlie would never know. Perhaps Claerwen had a word in his ear, for suddenly the big snake made himself visible. From Charlie's shoulder he lunged at Oddthumb, hissing like a steaming kettle. The troll, his eyes starting from his head, flung up his hands and the keys went flying through the air.

A dreadful sound came gurgling out of Oddthumb and he ran up the steps, stumbling and moaning in terror.

Charlie quickly scooped up the keys. The second one fitted the lock and the cell door swung open with a screech.

'We'd better hurry,' Charlie told the giant, 'or Oddthumb will be back with reinforcements.'

'It *is* you, Charlie Bone,' said the giant. 'I know your voice. But what are we going to do? How can I ever escape this place?'

'First of all, the boa will make you invisible,' said

Charlie. 'And then . . . then we'll find your wife before she dies, and you will be together.'

The blue boa needed no instruction this time. He seemed to know, instinctively, what he should do. Otus watched himself disappear in horror and fascination. It was only when Charlie began to direct his moth that he realised they would have to return the way they had come: through the painting of Badlock.

The boa looped himself around the giant's shoulders and Charlie held tight to his ancestor's arm. Claerwen spread her silver wings and, alighting on Charlie's head, she proceeded to take them through time.

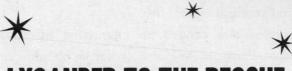

LYSANDER TO THE RESCUE

As usual, Charlie had given no thought to the flight ahead. Travelling with an invisible giant was not as easy as he would have wished. Otus might have been brave, but a journey to meet a wife he believed to be dead was a little daunting. If he had known he would be flying through nine hundred years, instead of twenty, he probably wouldn't have agreed to come at all. As it was, he kept calling out to Charlie for reassurance. The tumbling and whirling aspect of their journey was very uncomfortable for a giant.

'Are we there?' Otus would cry. 'My legs are floating over my head. Woe, Charlie. Bring us to earth.'

'Hush, Otus,' Charlie would reply, as though he were speaking to a child.

'When will we arrive? Will we be too late to see Amoret?' The giant's voice quavered as a violent gust of time spun them into a fast descent.

'I think we're here,' said Charlie, as his feet scraped the ground.

When the giant touched down a second later, there was an earth-shuddering crash.

'Woe!' yelled Otus as his invisible feet plunged through the floorboards.

A long shriek followed the crash and a voice cried. 'He's here! He's here!'

'Where? Where?' called other voices.

Charlie found himself on the stage of the Old Chapel, staring out at a crowd of angry-looking people. He was very glad to be invisible. Mrs Tilpin thrust her face very close to his. 'You're there, aren't you?' She tried to poke him in the chest, but Charlie stepped sideways, just in time.

'Where am I?' roared the giant. 'My feet have gone.'

'They're stuck in the floorboards,' Charlie whispered. 'Pull them out, Otus.'

There was a sound of cracking, splintering wood as Otus heaved his big feet up through the floorboards. 'AWWW!' he bellowed.

'There's two!' A woman at the front of the crowd pointed at Charlie. Her bright red ringlets looked very odd framing such an old, wrinkled face. 'I can see them. One is a giant.'

'A giant?' screamed Mrs Tilpin, stepping back.

'Dolores has the second sight,' said a burly fellow in a black balaclava.

Standing just behind the balaclava man, Charlie caught sight of someone he recognised, but events were moving too fast for him to put a name to the man.

'Where's my wife?' the giant called plaintively. 'Where's Amoret?'

'Amoret?' Mrs Tilpin turned to the crowd. 'Friends, this giant is the shadow's prisoner.'

The crowd surged forward and began to climb on to the stage. Charlie grabbed the giant's hand and tugged him to the green curtains at the back.

'There! There!' shouted Dolores, her black-gloved finger following Charlie as he pulled the giant towards the door at the side of the stage.

The crowd closed in. Coarse, deep-throated oaths filled the air as a dozen tall figures surrounded Charlie and the giant.

'There be monsters in your world, Charlie boy,' said the giant, 'but they shall not have us.' And he thrust out his big foot, pushing two of the men to the ground.

The others stepped back, staring in horror at the giant's shoulders, for the blue boa had made himself visible. He was thrusting his head out at the crowd, his open mouth revealing dreadful shining fangs.

'Dolores, do something!' screamed Mrs Tilpin.

As Dolores reached into her pocket, Charlie heard drumbeats. They grew louder and louder until the sound filled the chapel. The crowd looked round, trying to see where the drumming was coming from. But nothing could distract Dolores. Raising a small silver catapult, she shot a stone straight at the giant's forehead. He crashed to the floor with a groan.

'Otus, I'm sorry. I'm sorry I brought you here,' cried Charlie, falling to his knees beside the giant. The distressed boa wrapped himself round Charlie as though to comfort him. Too late, Charlie realised that he was becoming visible. He waited for Mrs Tilpin's sharp fingers to grab him by the neck. But nothing touched him.

Charlie looked up. The crowd was backing away, men and women falling over each other in their haste to leave the stage. Even Mrs Tilpin was moving down the steps. Her eyes were fixed on the wall behind Charlie, her face contorted with fear. Following her gaze, Charlie looked behind him and saw a line of ghostly forms, half hidden in a swirling mist. Their faces were undefined, but their brown arms were all too clear. Every hand held a long, gleaming knife.

'Lysander!' said Charlie.

'You bet!' Lysander came striding through the stage door. He swept his arm in an arc above his head and pointed at the crowd.

Lysander's spirit ancestors, their weapons held aloft, advanced on Mrs Tilpin and her sinister followers. Many of them held their hands over their ears, the drumbeats were now so loud. They jostled and moaned as they pushed their way to the door that opened on to Piminy Street. And then they were through and, above the drumming, their heavy feet could be heard pounding down the street.

The giant groaned.

'Whatever was that?' Lysander stared at the floor.

'A giant,' said Charlie. 'And he's alive. Thanks, Sander. Thank you, thank you. You saved our lives.'

'A giant,' said Lysander. 'I expected Billy.'

'Billy,' sighed Charlie. 'He wouldn't come.'

Lysander stared at Charlie in disbelief and then, studying the floor where the groaning was coming from, he said, 'We'd better get that giant out of here. I'm sure *they'll* be able to see him, even if I can't.' He beckoned his spirit ancestors.

The tall, wraith-like forms lowered their knives and tucked them into glittering belts. Charlie got to his feet as they came towards him. There were seven of them, their dark features appearing briefly and then receding into the mist that seemed to accompany them. They bent down and lifted the giant on to their shoulders, as easily as if he'd been an empty sack. At least Charlie assumed that was where the giant was, because his groaning voice was coming from somewhere just above their heads.

Lysander led the way through the door and round the back of the chapel. Charlie came last, with the blue boa hanging round his neck. He took a quick look back into the chapel before he closed the door. The painting of Badlock was lying on its back, facing the ivy-clad ceiling. Charlie was tempted to destroy it, knowing what it could do. And then he remembered Billy.

Charlie slammed the door of the chapel and raced round into the alley. He could hardly believe his eyes. Uncle Paton's camper-van was parked in a space no camper-van should occupy. Luckily, the back doors were right beside the opening in the chapel wall, and the ancestors had no trouble in depositing the giant on the floor. When this was done the tall figures slowly melted away. Lysander made a bow in their direction, and closed the van doors.

'Uncle Paton, when did you get here?' Charlie clambered in beside his uncle, who shied away from the boa and started the engine.

'An hour ago,' said Uncle Paton. 'You don't need to tell me where you've been.'

Lysander leapt in beside Charlie and said, 'Let's go, Mr Yewbeam!'

They sped up to the top of the alley and turned into a road that would eventually take them into Filbert Street.

'Is young Billy hurt?' asked Uncle Paton as he drove, rather too fast, along Park Road. 'He's making a devil of a noise.'

'It isn't Billy,' said Charlie.

'No?' Uncle Paton glanced at Charlie. 'Who then?'

Charlie hesitated and Lysander said, 'Mr Yewbeam, you have a very large man in the back of your van.'

'WHAT?' Uncle Paton's foot slipped on to the brake and everyone lurched forward rather sickeningly.

A dreadful groan came from the back, and a melancholy voice called, 'For pity's sake, what monstrous machine is eating me?'

'How large is this very large man?' asked Paton in a low voice. 'Are we talking of giants?'

'He's not strictly a giant,' said Charlie. 'He's only about eight or nine feet tall.'

Uncle Paton sighed. 'May I ask why he is here?'

'He's from Badlock,' Charlie told his uncle. 'He's my ancestor, and yours. I *had* to rescue him, Uncle P.'

'Of course you did,' Uncle Paton said wearily. 'And may I ask what you propose to do with such a very tall person, nine hundred years out of his own time?'

Charlie grimaced. He couldn't bring himself to tell his uncle that he planned to take Otus to the Castle of Mirrors. He knew it would sound ridiculous.

Lysander leaned forward and said quietly, 'The giant is at present invisible, Mr Yewbeam.'

'Oh, great.' Paton glanced at the blue boa. 'I suppose that makes everything all right, doesn't it?' He put his foot down hard on the accelerator and they whizzed up Filbert Street, coming to a screeching halt outside number nine.

Charlie wasn't quite sure what to do next. His uncle sat in the driving seat, scratching his head and looking stressed.

'I'll get the Browns.' Charlie raced over to number twelve to explain the situation to the Browns.

Uncle Paton eventually roused himself and joined Lysander, who had opened the van doors. The giant had fallen silent.

Mr and Mrs Brown came running across the road, followed by Benjamin, Charlie and Runner Bean. They all crowded round the back of the camper-van, Runner Bean barking with excitement.

'How interesting!' Mr Brown peered into the van,

accidentally resting his hand on one of the giant's feet. 'Ooops! There he is.'

'Charlie, open the front door, quickly,' ordered Uncle Paton.

Charlie leapt up the steps and opened the door, calling. 'Hi, Grandmas, we're just bringing a carpet in.' When he looked round, Lysander, Uncle Paton and the Browns were carrying the giant, wrapped in the van's carpet, towards the house.

With much huffing and puffing, the carpet was lifted up the steps and into the hall, where it was lowered, rather fast, on to the floor. There was a bump and a voice from the floor cried, 'Mercy! Let it end now, I beseech you.'

Charlie quickly shut the front door and let the boa slide inside the carpet. Maisie appeared in the kitchen doorway and said, 'There you are, Charlie. I see your uncle found you. I wondered what on earth had happened.'

Charlie gave her a sheepish grin. 'Sorry, Maisie. Got held up.'

'That's a very shabby carpet,' she said and, before anyone could stop her, she gave it a little kick.

The deep groan from the carpet sent her reeling back into the kitchen. 'There's someone in there,' she cried.

They all followed her into the kitchen. Charlie made her sit down and Uncle Paton put on the kettle. Runner Bean slid under the table and everyone gathered round Maisie. No one knew quite what to tell her, so Charlie sat beside his grandmother and began at the beginning. When he had finished, Maisie took a very deep breath and said, 'Well, you'd better do something about that poor man. Grandma Bone will be back from lunch in a minute.'

It was decided that Charlie should talk to Otus. The giant would not be so alarmed if someone he knew explained things to him.

'It would be a great advantage if the fellow could be seen,' said Mr Brown.

'Not with my sister about,' Paton told him.

They didn't realise that the blue boa had made his own decision until they opened the door. There stood the giant, every hair, every whisker completely visible. The boa had wrapped itself comfortably round his neck.

'Charlie,' cried Otus. 'What manner of place is this?'

Charlie was relieved to see Otus on his feet, but a little concerned about the huge bruise on the giant's forehead. 'Shall we go upstairs, sir?' he said. 'I've got things to tell you, and we might not be safe here.'

The giant gazed round at the framed photos on the wall, at the hall light in its stained glass shade, hanging beside his head. 'Yes, yes,' he murmured. 'It is very strange here, Charlie.'

And then Runner Bean ran out of the kitchen wagging his tail, and the giant beamed with pleasure. 'We meet again, dog,' he said, bending to stroke Runner Bean. 'Good dog. Best of all dogs.'

Runner Bean licked the big hand and barked delightedly.

Mrs Brown poked her head round the door and said,

'We'll be off now, Charlie. I'm sure you've got a lot to arrange. It's been nice meeting you, Mr Yewbeam.'

The giant inclined his head.

'Nice to meet you,' said Mr Brown, tiptoeing for some reason towards the door. 'Come on, Ben.'

Benjamin stared up at the giant's smiling face. 'Hi,' he said.

'Hi!' the giant repeated.

'I'd better be going, too,' said Lysander, holding his hand out to the giant. 'It's been a pleasure to meet you, sir.'

Otus solemnly took Lysander's hand. 'You are a powerful boy,' said the giant. 'I know this. And I thank you.'

When Lysander and the Browns had gone, Charlie led the giant upstairs. Uncle Paton suggested his room would be safer than Charlie's, as it was strictly out of bounds to Grandma Bone.

Otus ducked beneath the door lintel and sank on to Uncle Paton's bed, which was covered in papers. Otus didn't seem to notice, nor did he pay any heed to the loud twangs the bed made, as though several springs had broken.

'You've made a mistake, haven't you, Charlie boy?' said the giant.

'Sorry.' Charlie moved some of the papers and sat next to his ancestor.

'Shall I never see my wife?' asked the giant in a forlorn voice.

'I hope you will.' Charlie smiled encouragingly. 'The thing is, I had to come back here first, because the painting of Badlock was here, and it's what I do: travel into paintings.'

'There is no painting of my wife,' said Otus.

'No – but – I think I have seen her.'

'You . . .!' The giant's face came very close to Charlie. His large hand clutched Charlie's shoulder. 'How is that possible?'

'The castle where she died still stands, but the walls were turned to glass.'

'I heard that snow fell,' Otus murmured, almost to himself. 'Snow sent by a magician, but it came too late.'

'Too late to save them,' Charlie agreed. 'But it was a wonderful spell in its way, because now the walls are like glass, but they are also mirrors. Perhaps you haven't seen a mirror.' He pointed to the mirror on Uncle Paton's dressing-table, and the giant, seeing himself reflected there, smiled and said, 'Ah! A mirror!'

'When I went to the castle,' Charlie continued, 'there was a wall that showed me a time picture, not a painting but, well, it was like a memory, like the walls had kept the memory of the people who lived there. I saw a family: Amadis and his wife and children, and a beautiful woman with black hair –'

'Yes, yes . . .' Otus exclaimed.

'And they called her Amoret.'

'And you saw her . . . truly?'

'She talked to me.' Charlie looked into the giant's incredulous face. 'I went in.'

'You went . . . *in?*' Otus lifted his head and stared at the ceiling. He looked round at the shelves of books, the pictures and the calendar. He looked at Uncle Paton's desk with its jars of pens and pencils, and he didn't seem surprised by any of it. 'So you could take me?' he said.

'I think I could, with Claerwen's help. After all, she was a magician's wand. The magician that sent the snow, I think.'

The giant stood up, and the bedsprings twanged into place again. 'When do we travel?' he asked.

'Um . . . I haven't told my uncle yet,' said Charlie. 'It'll be up to him.'

Uncle Paton opened the door just then, and said, 'We've got a visitor.'

Mrs Kettle, carrying a large basket, pushed past him into the room. She gave a little start when she saw the giant's face so very far above her, and the giant obligingly sat down again.

'I'm so very thrilled to meet you, Mr Yewbeam.' She held out her hand. The giant took it and leaned forward, bending his head as though he would have made a bow, if he'd been standing up.

'My name is Mrs Kettle,' the blacksmith went on, 'and I've been caring for . . . ah, there he is.' She spied the blue boa, curled up on a pile of Uncle Paton's clothes. 'Come on, Solomon darling, time to go home.'

'A wondrous snake,' Otus remarked as Mrs Kettle approached the boa with her basket.

'I wouldn't like him to get into the wrong hands,' said Mrs Kettle, helping the snake to curl himself into the basket. 'There.' She closed the lid and smiled round at everyone. 'Well, this is a most incredible event, and I am very happy to be part of it. There is some good news which I don't suppose Lysander told you, Charlie?'

Charlie shrugged.

'No, I thought not. I imagine it's been very busy here.' She glanced at the giant. 'Anyway, Gabriel Silk has obtained so many signatures on his petition for re-opening the Pets' Café, it is likely that the Onimouses will be successful.'

Instead of giving her a happy smile, Charlie suddenly leapt up, clapping his hand to his head. 'Oh no,' he cried. 'I've remembered.'

'What have you remembered?' Paton came further into the room and closed the door.

The giant stared anxiously at Charlie as he paced towards the window. 'Norton Cross, the doorman at the Pets' Café,' Charlie said. 'I saw him in the Chapel. He must be one of the shadow's followers. Perhaps he even caused the Onimouses' accident.'

'We'll just make sure he doesn't go back there, m'dear,' said Mrs Kettle calmly.

'You don't understand.' Charlie clutched his tangled hair. 'I told Mr Bittermouse to contact Norton, to help with mending his door. And now I've put him in danger.'

'He was in danger already, Charlie,' said Mrs Kettle.

'But we'll make sure that he's safe. Don't you worry your head about it. You've got enough on your plate.' She smiled at the giant, who was sitting very still with a faraway look in his eyes. 'I mean no offence, Mr Yewbeam, m'dear, but I'm sure Charlie's been making plans for you.'

'Er, yes,' Charlie muttered.

'And what are they, m'dear? Will you let me into your secrets?'

'Um . . .' began Charlie.

The giant said, 'He is taking me to my wife.'

Not by a single twitch did Mrs Kettle show her surprise. 'How wonderful,' she said. 'I'll be off now and let you get on with things. Good luck, all.' She slipped out, closing the door very quietly behind her.

Unfortunately, Uncle Paton was so flabbergasted he staggered to a chair and sat down rather heavily. 'Can I believe my ears, Charlie? Did you tell Mr Yewbeam here that you were taking him *to see his wife*?'

'I'm sorry I didn't mention it before,' said Charlie.

'But . . .' Paton looked at the giant and shook his head.

Charlie felt deflated and helpless. It was several seconds before he realised that the giant was speaking. Otus Yewbeam's deep voice stole so softly into the room, Charlie and his uncle felt they were listening to a voice from another world.

'I know what awaits me, sir. I know the fire was fierce and that Amoret died most horribly. I have known this for many years. I have thought of it every day since I learned the nature of my wife's passing; every day that I spent in that hell, for Badlock is hell, my friends. And I thank you, most fervently, Charlie, for bringing me out of it. I would not have wished to die there. I know what my end will be if I am with my wife, but one day, one hour, one minute spent with her would, at a stroke, wipe away the memory of all those bitter years. So I beg you, Sir Paton, Uncle of Charlie, please help Charlie to take me to my wife.'

Uncle Paton had been looking at the giant as though struck by an amazing revelation. 'It will be a pleasure, sir,' he said.

There was a crash from below as the front door was flung open, and a voice called, 'WHERE IS IT, THEN? I've heard from my friends in Piminy Street, that there is most likely a giant in my house.'

'Grandma Bone!' Charlie whispered.

'An ill-disposed voice,' remarked the giant.

'Exceedingly ill-disposed,' Paton agreed. 'But don't let it worry you. Stay here, with Charlie. I'll deal with this.'

Uncle Paton left the room, calling, 'Good afternoon, Grizelda. Are you grumbling again?'

'I most certainly am.' She stared up at her brother, her features twisted with spite. 'Where is it?'

'IT? IT?' shouted Paton, descending the stairs. 'There is no IT here, unless you mean your sorry self.'

Grandma Bone stamped her foot. 'Don't try and be clever, Paton. I won't have it in my house.'

'*Your* house, Grizelda?' Paton poked her in the chest.

'*Your* house? It's half mine, and I won't have you poking your nose into my business.'

'Don't do that!' Grandma Bone found herself backing down the passage as Paton poked and poked at her.

'Stop it!' she shrieked.

They had reached the cellar and, in one swift movement, Paton opened the door and pushed her in. She slipped down the first two steps, steadied herself and screamed, 'H-E-L-P!'

Paton slammed the door. As the key was not readily available, he quickly pulled a heavy oak chest in front of the door.

'What's going on?' asked Maisie, looking at Paton in alarm.

'I've temporarily imprisoned my sister,' Paton told her. 'Don't worry, Maisie. She'll lose her voice in a minute. We've got a very long journey ahead of us, so I'd like you to make sure Grizelda stays put until we get back.'

'Are you taking . . .?' Maisie hesitated and looked up the stairs. 'The other Mr Yewbeam?'

'We are indeed. We are taking him somewhere safe.'

'I'm so glad. I was very worried about him. But I thought that little Billy would be coming back. Is he still . . . there?'

'Still there, Maisie.' Paton frowned. 'And I'm not sure how we'll get him out.'

'But get him out you will,' said Maisie sternly.

The light was already leaving the sky. Soon it would

be dark. Uncle Paton decided he would have to put out the street lamp if the giant wasn't to attract too much attention when he left the house.

The giant waited patiently on Uncle Paton's bed. He had fallen silent and a mysterious half-smile touched the corners of his mouth. Was he thinking of the past? Charlie wondered. Or was he imagining the moment when he would see Amoret again? The house was very quiet. Grandma Bone had stopped screaming, just as Paton had predicted.

When the first star showed, Paton put on his black fedora and stepped down into the street. With his hand on the lamp post, he murmured, 'Let it happen, then, but quietly please.'

There was a small 'popping' noise; the lamp went out and Paton's fedora was covered in a silver dust. 'Many thanks,' he said, though he wasn't sure who or what he was thanking. He removed his hat and shook the glass fragments into the street.

Watching from the window, Charlie saw his uncle open the back doors of the camper-van and slide the carpet back into place.

'It's time to go,' Charlie told the giant.

Otus stood up and stretched his arms, scraping his knuckles on the ceiling. He laughed and said, 'This house would never suit me, Charlie Bone.'

'No,' said Charlie. 'They don't make houses for giants any more.'

'They never did,' said Otus.

The giant's heavy feet thumped on the treads as he followed Charlie downstairs. Maisie handed him a box of food and he made a low bow.

'Good luck, Mr Yewbeam,' she said. 'I wish we could have spent a bit more time together.'

'I agree, my lady,' said Otus, tucking the box under his arm. 'You are very gracious.' He took her hand and planted a kiss on it.

'How chivalrous,' said Maisie, blushing with pleasure.

'Hurry up,' called Uncle Paton.

Otus walked down the steps and then stood on the pavement, gazing at the passing cars, the street lamps and the lighted houses. An aeroplane passed overhead, its tail light twinkling among the stars.

'Oh,' sighed the giant, 'what a wondrous thing this new world is. I wish I had known it better.'

Charlie took the box and put it in the back of the van. 'It's time to go, Otus,' he said quietly. 'I'm afraid we'll have to travel in this machine again.'

'I am not afeared.' The giant took a large step into the back of the van and Charlie closed the doors. Uncle Paton started the engine and Charlie climbed up beside him.

Maisie stood waving from the door as though she might never see them again. But Charlie's confidence didn't waver until they drove out of the city and into the night. And then a voice in his head began to ask, 'What if I fail? What then?'

AMORET

The way to the Castle of Mirrors was long and difficult, but after his last journey there, Uncle Paton had made a map of the route. The road followed the river for a while and then, at a crossroads five miles outside the city, they turned on to the coast road. Otus had never seen the castle though he had heard much about it.

'They said it was the finest castle in the world.' The giant's voice rumbled softly from the back of the van. 'Borlath, the eldest prince, envied Amadis in all things, and the shadow stoked the fires of his envy. Anything Borlath could not have, he destroyed.'

After a long pause Charlie asked, 'Where did you live, Otus?'

The giant chuckled. 'I was born in a house of living yew. My father dug a pit in the centre of an ancient grove. So wide were those yews it needed but a few beams driven between them to give us our walls. Above we had a roof of hides, tied to the highest branches. We never touched the leaves or berries for they are poisonous, but they kept the wolves at bay.'

'Yewbeam,' Charlie murmured. 'So that's how the name began.'

'Aye,' said the giant.

'Well, I never found that out,' Paton declared, 'in all my years of research. How very interesting. And did your wife live in this house of yew?'

'Faith, no.' Otus sounded quite indignant. 'I built my Amoret a fine house from stone and pine, with bleached walls and a floor of slate.'

'Naturally.' Paton gave a small apologetic cough.

After this they all fell silent and Charlie drifted off to sleep. When he woke up they were driving through a valley. On either side, mountains rose, dark and sheer, into the moonlit clouds. A flash of white caught Charlie's eye and he looked into the wing mirror. His heart missed a beat for there, reflected in the mirror, was a white horse. Behind the flowing white mane sat a knight in armour.

'They're here,' said Charlie. 'The Queen and the Red Knight. They're following us.'

'Are you sure?' Paton frowned at the mirror. 'Ye gods, Charlie, you're right.'

'The Queen?' Otus heaved himself to the small window in the back door, and the van rattled and shuddered. 'I see no queen, there is but a knight and his horse.'

Charlie realised that, to Otus, a knight on horseback was quite an everyday sight. 'It isn't an ordinary horse,' said Charlie, and he explained how Ezekiel Bloor had unintentionally brought Queen Berenice back to life, in the body of her favourite mare. 'He's not a very good magician,' Charlie went on. 'He meant to bring Borlath into the world again.'

'Be thankful of the mistake,' grunted Otus.

For the rest of the journey, Charlie drifted in and out of sleep, and in his waking moments, the knight and his white horse were almost always there; if he couldn't see them in the mirror, he would hear the hoofbeats, not too far behind. When the moon was at its zenith, they parked beside a cliff and ate some of Maisie's food. Then Uncle Paton slept for a while, before driving the last few miles.

They turned off the main road at dawn and parked on a track that led to the sea.

'I believe this is the place,' said Uncle Paton. He climbed out of the van and stretched, breathing in the sea air.

Charlie got out and ran to open the doors for Otus. He found that the giant was still fast asleep. The big man lay curled on the floor, with his cheek resting on his hands.

'Otus!' Charlie shook the giant's foot.

Otus opened his eyes, sat up and gave Charlie a broad smile. 'I think this day will be kind to us, Charlie,' he said, levering himself out of the van. Then, seeing a faint blue line of water beyond the cliff, he ran to the edge, while Paton shouted at him to take care. Otus was a heavy man and the cliff had already subsided in several places.

'Where is the castle?' cried Otus. 'I do not see it.'

Charlie came to stand beside him. A feathery mist covered the sea and Charlie remembered that this had happened before. 'It is there, I promise you, Otus,' he said. 'When the sun burns through the mist, we'll see it.'

'It's happening.' Uncle Paton had joined them and, in a few minutes, all three saw an island emerge half a mile out to sea. 'The island of a thousand blues,' said Uncle Paton. 'Soon we'll see its crown.'

The giant clutched his chest. His heart was beating so fast and loud, Charlie was afraid that it might stop altogether. Gradually, the mist evaporated and small patches glittered in the light. As the sun rose higher, the last traces of mist melted away and the castle of shining glass appeared.

'Ahh!' breathed the giant. 'It is there.' He began to stride down the perilous path to the beach, while Charlie and his uncle slipped and staggered in his wake.

'There is a boat, kept in a cave,' said Uncle Paton, 'but . . .' he looked at the giant, 'I'm not sure that it'll take your weight, Otus.'

The giant opened his mouth and let forth a great gust of laughter. 'A boat? I do not need a boat, Sir Paton,' he roared and, without another word, he rushed into the sea. His joyful laughter echoed back to the beach as he strode through the waves, and then he was treading water, his white head bobbing among the seagulls that floated on the surface.

'We'd better get that boat,' said Uncle Paton.

The boat was just where Charlie had found it before: at the back of a deep cave. They soon had it afloat and Uncle

Paton, his back to the castle, rowed as fast as he could, while Charlie gave directions. When they reached the island, the giant was sitting on the shell beach, wringing water out of his shoes.

Uncle Paton chose to stay with the boat, while Charlie took Otus up to the castle. The sun had risen and Charlie and the giant could not look at the blazing glass, as they tramped through the stony scrubland that surrounded the castle. They walked round to the north, where the sun couldn't reach the mirrored walls, and the giant had another good laugh at their reflections, one almost twice the size of the other.

There was no door. They had to squeeze through a narrow tunnel that led under the walls. Twice the giant got stuck but his laughter only increased as he heaved and struggled to get himself free. At last they stood in a wide courtyard paved with shining cobbles. In the centre, a flight of steps led up to a door in the keep: a tall square tower.

'The walls of history are up there.' Charlie pointed to the top of the tower.

'And that is where we shall say farewell,' said Otus.

The steps were made of coarse glass and they climbed up to the door without slipping. The room they entered was walled in long rectangles of misty glass, and their reflections became coloured fragments that wavered and parted whenever they moved.

Beside the door a staircase led to the top of the tower. 'I'll go first,' said Charlie. 'It's a long climb.'

The giant smiled and tapped Charlie's shoulder. 'Lead on, Charlie.'

The steps were narrow and uneven and Charlie wondered how the giant would manage as the stairway wound upwards. Claerwen flew out of Charlie's pocket and lit the way, or they would have been climbing in the dark. Charlie could hear the giant grunting and shuffling as he hauled himself up the rough glass steps and then, at last, they were in the extraordinary room at the top of the tower where Claerwen's light was reflected a thousand times, bouncing from wall to wall, on and on, through the shining glass.

'Where is Amoret?' Otus whispered.

Charlie wanted to tell the giant to have patience, but couldn't bring himself to utter a word. He felt anxious and afraid. Suppose the walls had lost their memory? Suppose there was nothing there? I can travel, he told himself, and Claerwen is Mathonwy's wand.

Deep in the shimmering glass before him a fragment of colour moved, a soft red. A hint of green appeared, followed by browns and a mellow gold. And now the fair-haired Amadis could be seen in his silver-grey armour.

Still gazing at the wall, Charlie reached for Otus with his left hand. The giant's fingers closed over his. Now holding out his right hand, Charlie said, 'Claerwen, 'dwi isie mynd mewn.'

The white moth fluttered on to Charlie's forefinger and he began to move closer and closer to the tantalising shapes and colours; through a fog of stifling air, through clear then stormy weather, on and on, his face now warmed by the sun, now brushed with snow. He could feel the giant's fingers crushing his own and then, as though breaking through the surface of a frozen pond, Charlie found himself in that ancient room again.

They were sitting at the table, just as they had been before: Prince Amadis at the head, his wife and daughter gazing at Charlie. Another child sat with his back to Charlie; the third, with hair as white as snow, turned to look at him. And then Charlie saw Amoret; she was standing beside Amadis, her black hair framing a sad, pale face.

High above him Charlie heard a voice call, '*Amoret*!'

She looked up and a smile of astonishment lit her face.

Charlie felt the giant's fingers slipping away from him and he knew he must go back. 'Let's go,' he said, bringing Claerwen closer to his face. 'God 'ni fynd.'

As he floated away from the scene, he saw a tall young man take Amoret in his arms. He swung her round and the hem of her red dress swirled over his hands. She buried her head in his shoulder and he laughed with happiness. The man had chestnut hair and strong, handsome features. He was exceptionally tall – a giant, in fact.

Before Charlie lost sight of them the giant caught his eye and deep, muffled words broke through the waves of time. *I thank thee.*

And then Charlie was alone in the room where the

shining walls of history kept their secrets. He should have felt elated. He did, he told himself, for he had been successful, and yet, as he stumbled down the narrow stairway, a sense of failure spoiled his happiness. The last time he'd been in the Castle of Mirrors, Billy had been with him.

Charlie stepped into the room where he had met the man he had mistakenly thought to be his father. 'Why are you never here, Dad?' he said to his own reflection in the mirrored walls.

Claerwen fluttered to the door and Charlie followed her, down the rough glass steps, across the glittering courtyard and into the tunnel under the walls.

Uncle Paton was sitting on a rock, close to the boat. When he saw that Charlie was alone, he stood up and waved. 'You were successful, then,' he called.

Charlie nodded.

'You seem unsure,' said Uncle Paton, when Charlie reached the boat. 'Didn't things go according to plan?'

'Yes,' said Charlie. 'It was fantastic. The giant was young again and Amoret was smiling.'

'Well done.' His uncle patted him on the shoulder. 'I have to admit I had my doubts. It was an extraordinary undertaking. You're tired, I expect.'

'A bit,' said Charlie.

They got into the boat and Uncle Paton began to row away from the island. They hadn't gone far when a huge wave slapped the side of the boat, tipping it dangerously.

The sun had disappeared and the sky was filled with dark, angry clouds. There was a sudden crack of thunder, followed by a torrent of rain.

'Dagbert didn't follow us, did he?' Charlie looked at the heaving waves.

'Could be the other one, his father,' said Uncle Paton. 'Mrs Tilpin and the shadow have been gathering their forces, no doubt.'

And they'll be angry about what I've done, thought Charlie.

The waves rose higher; great walls of water lifted the flimsy boat and tossed it down as though it were a toy.

'I should have thought of life-jackets,' shouted Uncle Paton through the roar of water.

The next wave sent the boat rolling on to its side. Charlie lost his grip and felt himself sliding into the sea. He's not going to let me get away with it, he thought, as the waves closed over his head. But at least I got one thing right.

'Charlie! Charlie, hang on!'

As he came up for air, Uncle Paton grabbed his wrist. 'Come on, come on, Charlie. Don't let go,' he shouted. 'We'll get there, don't give up!'

Charlie felt his uncle's hands pulling the back of his jacket, but the waves kept washing over his head and he knew that they wanted to drown him. And then, beneath his feet, the water began to force him upwards. A strong current wrapped itself around his legs and held him steady. Gradually his body was carried upwards and, as he scrabbled to get a hold on the boat, he was firmly thrust over the side into it.

Uncle Paton picked up the oars and smiled down at Charlie, lying on the bottom of the boat. 'We'll get there, old man,' he said.

Hauling himself on to the seat, Charlie saw that they were moving through a wide path of smooth, tranquil sea. On either side the waves still rose and fell in threatening banks of water, but they seemed incapable of touching the boat.

The sea around the boat sparkled in sunlight and, in the same bright rays, Charlie suddenly saw the figure on the cliff. His windblown cloak and feathers looked like a burning cloud.

'The Red Knight,' cried Charlie.

'What was that?' called Uncle Paton, pulling on the oars; his coat was soaking, Charlie noticed.

'It's the knight. The Red Knight. I think he saved us.'

Uncle Paton looked over his shoulder. 'I can see him now. Perhaps you're right, Charlie.'

I know I am, thought Charlie. The Red Knight saved us.

Their passage was smooth from then on. They reached the shingle and drew the boat into the cave. Charlie felt he would never make it up the steep cliff path, but with Uncle Paton's persuasive voice urging him on, he eventually tumbled on to the wet grass at the top.

The Red Knight had gone.

'What happened to his horse?' Uncle Paton wondered aloud.

'She can't look at the island where her children died,' Charlie told his uncle.

Uncle Paton frowned. 'How would you know that?'

'Billy understands her.'

'Ah, Billy,' said Uncle Paton.

'I wish I could have brought him back, Uncle P, but he's spellbound, I know it.'

'Spells can be broken,' said his uncle.

When they got to the camper-van they dried themselves and had a rest. Paton made Charlie wear some of the travelling clothes he kept in the van. Charlie rolled up the long trousers and tucked them into the equally long woollen socks. He hoisted up the shirt with a belt, but Uncle Paton's spare jacket hung on him like an outsized overcoat.

'You'll do,' said Uncle Paton. 'At least you're dry. If we set off now, we'll be in the city by supper time.'

It wasn't something that Charlie looked forward to. He missed the giant and he missed Billy. But most of all he dreaded returning to the place where his mistake had caused a drowning; a place where he would never see Tancred again.

They broke their journey at a country inn and bought fish and chips. Charlie, in his outsized clothes, received a few odd looks from the locals, but their attention was diverted when the lights above the bar exploded, and

Uncle Paton apologised for the inconvenience.

''Tis only a power cut, sir,' said the barman.

'I think you'll find that's not the case.' Uncle Paton gave the man a warm smile and he and Charlie marched out, clutching their fish and chips.

As they sat in the van eating their delicious hot food, Charlie asked his uncle what had taken him so far away, and for so long.

'I've been following a trail,' Uncle Paton replied. 'It's taken me to places I never knew existed, but I think I've discovered something quite . . . well, sensational.'

Charlie looked up expectantly. 'What?'

'I believe that Billy Raven should have inherited the Bloor fortune. It's a long and complex story, and I know we shall have trouble in proving it. But I relish the challenge. Billy shall have his fortune.'

'Then I'll have to bring him back,' said Charlie.

Uncle Paton regarded his great-nephew fondly. 'I'm sure you will, Charlie.'

After they had eaten Charlie fell into a deep sleep. He didn't wake up until they were approaching the city. Glancing in the wing-mirror, he saw the Red Knight and his horse stop at the end of the stone bridge. And then Uncle Paton turned off the main road and the knight disappeared from view.

'Where are we going?' Charlie sat up and looked at his uncle, for they were driving up the hilly road they called The Heights.

'We've been invited to supper,' said Uncle Paton. 'Had a call on my mobile. I'm told it's a celebration.'

'A celebration of what?' asked Charlie.

'I imagine we'll find out when we get there,' said his uncle.

They passed the Looms' house where their headlights were reflected in the glassy eyes of two Rottweilers, staring through the barred gate. And then they were beside the walls of the Sage mansion where Lysander lived; on and on, up and up, until they reached the yard leading to the ramshackle house and barns, where Gabriel and his family kept ducks and geese, goats and gerbils. Charlie expected his uncle to drive into the yard, but he kept going up the steep road until a dark forest came into view.

Charlie could see the gate leading to the Thunder House. As they drew nearer, the headlights picked out four, no five, figures leaning on the top bar. Lysander towered above the others, but Charlie quickly made out the rest: Gabriel, Fidelio, Olivia and Emma. And then he saw a sixth, perched at the very end of the gate, his arms waving, his jacket swirling in a breeze that wasn't there and his blond hair as bright as a crown of stars.

'Tancred!' Charlie shouted.

TO BE CONTINUED . . .

Read about Charlie's next adventure in:

CHARLiE BONE

AND THE RED KNIGHT

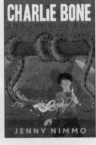